MW00881783

SKYRIDERS

SKYRIDERS

POLLY HOLYOKE

VIKING

VIKING

An imprint of Penguin Random House LLC, New York

First published in the United States of America by Viking,
an imprint of Penguin Random House LLC, 2023

Library of Congress Cataloging-in-Publication Data

Names: Holyoke, Polly, author.
Title: Skyriders / Polly Holyoke.
Description: New York : Viking, 2023. | Series: Skyriders ; book 1 | Audience: Ages 8-12. |
Audience: Grades 4-6. | Summary: When monsters emerge to attack the empire, it is up to
twelve-year-old Kiesandra and her beloved winged horse N'Rah to prove to herself and the
imperial army that she has what it takes to lead them to victory and survival.
Identifiers: LCCN 2022027498 | ISBN 9780593464410 (hardcover) |
ISBN 9780593464434 (paperback) | ISBN 9780593464427 (ebook)
Subjects: CYAC: Winged horses--Fiction. | Human-animal communication--Fiction. |
Monsters--Fiction. | Friendship--Fiction. | Fantasy. | LCGFT: Fantasy fiction. | Novels.
Classification: LCC PZ7.H7435 Sk 2023 | DDC [Fic]--dc23
LC record available at https://lccn.loc.gov/2022027498

Printed in the United States of America

ISBN 9780593464410

1 3 5 7 9 10 8 6 4 2

BVG

Design by Lucia Baez • Text set in Centaur MT Pro

For my brave Sarah and Jessie,
who fight the storms of injustice
and dive into the challenge of helping others.
I am so proud, and I love you both so much.

CHAPTER ONE

Junior Sky Courier Kie Torsun sighed in relief as she and her skysteed, N'Rah, shot out of the black rain clouds into the bright sunlight. She checked to make sure her mail packet and harness were still secure. Once again, they had survived a wild, gut-twisting flight through the mountains.

"You were amazing back there," she told N'Rah warmly and hugged his neck.

A little weather just makes our day more interesting. How is our time? N'Rah asked. She heard his words clearly in her mind as wind ruffled his damp golden mane. His long wings swept up and down in the steady travel pace he could hold all day.

Kie wiped raindrops from her flight goggles and pulled her timekeeper from its waterproof pouch. "We're tight," she admitted, her belly clenching. They *couldn't* be late delivering an emergency dispatch.

We can make it. N'Rah snorted and flew faster, his wings glinting gold in the sun.

Trying to help, Kie hunched low against his neck. "If we rack up another on-time arrival, we'll earn five silver dashins, which could pay for more of Uncle Dugs's heart medicine. I'm afraid he's been stretching it again."

He did look a bit gray when we left. N'Rah peered back at her, and she felt the concern in his mental voice. Her skysteed loved her stubborn old uncle almost as much as she did.

The green foothills below slid past rapidly, and soon they reached the dusty yellow plains. The sun-seared air became so hot that Kie shrugged out of her flight jacket and tied it around her waist. Out of nowhere, a downdraft grabbed them.

Hold on, N'Rah warned her as the air currents sucked them down. Kie clutched the dive strap across his withers. Instead of fighting the draft, N'Rah folded his wings and dove into it. They plummeted toward the yellow grass below like a kyr hawk swooping down on its prey. The ground came rushing at them. Kie's whole body tensed. Would N'Rah be able to pull up in time? He soared out of the draft a hundred feet above the ground and used the extra momentum to speed them on their way.

Kie let go of the breath she'd been holding. "You reckless horse," she teased when her heart had slowed a little. "I just left my stomach five hundred feet above us somewhere."

N'Rah bucked playfully. *I am NOT a horse.*

"I'll remind you of that the next time I'm feeding you sweet oats and shoveling up your road apples."

I see N'Meary and Topar waiting for us to relay, N'Rah announced happily.

Much like hawks and eagles, skysteeds had incredible distance vision. Before long, Kie spotted N'Meary's white wings stroking the air as she hovered above the relay station. The stationmaster would be outside, ready to clock their time.

"We'll make it, two minutes ahead of schedule," Kie

announced with relief after she glanced at her timepiece again.

They flew up beside Topar and his pretty palomino mare. "You look like a drowned rat," he said with a grin. Because his mother was a Ledari from the Western Desert, Topar had brown skin and wore his black hair in a ponytail after the Ledari fashion. Unlike the Ledari, he had bright green eyes, which must have come from a mysterious father he never mentioned.

"You'd look like a drowned rat, too, if you'd just flown through the mountains in a thunderstorm," Kie said, bristling at the comparison.

Topar's smile vanished as he glanced back at the dark clouds shrouding the jagged peaks in the distance. "I'd never fly through a mountain thunderstorm. We'll take the dust tornadoes and grytoc attacks on the plains and desert any day."

"Guess that's why we fly the mountain route," Kie said as she pulled the mail pouch from her saddlebags. "I've got an emergency dispatch here. Ready to catch?"

Topar's eyes widened. "I've never carried a red dispatch before, but I heard a senior courier say she flew one from Terkann addressed to the Emperor two days ago." Even as he talked, Topar urged N'Meary downward until she hovered beneath N'Rah. Within moments, the skysteeds had synchronized their wing strokes.

"Ready," Topar called up to her.

Kie leaned over and dropped the pouch into his outstretched hands. When she was sure he had the pouch, she let go of its security line, and Topar tucked the pouch into his own saddlebags.

"I bet you took a peek," Topar said slyly.

"I'd never open a dispatch," she said, bristling again.

"Glad to hear it," Topar said with a straight face after N'Meary flew up beside N'Rah again. "I'd hate to think Stationmaster Riken's favorite sky courier was breaking the rules."

"Riken doesn't have favorites."

"He favors couriers like you who fly their routes on time."

"Which is why you should be off instead of nattering on at me. Your timer's already ticking."

He was just teasing you about opening the dispatch, N'Rah scolded her as N'Meary pivoted and started the long flight across the plains.

Her cheeks heated as she watched Topar fly away. How come her skysteed had better people sense than she did?

"Fly safe, fly free," she called after them. Truly, she did wish them a safe flight. His desert route could be just as dangerous as her mountain one. Topar looked over his shoulder and flashed her a smile in acknowledgment; Kie waved, and soon he and N'Meary were nothing but a black dot in the bright blue sky.

Kie shifted her weight, and N'Rah spiraled down to the relay station. He landed nimbly before the front porch, showing off a bit to his fellow skysteeds in the nearby paddock. The stationmaster, a small, lean man with a face lined from years of flying courier routes, strode out to meet her. He had the copper skin, red hair, and green eyes common among the Rosari, the richest, most powerful class in the Empire.

"Looks like it might have gotten tricky back there," Riken said, jerking his thumb toward the mountains.

"Nothing N'Rah couldn't handle." Kie patted her skysteed's neck proudly.

"Wish we had a dozen more like him," Riken said with a smile.

"We pushed it because we carried a red emergency dispatch marked for the commander of the garrison at Terkann. The stationmaster told me it carried the Emperor's own seal."

"Did it now? That's the second we've seen this week. The first was from the garrison at Terkann and addressed to the Emperor himself." Riken stared off to the west, his ruddy eyebrows drawn together in a frown, but then he seemed to remember Kie and focused on her again. "Well, here's your pay. You'll have three days off before I send you back across the mountains. You two have earned it."

"Thanks," she said and pocketed the precious dashins. Most couriers hung around the station to boast about their flights, but she wanted to get home to check on Uncle Dugs. First, though, she needed to let N'Rah drink. Mountain bred, he preferred the clean water from the town well over the muddy stream behind the relay station.

She led her tired friend down the dusty yellow street of Durwen Town, past dozens of sunbaked wooden shops and shacks to the town well. Under the sparse shade thrown by scraggly trees, a half dozen town girls and women waited in line. They were all neatly dressed in long skirts and wore their hair in tidy buns and braids. Feeling like a damp, windblown mess in her flight jacket and courier pants, Kie led N'Rah to the back of the line.

Almost at once, though, the middle-aged woman standing in front of her smiled and curtsied. "It looks like you had long, hard flight today, Courier Torsun. Please take my place in line."

"Thank you," Kie said, her cheeks starting to heat. "My sky-steed is very thirsty."

"Then take my place as well," the next woman said with less enthusiasm, but still she stepped aside.

Kie's heart fell when she saw a striking girl with dark red hair done up in a fancy braid standing next in line. Their fathers had been friends long ago, but now Betta's father was the mayor, and she lorded it over all the young people in town.

"Well, I'm not giving up my place in line to some grimy hill girl," Betta said with a sneer. "And that"—she gestured toward N'Rah—"should drink from the town trough just like all the other livestock."

Anger blazed through Kie as she faced the girl who had made the years she'd gone to Durwen's school so miserable. She stood straighter and tossed her soggy braid over her shoulder. Betta could say what she wanted about her, but *no one* insulted N'Rah.

"Then I claim my skysteed's first right to this water."

CHAPTER TWO

BETTA'S EYES WIDENED AND HER face flushed with fury. Kie glared at her, daring her to defy centuries of tradition. After a long moment, the town girl gave a strained laugh and gave up her place in line. "Oh, go ahead and let your stupid horse drink."

"Thank you, and he's *not* a horse," Kie said through clenched teeth. She stepped past Betta and the girls who had been in line before her and cranked the well handle. Her face burning, she pulled up the bucket and poured it into a nearby stone trough carved with flying skysteeds. By order of the first Emperor, a trough like this one stood beside every town and city well in the Empire, to honor the skysteeds for saving Prekalt from the monstrous chimerae three hundred years ago.

N'Rah lowered his head and drank deeply. The girl who had just filled her water jars poured them both into the skysteed trough, too. Surprised and touched by the generous gesture, Kie glanced up. It was Sheri, one of the few students who had been kind to her when they'd been in school together. Her brown hair and golden skin meant she was Mosai, like Kie and most of the poor settlers out here on the wild fringes of the Empire. Unlike Kie, who was small and strong from working in her orchard, Sheri was taller and starting to grow curves.

"Thank you," was all Kie could think to say as they stood watching N'Rah drink.

"It was my honor, Courier Torsun," Sheri said formally, but her brown eyes were warm when Kie met her gaze. "Your skysteed is so beautiful. I love the copper color of his coat and his golden wings."

Kie smiled as she studied N'Rah. His body looked much like a horse's, but it was lighter and more graceful. He had an arched neck and dark, intelligent eyes, and she loved his wandering white blaze, with its white snip on his muzzle that gave him an alert and curious look. His golden mane and tail were lovely, but she could see why Sheri was most impressed by his shining wings that sprouted from his shoulders and stretched fifteen feet from tip to tip.

"Can't you tell the difference between a real skysteed and a scrub?" Betta asked scornfully. "This animal is too small to be a proper skysteed."

"And you still dye your hair with tada root so people will think you're a proper Rosari," Kie shot back at her. Betta gasped and Sheri smothered a giggle. Kie felt like gasping, too. She'd *never* stood up to Betta back in their school days.

"You dishonor yourself and our town by insulting a skysteed," the older woman at the back of the line chided Betta.

"And Kie and her skysteed are the fastest, most reliable courier pair posted here," Sheri said. "I heard the stationmaster say so."

Kie shot Sheri a grateful look and searched for something nice to say to the town girl. Should she compliment Sheri's hair or her skirt? But what if her skirt was an old one and her compliment insulted Sheri? Her cheeks heating again, Kie said nothing and stared hard at N'Rah instead. She could find her way through a mountain blizzard, but when she tried to navigate town ways and town talk, she always got hopelessly lost.

As soon as N'Rah had drunk his fill, Kie nodded gratefully to Sheri and the others who had given up their places in line. Then she and N'Rah hurried down the street to the healer's shop.

I am happy I got to drink, N'Rah said with a wistful glance back at the well, *but now that girl Betta will never let you join her herd.*

"I don't want to join her herd," Kie replied, but she did wish she had thought of something nice to say to Sheri.

I think you would be happier if you had a herd of your own. You spend too much time by yourself.

"We've been through this before," Kie said with a sigh. "I like being by myself."

The healer's shop was quiet, and Kie used three of her precious dashins to buy Uncle Dugs's heart medicine. When she stepped outside again, a small group of awestruck children had gathered around N'Rah where he stood with his wings partially folded, dozing in the sun. He wouldn't fold his wings tightly in Durwen or in any place he didn't feel completely safe.

After warning the children with a stern glance not to bother her tired skysteed, she strode on to the general store and used her last two dashins to buy a loaf of bread and some of Uncle Dugs's favorite tea and cheese. She was headed back to N'Rah when her uncle's old skysteed, N'Tor, touched her mind.

Come quickly! N'Tor urged her. *Your uncle is sick again.*

His panic made her stomach lurch. *We'll come right away. We're in town and we have his medicine,* Kie tried to assure N'Tor as she broke into a run and called N'Rah. He met her halfway down the street. She jammed her purchases into his saddlebags and vaulted onto his back. Without her urging, N'Rah surged into a gallop, pounding between several startled townsfolk in the street. Within moments, she and N'Rah were airborne and winging toward home.

What happened? she asked N'Tor as she clipped herself into the flying harness.

He was pulling rocks out of the vegetable garden, and then he staggered over to the wall and sat down. His eyes are closed and he will not talk to me, but he still breathes.

I told him not to do any more work like that, but he never listens to me, Kie sent back, her eyes filling with tears.

The medicine will help his heart, N'Rah tried to comfort her as they raced between thin white clouds. *It always has before.*

It had better. I'm going to kill Uncle Dugs if he dies on me.

You humans make no sense sometimes. N'Rah shook his golden mane.

Please, just fly faster, she begged, and lay against his neck to reduce every bit of wind resistance she could. At last they left the yellow plains behind, and the green foothills appeared beneath them. A lifetime later, they flew over the first dayan trees on the lowest portions of her father's orchard. As she snatched the heart medicine and a water flask from her saddlebags, N'Rah dove past the sturdy stone cottage built into the hillside and landed in the vegetable garden.

Uncle Dugs sat slumped against the wall near the carrots they grew for the skysteeds, his face a shade of gray that made Kie's own heart seize in her chest. N'Tor stood over him, nuzzling his straggly white hair.

After she jumped from the saddle, she sprinted to her uncle's side. His chest heaved as he labored to breathe, and his bushy gray eyebrows were drawn together in a scowl of pain.

"Uncle Dugs, you've got to take your pill." She forced the words past the fear closing her throat. Remembering his hearing had gotten worse this past year, she shouted, "Uncle Dugs, *please*, you've got to wake up!"

His eyelids fluttered open, and his light brown eyes focused on her. The effort he made to smile made her eyes well with tears again.

"Now open your mouth."

Obediently, he opened his lips, and she placed one of the pills on his tongue. Her hands shaking, she raised the flask to his lips. He managed to gulp down two swallows. Then she rocked back on her heels and watched his sweaty face, willing the color to come back to it. He'd had spells before, but he'd never looked *this* gray.

If only she'd come home sooner. If only he wouldn't try so hard to help her with the work around here. She couldn't bear to lose the very last person in all of Prekalt who loved her. She dashed away another wave of tears because they kept her from seeing him clearly.

N'Rah rubbed his head against her shoulder. *I love you.*

"I love you, too," Kie said and raised a hand to stroke his jaw. But she was frightened to think she might not have a single human left to care about her.

Slowly the color crept back into Uncle Dugs's cheeks.

He tells me his chest feels less tight, N'Tor relayed to her.

"More water," Uncle Dugs said hoarsely, and she held the flask to his lips again. This time he managed several swallows and sat up straighter.

She couldn't hold back the question any longer. "What were you thinking, trying to dig rocks out here in the hot sun?"

"I was thinking we could grow more tubers and carrots if there were fewer rocks in this cursed dirt," he replied. "Why your father chose to be a settler out here, hundreds of miles from any proper city, is beyond me."

She smiled in relief. If Uncle Dugs was back to complaining, he had to be feeling better. "We've enough carrots and only one of you. And leave Da out of it. Now, if you're feeling strong enough, let's get you back to the house."

She put an arm around his waist and helped him to stand.

"You scared N'Tor, you know," Kie scolded her uncle as they started for the house. N'Tor walked right beside his rider, trampling a whole row of beets, but she didn't have the heart to admonish the old skysteed. N'Tor wasn't the one who'd been so foolish today.

"I am sorry, old friend," Uncle Dugs said, giving his skysteed a pat, and N'Tor whickered in reply.

After they stepped inside the cool main room of the house, she settled Uncle Dugs in his rocker. Then she went out and gave N'Rah a good rubdown along with a double ration of sweet oats. Back indoors, she lit the stove and set about toasting some bread and cheese for their supper. Once she'd placed his plate on her uncle's lap, she sat down at the wooden table across from him and devoured her own toast.

"Your flight go well?" he asked. "I saw storm clouds gathering over your route and worried some."

"It had to go well, because we carried an emergency dispatch with the Emperor's own seal on it," she replied between bites. "Flew it through those storms you saw and delivered it on time."

"Did you, now?" Uncle Dugs sat up straighter in his chair. "Where was it headed?"

"Out to Terkann," she admitted, and then decided she had best tell him all of it before he found out from the stationmaster, who was an old friend. "Riken said another red dispatch came through relay two days ago from there, addressed to the Emperor himself."

Her uncle lowered his toast, his face flushing with excitement. "This could be it. The chimerae could be returning. Terkann would be the first town to be destroyed in their advance out of the Broken Lands. You've got to take my great-grandfather's manual on fighting chimerae to the capital and tell them. You've got to show them how wrong they are to waste their time on tournaments."

"I'm not going anywhere." Kie stared hard at her plate. She refused to stare at the wall over his head, for he'd decorated it with three chimerae trophies from olden times that gave her the shivers—a set of sharp bloodgoat horns, a mounted lion's head, and an old sand dragon skull with curved yellow fangs. She hated fighting with Uncle Dugs, and they'd argued about this so many times before.

"The chimerae are never coming back, and I have you and the skysteeds and the orchard to tend. Dayan trees don't prune themselves."

"Forget about those blasted trees, Kiesandra." Uncle Dugs slammed the table with his palm. The noise startled her into meeting his gaze again. "The safety of the entire Empire could be at stake."

"Please, you mustn't get yourself so worked up," she warned him, but of course he ignored her.

He lifted his hand to slam it again, and then his breath caught, and he jerked back in his chair. He started panting, and that awful gray color seeped back into his face again.

"Easy, now." Kie snatched another pill from her pocket. "Take this, and let's get you to bed."

His hands trembling, he took the pill, and gradually his color improved. She helped him from the table, and soon he was tucked into his bed near the stove. As she tidied the cottage she'd lived in all her thirteen years, she felt his gaze on her, but she was grateful he didn't bring up the manual again.

"We've got to practice tomorrow before it gets hot," he did say before she could slip outside to check on the skysteeds.

"You know what the healer said. You're to take it easy after you've had a spell."

"All right, then. I'll watch and you'll practice."

She thought of all the chores she had to do tomorrow around the orchard, and she sighed. But if her doing skyfighting drills kept Uncle Dugs from badgering her about taking his great-grandfather's manual to the capital, it would be time well spent.

"Have it your way, you obstinate old geezle gop," she said, making sure he could reach the water mug on his bedside table. He reached out, caught her hand, and squeezed it.

"Thank you for bringing the medicine. I am sorry I scared you, along with N'Tor," he said gruffly. "Scared myself, too. Thought I was a goner this time for sure."

She leaned over to press a kiss on his forehead. "You're too ornery to die anytime soon." She hoped.

Quietly, she slipped outside to check on the skysteeds. N'Tor stood dozing by the window she'd kept open so he could keep watch over his beloved rider. N'Rah slept standing beside him. Her lips twitched. N'Rah looked like a pony beside majestic N'Tor, who was a third wider and taller from the tips of his white wings to his broad gray chest.

Bred for tournaments where the Rosari nobility won and lost

fortunes, N'Tor had carried her uncle to three championships before the tragedy that had made them turn their backs on the aerial games forever.

She wandered past the skysteeds to the first row of dayan trees that surrounded the house. The sun had already set over the plains, but its last rays transformed the clouds overhead into bright orange and red sailing ships voyaging across a lavender sky. Unlike her restless mother, who had left her family, Kie didn't want to voyage anywhere. Breathing in the scent of earth and the tangy smell of dayan bark, she pulled down a branch and inspected the clusters of small apples growing along it. For midsummer, the fruit looked good. Her father's orchard produced some of the finest apples in all the Torgaresh foothills.

"Da, I hope you'd be proud of how I've kept the place up." She said the words aloud because she liked to imagine a part of his spirit had lingered among the trees he'd loved so. It had been two winters since lung fever had taken him, and she still missed him every day.

If only Riken would promote her to senior courier. Then she'd earn double the dashins on every route she and N'Rah flew. With twice as much income, she could also afford to hire workers, rather than trying to bring the whole crop in by herself. More importantly, she could ensure that Uncle Dugs didn't have to skimp on his medicine.

Her bones aching from hours of flying, she forced herself to face the truth. She'd come *way* too close to losing him today. As much as she liked time by herself, being completely alone terrified her. But Uncle Dugs's heart kept getting worse, along with his obsession with the chimerae. Surely the emergency dispatches going back and forth to Terkann were about some other crisis. The cruel monsters from the heart of the Broken Lands and the evil mage who had created them were long gone.

But as Kie trudged back to the house, she found herself rubbing her arms against a chill.

CHAPTER THREE

IN THE MORNING, UNCLE DUGS insisted on making her breakfast, and his color was much better. Kie, though, felt tired and grumpy because she'd gotten up twice in the night to check on him. She barely had time to finish her oatmeal topped with dayan apple and braid her thick hair before he hustled her out the door into the cool, clear morning.

He wants us to practice fighting the Foul Ones again, when I've a dozen chores to do, she complained to N'Rah as she stomped toward his paddock.

I like to practice fighting the Foul Ones, he replied cheerfully. *I think we are very good at it.*

She'd asked N'Tor once about the origin of this name, and the old skysteed had explained, *We call them the Foul Ones because the chimerae were tormented creatures that should never have existed.*

"We should be resting up for our next courier run," Kie grumbled, loudly enough for Uncle Dugs to hear as she entered the paddock, but he ignored her.

I do not need more rest. I had a good sleep and plenty of sweet oats. N'Rah bucked to prove his point and then raced in mad circles while N'Tor watched him tolerantly.

"If you're done acting like a loony rabbit, I'd like to groom and saddle you," Kie said, his antics making her smile. She was glad that her friend, at least, was in such a good mood this morning. "It looks like you slept in a burr bush last night. Here's your breakfast."

While N'Rah and N'Tor chomped on their sweet oats, she and Uncle Dugs brushed their skysteeds until they shone. After they saddled and harnessed them, they headed for the training area on the hillside above the house. The last of Kie's grumpiness vanished as they soared into the blue sky, startling a flock of cheechees. The yellow birds circled them in a bright chittering swirl before they scattered into the fresh foothill morning. As much as she longed to tend her orchard, flying with N'Rah would always be her very favorite thing to do.

They landed by a shed that contained an impressive array of old skyfighting gear.

"First bow practice and then triwire practice," Uncle Dugs said eagerly, handing her a quiver of arrows and a handsome bow made from deerhorn and dayan wood. Smaller than the longbows Imperial soldiers carried, the skyfighter bow was still powerful enough to pierce a chimera's thick leathery hide.

Catching Uncle Dugs's eagerness, she slung the quiver across her shoulders and vaulted onto N'Rah's back. The moment she clipped into his harness, he leaped into a canter, his golden wings swept up and down, and they were airborne. They flew toward the tall old pine where Uncle Dugs had hung painted heads of a bloodgoat, a sand dragon, and a lion, with battered straw targets beneath each. Real chimerae had three heads and three separate hearts, because they had been created from three fierce desert creatures merged together in a terrible, dark binding magic.

As Kie and N'Rah circled over the pine, she strung the bow, no easy task on the back of a skysteed. But the real challenge in skyfighting with a bow, she thought as they climbed upward for their first pass at the target tree, was avoiding your own skysteed's wings.

"Let's go for the bloodgoat heart first on a direct pass," she told N'Rah as she nocked her first arrow. When she judged they were a hundred feet above the tree, she shifted her weight and squeezed her legs.

Neighing in excitement, N'Rah dove straight at the tree. Carefully, she sighted the bow over his head. She released her bowstring when they were still twenty feet away, well out of the range of the imaginary chimera's talons and spiked tail. The arrow thudded home dead center of the heart target. She grinned and reached for another arrow.

Nice shot, N'Rah congratulated her as they skimmed past the tree and flew upward once again.

"Thanks," Kie said and patted his neck. "You set us up perfectly."

"Try a side pass this time," Uncle Dugs shouted from the ground.

Side passes were trickier. She had to shoot during the brief moment N'Rah's wings swept downward and she had an open field of fire.

"Let's kill the lion head," she told N'Rah. This time they swooped down at the chimera tree from the side, and N'Rah tilted inward to give her a clearer shot. *Thwoosh!* The arrow flew straight and true. It had just pierced the lion's eye when N'Tor called out, *Apprentice Courier Sanny comes.*

Kie swore under her breath and spun N'Rah away from the chimera tree. Her cheeks burned as she slipped the bow over her shoulder and flew down to the meadow, where Sanny had landed next to Uncle Dugs.

I do not understand why practicing the old ways of fighting the Foul Ones embarrasses you so much, N'Rah said.

"Because sky couriers deliver dispatches. Skyfighters joust with each other in tournaments, and it's a waste of time to practice fighting an enemy that's long gone." She struggled to tamp down her temper. It wasn't N'Rah's fault that Sanny'd caught them practicing skyfighting, but Kie worried she might tell the other couriers at the station what she'd seen. They thought Kie and her uncle were strange enough already.

"Riken needs you to deliver another emergency dispatch," Sanny announced the moment N'Rah landed beside her brown skysteed. "He wants you to come right away, and you're to fly the desert route out to Terkann this time."

"But we just made our mountain run yesterday," Kie protested. "He has to have a courier pair better rested than we are."

"Riken wants you. He said to tell you that you'd be a big step closer to making senior courier if you two can complete the flight in time."

"Time's already ticking," Uncle Dugs said quickly. "We'll be fine. I've plenty of my medicine now, and I promise I will laze like a pig in mud while you're gone."

"But I can't leave you."

"N'Tor will look after me. If Riken wants you, this message must be important. You swore an oath to serve the Empire. Take the bow and these triwires." Her uncle pressed three packets into her hands. "They're better than standard courier weapons if you run into a flock of grytocs."

"All right," she said reluctantly. Uncle Dugs did look much better, and when he took his heart medicine regularly, he didn't have spells. "I have to pick up my flight jacket and another water flask," she told Sanny.

"Time is ticking. Take mine." Sanny tossed her a jacket and a flask and then urged her skysteed into a gallop. Moments later, they were winging their way toward Durwen Relay.

"We're not going to let an apprentice beat us to the station, are we?" Kie asked N'Rah with a grin.

N'Rah reared up on his haunches and leaped straight into the air, a maneuver the bigger, heavier skysteeds like N'Tor couldn't manage. Kie leaned low against N'Rah's neck and relished the cool air rushing past her face as her skysteed quickly reached racing speed.

Kie reached out to N'Tor. *You will try to keep my uncle from doing anything foolish?*

I will do my best, N'Tor promised her. *Yesterday scared him enough that he will be careful, for a time anyway.*

She hoped with all her heart that N'Tor would be right and that Uncle Dugs would rest up while she was gone. Despite their head start, N'Rah caught Sanny and her skysteed a few miles before the station. Sanny grinned ruefully and called out, "Fly safe, fly free" as N'Rah flashed past the pair.

Dressed in flight gear, Riken waited for them in the air above the station on his bay skysteed. He must have been planning to fly the route himself if she refused.

"Glad you said yes," Riken called to Kie, and motioned they should sync for relay. "If there's trouble brewing, I should be here making sure the mail keeps moving along all our routes."

N'Rah flew under N'Deve, and the skysteeds matched their wing strokes. She was bursting to ask Riken what he thought might be happening out in Terkann, but he was already giving her instructions.

"Watch for grytocs out by Shiprock and for skyriders all along your route." Riken spoke quickly as he lowered the red dispatch into her hands. "Our courier from Terkann is overdue, and an Imperial trade mission, including the Emperor's youngest son, Prince Shayn, is late as well. You're to offer aid if they need it, but first and foremost, get that dispatch to the garrison commander. Your time starts now."

Kie caught the red dispatch bearing the skysteed seal of the Rathskayan emperors. Amazed she was holding a dispatch the Emperor himself may have written, she tucked it carefully into her mail pouch and clicked her own timepiece. N'Rah pivoted in the air toward the west and Terkann, and they were away.

As the yellow plains slipped past below them, N'Rah fell into the swift travel rhythm he could maintain all day. To score an on-time arrival, they had to reach Terkann in ten hours, which they should be able to do unless they encountered strong headwinds or ran into trouble.

Anxiously, Kie braided and unbraided a section of N'Rah's mane. What could be happening out in Terkann? Could the desert tribesmen be threatening the town again? Three hundred years ago, when the chimerae had threatened to devour whole tribes and all their livestock, the tribesmen had pledged fealty to the first Emperor and became some of his best skyfighters. But with the chimerae threat gone, many Ledari tribes had returned to raiding settlements on the western borders of the Empire.

As N'Rah flew west, the yellow plains gave way to beige sand, sparse patches of dry grass, and prickly green-gray alai that came in a variety of shapes. When the sands beneath them grew hotter, N'Rah climbed higher, where the air would be cooler for them both. Kie still had to take off her flight jacket, and sweat began to darken N'Rah's neck.

She adjusted the brim of her flight cap to keep the sun from burning her face. "Please keep an eye out for that trade delegation that might be lost out here somewhere," she said. "They probably dropped their compass in the sand. I wonder what that prince is like. Uncle Dugs said the older Imperial princes were a wild lot."

It might not be so easy being a prince or having four brothers, N'Rah said thoughtfully.

"Like having servants and being waited on could be so hard?" Kie scoffed. "He's probably never done a day of real work. Speaking of work, I should be pruning all the trees in the lower orchard this afternoon."

I am glad we are flying together.

N'Rah's comment made her smile through her worry. "I'm glad, too," she admitted, and patted his silky shoulder. Still, it was hot and dusty out here, and attacks from grytocs, large flying reptiles with razor-sharp beaks and slashing talons, were always a danger. Uneasily, she checked her weapons and scanned the horizon, even though N'Rah would probably spot a grytoc long before she could.

She waved at a goatherd, who was waving at them from the ground. He must be one of the older folks who still believed seeing a skysteed in the air brought good luck.

They were a third of the way to Terkann and several miles past the Mrai oasis when she felt N'Rah tense.

I see many grytocs circling ahead. I think they are attacking some skyriders. Without her urging, he flew faster.

Her pulse hammering in her ears, Kie sat up straighter in her saddle. "That might be Riken's lost trade delegation. He said we were supposed to help them if they needed us, but we're also supposed to reach Terkann on time." Somehow they *had* to find a way to do both.

She wiped the sweat from her forehead and strained to peer through the shimmering heat waves rising from the sand. At first she couldn't see anything, but then she spotted a flash of light above the horizon, and then another, as if sunlight were reflecting off weapons in the distance. She and N'Rah were miles from Shiprock yet, but clearly some sort of aerial battle raged ahead.

Her stomach tightening, she shifted her quiver of arrows so she could reach it easily and untied her bow from her saddle. After a moment's hesitation, she slung all three triwire packets from her saddle pommel as well. The last time they'd fought off a half dozen grytocs, one had managed to claw N'Rah's haunches, and he still carried the scars. She was *not* going to let one of those awful creatures hurt her skysteed again.

Her mouth grew dryer than the desert sand below as N'Rah carried them closer to the fight.

"Can you tell how many they're fighting?" she asked. Grytocs usually hunted in small flocks of four or five, but couriers had reported being chased by much larger flocks recently.

I think there are only five of them, but they are very big for grytocs, N'Rah replied, and she could sense his uncertainty.

"Let's gain some altitude and come at them from above." She double-checked her flying harness and nocked an arrow.

Suddenly, N'Rah let loose a wild, clarion neigh and laid his ears back.

"What's gotten into you?" she asked in bewilderment.

The skyriders do not fight grytocs, he replied. *They fight chimerae!*

Chapter Four

Kie stared into the distance, her innards churning as she blinked her dry eyes against the hot desert wind. N'Rah had to be wrong. Those skyriders *couldn't* be fighting chimerae! All the monsters had been killed centuries ago.

But now N'Rah had flown her close enough that she could see several large tawny shapes wheeling around a band of sky-riders. For a moment, the nearest winged beast was silhouetted against the blue sky, and it had . . . one, two, *three* heads! And then the desert wind brought with it the deep, rumbling roar of a lion.

"You're r-right," she stuttered, even as cold terror seized her. "Should we run for Durwen station and warn Riken? He has to know. He has to warn the Empire!"

But as N'Rah raced closer, it became obvious that the fight was not going well for the skyriders. At the center of their band, a gray skysteed fought to stay aloft, its damaged wing flailing at the air. Another rider slumped forward, unconscious, against his skysteed's neck while two more riders struggled to protect their injured. The air thundered with the full-throated roars of lions and the harsh cries of the bloodgoat heads as they tried to tear at the skysteeds with their sharp black horns.

We have to help them! N'Rah cried.

"All right," Kie said. Abruptly, the panic making her thoughts tumble about disappeared, and a strange calm took its place. "Take us higher. I want the sun in the chimerae's eyes."

Three wing strokes later, they hovered above the fight. The rider on the injured skysteed fired arrows at the chimerae, and a second skyrider sliced at the beasts with a sword. When one of the chimerae advanced on the injured gray, a third rider on a smaller pinto skysteed darted past the monster, obviously trying to distract it. The chimera chased the pinto for several wing strokes, but then it turned back toward the stricken skysteed again.

"Let's try to hit the sand dragon's heart." She turned N'Rah toward the chimera menacing the injured skysteed. A hit to the largest of the chimera's hearts could, in theory, kill the creature outright.

She sent N'Rah into a dive and pulled her bowstring back. They flashed closer until the chimera's tan-and-black wings flapped below them. N'Rah swooped beneath its left wing into the creature's blind spot, and a wall of sand-colored hide slipped past. She gripped her bow tighter. The monster seemed so much bigger than Uncle Dugs had described! It was twice as tall and twice as long as N'Rah, and three arrows already protruded from its side.

As they skimmed past the beast, Kie turned back and fired into the center of its chest. The lion head, surrounded by a thick brown mane, twisted on its strong neck and roared at them so loudly that her whole body vibrated from the sound. A second later, the stench of the rotting flesh caught in its teeth made her gag. The sand dragon head, on a much thinner and longer neck, struck at them in a blur of black scales and yellow fangs, but N'Rah had already carried them beyond its reach. The fury in the chimera's hiss made her tremble.

"We have to use the triwires," she gasped to N'Rah as he climbed swiftly above the fight again. "That thing has four arrows in it, and it's still flying." Which meant she must have missed her heart shot. She slipped the bow over her shoulders and ripped the first triwire from its packet. Three razor-sharp wires, four feet long and weighted with spiked metal balls at their ends, were joined at the center with a small wooden handle. Careful to keep the wires away from N'Rah's wings, she whirled the triwire over her head until it hummed.

Concentrating hard, she gauged the chimera's wing strokes. Her timing had to be perfect. With her seat and legs, she sent N'Rah into another dive. This time they skimmed past the chimera on its right, and as its wing reached its lowest point, she threw the triwire. It went spinning through the air, sunlight glinting on its sharp copper strands. One wire sliced halfway through the chimera's thin wing hide. The second wrapped around the talon protruding from the wing's leading edge. The last caught the monster's front leg. Then they were past it.

She glimpsed movement behind them and leaned hard to the right. N'Rah dove right as the chimera's spiked tail whistled through the space where they'd been moments earlier.

"That was close. You all right?" she asked breathlessly as N'Rah pumped his wings to gain them altitude once more.

Yes, but the Foul One is not, N'Rah replied with fierce satisfaction.

She glanced down. The triwire had bound the chimera's damaged wing to its leg. Screeching frantically, the monster beat at the air with its good wing as it plunged in tight circles toward the ground. One of the remaining four chimerae broke off the attack and dove after it.

Moments after the first one crashed, the second one landed on top of it and began to feed.

Kie ripped the second triwire from its packet. When she looked up again, a slim boy seated on the pinto skysteed hovered beside them. He had bright red hair and a thin sunburned face, and he was dressed as simply as a sky courier, except that he didn't wear a blue uniform shirt.

"Toss me that third triwire," he said.

"If you've never used one, you could slice your skysteed's wing off."

"I know how to use a triwire," he said impatiently.

Something in his level green gaze convinced her. She backed N'Rah closer to the pinto so their wings wouldn't tangle. Kie stretched out her hand, and the boy grabbed the packet from her.

"We should probably save the prince." She gestured toward the boy below them on the injured skysteed. She guessed he must be the prince because of the fancy maroon uniform he wore.

"I'm all in favor of saving princes," the boy said as he ripped the triwire from the packet. "I'll take the chimera on the right. You take the one on the left. The captain is chopping apart that third one."

Even as she watched, the woman with the sword severed the

bloodgoat head from the neck of a chimera attacking the group from the west, and dark purplish blood sprayed through the air.

"All right." Kie took a deep breath and forgot about the boy. She concentrated on the chimera trying to gut the injured skysteed and the prince who rode him. She whirled the triwire and sent N'Rah into another dive.

Focused on the injured skysteed, the chimera's heads didn't spot them as they glided along beside it. The moment the chimera's wings flashed downward, she flung the triwire. While the weapon still spun through the air, the monster lunged toward the gray skysteed. The triwire sliced into the chimera's foreleg but missed the wing completely.

Screaming in pain and fury, the creature whipped around. Now Kie faced all three heads of an angry chimera. *This thing looks nothing like Uncle Dugs's target tree!* she thought. Then the lion head roared so loudly that her ears rang with the sound, and she couldn't think at all.

Just as the sand dragon head struck at them, N'Rah twisted backward. *At least I am keeping my wits,* he gasped. The fangs closed on the tip of N'Rah's wing, tearing several shining feathers loose. The bloodgoat head had baleful yellow eyes and a neck almost as long as the sand dragon's. Shrieking, it tried to impale them with its sharp horns, but missed.

"Did the sand dragon head bite you?" she asked frantically as N'Rah folded his wings and they dropped into a steep dive. Skysteeds had more resistance to chimera venom than humans, but it could make them very sick.

No, but it is still trying, he replied, his eyes rolling with fear.

She glanced over her shoulder. The chimera dove after them, so close that the sand dragon head snapped at N'Rah's tail.

Try shooting it!

Right. She unslung the bow and grabbed an arrow.

I am going to level off in a moment. You should get a good shot then.

She nocked the arrow and pulled the bowstring back. *I'll be ready,* she promised him. Right now, the chimera's angry heads blocked her shot as they wove back and forth in mesmerizing patterns. *Don't be distracted by their heads,* Uncle Dugs had always warned her. She watched and waited. She couldn't miss the sand dragon heart this time. N'Rah was counting on her!

He came out of the dive two hundred feet above the desert sand. The chimera had to pull up, too, flapping its wide wings and leaving its chest exposed. She fired. The instant after the first arrow left her bow, she nocked a second. Before the bloodgoat head dropped to block her shot, she sent a second arrow slicing into its chest.

The bloodgoat head screamed, and the lion head roared in pain, while the sand dragon head snapped and bit at the arrows. The chimera reared back, fanning its wings. N'Rah skimmed away from it and started to climb.

"I th-think we got it," Kie said, her voice shaking as she nocked another arrow and peered downward. The chimera thrashed about on the ground now, kicking up clouds of sand.

She forced herself to look away and focus on the main

fight. The pinto's rider and the prince fired arrows at a chimera entangled in a triwire. The woman with the sword sliced off the sand dragon head on the monster she'd been battling, and the creature plunged toward the ground.

Abruptly, something big blocked the sun overhead. Kie glanced up. A chimera dove toward them, talons outstretched, the lion's mouth open in anticipation.

She kicked N'Rah's sides and yelled, "Move!"

Startled, he sprinted forward. In desperation, she raised her bow and fired into the lion's mouth, but she knew she was too late to save them.

There was a flash of yellow, and a palomino skysteed dove at the chimera. It was N'Meary and Topar! He whirled a botan, a single weighted rope. Waiting until he was dangerously close, he loosed it. The botan caught the chimera's wing and bound it to its back leg. Roaring and screeching, the chimera lurched sideways, and something hit Kie hard across her shoulders, throwing her up onto N'Rah's neck.

He squealed in pain, and they began falling. All she could see overhead was sandy, leathery hide. They must be trapped under the chimera's left wing! She shoved at it, trying to push it away from N'Rah's wings.

"We've got to dive out from under it!" she cried to N'Rah, even as she wondered how much time they had before they crashed into the ground.

But he didn't listen to her. Panicked, he kept flapping his

wings, instinctively trying to stay airborne.

"DIVE, NOW!" she yelled with her mind and her voice, and yanked on his mane.

At last, he heard her. He folded his wings, tucked in his head and feet, and they dove. Within moments, they were falling faster than the chimera and left it behind and above them.

Kie gulped when the ground came rushing up. N'Rah opened his wings again. But were they badly damaged? She closed her eyes and prayed to the Messenger, the patron god of sky couriers.

Between her knees, N'Rah's muscles tensed as he extended his wings fully and soared out of the dive, skimming just above the desert sand. Behind them, she heard an awful *thud* and a coughing roar as the chimera crashed into the ground. Looking back, she saw it convulse several times and then lie still.

She scanned the sky above them. All five chimerae were grounded and dying. The fight was over for now, but were more chimerae on their way?

Chapter Five

The moment they landed on a ridge next to a twisted alai plant, Kie started shaking in reaction. She unclipped her flight harness and slid from the saddle. Was dear N'Rah hurt? On rubbery legs, she walked around her skysteed to check him for injuries.

"A-are you all right? I'm so sorry. It was my job to look up and watch for chimerae. Uncle Dugs told me never forget to look up." She apologized to N'Rah again and again.

I think I am fine, he said, stretching his wings out and sounding shaken himself. Other than some missing primary flight feathers on his right wing, he didn't appear to be injured.

With a huge sigh of relief, she wrapped her arms around N'Rah's sweaty neck, and he leaned into her.

"We're only alive because you're so quick," she told him. "And you kept your wits."

We did well for our first fight against the Foul Ones, he said.

She shuddered as she glanced at the closest chimera sprawled on the sand, one of its sand-colored wings, veined with black, tilted drunkenly into the air. Would they have a second fight against these monsters? How could they even exist?

Maybe the other skyriders would know more. N'Rah was sweating and breathing hard, and he needed to walk. Glancing at the sky again, she led him across the baking sands to where the other skyriders had gathered in a group. Topar hurried to meet her. He had a bloodstained bandage wrapped around his upper arm, and his expression was serious.

"I thought that chimera had us for sure," she told him. "Thank you for saving both our lives. But are you and N'Meary all right?"

"Yeah. We're just a little cut up. We had a fight with a big flock of grytocs outside of Terkann. The scent of the dead there are attracting scavengers from all over."

"What dead? *What* is going on?"

"You should come meet these people. They know more than I do." As they walked, Topar shot her a curious glance. "They say you killed two chimerae all by yourself."

"N'Rah and I got lucky." Despite the desert sun scorching her shoulders, she shivered to think just how lucky.

"Yeah, and maybe all that training your uncle made you do wasn't so crazy after all."

They had reached the small group now. A woman knelt next to an older man lying on the sand. They both wore the maroon-and-gray uniform of the Imperial Skyforce, and the silver braids on their shoulders meant they were officers. The tall, fair boy, who wore a simpler maroon uniform, examined the injured wing of the gray skysteed. The shorter boy, who flew the pinto, hurried to greet her.

"I'm Prince Shayn, that's Captain Nerone"—he gestured toward the woman—"and that's Jann Mackson, senior skyfighter cadet." The prince nodded toward the older boy. "We owe you our lives. If you hadn't shown up when you did with your triwires, we'd all be dead. I thank you." Then he bowed deeply to her.

Kie blinked in surprise. Was this boy really the prince? He was definitely Rosari, but princes weren't supposed to be so skinny and have peeling noses. Should she curtsy? She'd probably look ridiculous if she tried to curtsy wearing pants. Instead, her face burning, she ducked forward in an awkward imitation of his bow.

"My name is Kiesandra Torsun," she replied, "and you're welcome. But where did those chimerae come from?"

"They followed us out of Terkann," the prince replied. "We were trying to escape the slaughter there and warn my father."

"Wh-what slaughter?" Kie asked, unable to keep a tremor from her voice.

"At least a half dozen scourges of chimerae descended on Terkann yesterday and literally tore it apart," he replied, looking somber. "They devoured every living thing they could catch. The town had so little warning that few people made it belowground into the old shelters."

It took her a moment to absorb his words. "But I thought we had a system of sentries to warn us if the chimerae ever returned. Those people should have had plenty of warning."

Captain Nerone rose to her feet. She was a strong, striking-looking Rosari with short chestnut hair and cool green eyes. "We did, until fifty years ago, when the nobles in the Grand Senate in all their wisdom voted to stop funding the outposts along our border with the Broken Lands."

"Now these monsters and whoever created them have surprised us," the prince said. "We need to get back to the capital and warn my father that the chimerae have returned." The pinto skysteed stepped closer to the prince, plainly ready to fly again. The pinto was almost as small as N'Rah. Surely an Imperial prince could afford one of the big skysteeds that fetched such high prices at auction.

"And I need to get back on my route now," Kie said, unable to hide her impatience any longer. She still wanted to score an on-time arrival, even if it meant dodging scourges of chimerae along the way. "I have an emergency dispatch for Garrison Commander Meem from the Emperor."

"I'm afraid he's Commander Meem." Prince Shayn gestured toward the unconscious man on the ground. The commander's face was ghastly pale, and his chest heaved. "He's suffering from sand dragon venom, and there is no garrison left in Terkann. You might as well give the dispatch to me."

Kie bit her lip. Should they fly on to Terkann anyway?

"Prince Shayn's right," Topar said. "There's no point in you taking the risk of finishing your route. There's no one left at Terkann station, either."

A courier was only supposed to hand off the mail to another courier or a stationmaster. Reluctantly, she handed the prince the dispatch. He tore it open and scanned the contents.

"There's a good healer in Mrai," Kie said to Captain Nerone while the prince read. "She might be able to help Commander Meem."

"And we could let the skysteeds drink," Topar said. "N'Meary needs water."

Prince Shayn crumpled the dispatch and flung it away from him. "My father says the garrison and my personal guard should protect the town at all costs if the chimerae threat proves to be real. That's what our soldiers and our skyfighters tried to do, but now there is no garrison and no town, and I have no personal guard."

His voice quivered with anger, but the haunted look in his eyes made her wonder how many people and skysteeds the prince had seen die yesterday. She cleared her throat. "Topar, you should lead them to the oasis, and I'll meet you there. I have to get my triwires back."

"That's an excellent idea," Prince Shayn said. "They're one of the few weapons that seem to work against these monsters. I'll help." He turned and marched toward the closest grounded chimera, which looked as big as a sand dune.

"Your Highness, wait!" Captain Nerone called out. "We need to cut off all three heads on each of the chimerae before you try to get those triwires back. If there's life in any of the three heads, the beasts could still be dangerous."

"Um, right. Thanks, Captain." The prince glanced back at them, his lips lifting in a sheepish smile.

"I'll stay and look after the skysteeds and Commander Meem," the senior cadet spoke up. Because of his fair skin and blond hair, she guessed he must come from the Northern Isles.

"I'll stay, too, and I can look at your skysteed's wing if you want," Topar offered. "I often help the healer at Terkann station tend injured skysteeds."

"Thank you," Jann said. "Neither N'Tal nor I can tell how badly he's hurt."

Kie tried to keep a wary eye on the sky as she followed the prince and the captain, but the closest chimera kept drawing her gaze. Twice the size of a large skysteed, it lay still, and the eyes of the lion and bloodgoat heads were half closed. But the sand dragon's cold yellow eyes were still wide open and seemed to stare at her accusingly.

It was the second chimera she'd downed. Two of her arrows protruded from its chest, and a triwire bound its front left leg. The stench of rotten flesh in the lion's teeth made her nauseous. She tried to breathe through her mouth instead of her nose, but that didn't help.

After approaching it cautiously, the captain cut the sand dragon head off with a single stroke of her sword. Captain Nerone had to be even stronger than she looked! She lopped off the other two heads and strode on to the next closest chimera.

"Good thing for us, she has a sword forged from amartine steel," Prince Shayn said, and reached for the triwire wrapped around the chimera's foreleg.

"Wait," Kie cried and pulled his arm back. He looked so surprised that she almost smiled. Was there a law against touching Imperial princes? "You need to use this glove." She handed the prince a light mesh glove from her belt pouch. "You'll slice your fingers if you don't wear it. These wires are sharp."

The prince shot her a curious look as he tugged on the glove. She tugged on the other, and they set to work unwinding the triwire as quickly as they could.

"I've only seen triwires in museums," the prince said. "I made one myself that N'Laure and I practice with, but it's not as sharp as these. How did you come to have three, and gloves made for handling them?"

"My uncle is very interested in chimera lore." She didn't want to admit that he was obsessed. Instead she asked, "Were you truly on a trade mission out here?" Prince Shayn appeared to be about her age, which seemed awfully young to have been given so much responsibility.

"Actually, my father had heard rumors from the Ledari that they'd seen some chimerae on the wing, and he knows I've spent a lot of time studying them," the prince said. "He sent me to find out if there was any truth to those rumors. I was talking to one of their clan chieftains when Terkann was attacked. We hurried back to help the town, but the scourges annihilated our force." His voice roughened with grief.

She wished she could think of something to say to comfort him, but what could she say that would make any difference to someone who had just witnessed a massacre? He handed her the triwire, and she wiped it free of dark purple chimera blood. Then they hurried on to the next carcass. She sucked in several deep breaths of untainted air along the way.

"Do you think this is the start of an invasion?" Kie looked away from the triwire she was coiling long enough to check the sky overhead anxiously.

"I'm not sure those scourges were supposed to attack Terkann, or at least, not yesterday," Prince Shayn replied as they approached the next chimera. Captain Nerone had already done her job here. The beast's three heads were severed from their necks, and the sand around them was stained blackish purple. "I saw several men riding on the biggest chimerae, yelling what sounded like commands at the rest, but they ignored those men completely."

"Maybe they were the scourge masters and they lost control of their scourges," Kie suggested as she unwound the wire from the chimera's wing while the prince freed the wire wrapped around the chimera's talon. "The old chimerae were created to feel terrible hunger, so they never felt full, no matter how much they gorged themselves."

She glanced up to see the prince watching her curiously again. "You know, I've read everything I could find in the Imperial archives about chimerae, and I've never read that."

Was this prince going to decide she was odd, too? Her face starting to warm again, Kie focused on cleaning the second triwire. She'd finished placing it in its packet when she felt the desperate touch of N'Tor's mind. He'd never been able to reach her across such a great distance before. Something must be terribly wrong!

You must help us! Two chimerae attack Durwen. We go to protect the people and give them time to reach the shelters.

"N'Rah, come!" she cried to her skysteed, her pulse racing and panic tightening her chest. "Durwen is being attacked by chimerae, and I have family there," she explained hastily to the prince.

"But how could you possibly know Durwen's under attack?" the prince asked. "It must be a hundred miles from here."

"I just know," she said, fear for her uncle making her voice shake. She couldn't take time now to explain that she could speak to her uncle's skysteed. "I *have* to go."

"I wish we could help your town, but my first responsibility is to get word to my father about these chimerae attacks."

"I understand. You should take the last triwire. You have to make it to Pedarth and warn them," she said as she vaulted into her saddle.

"If you and I survive the next few days, come find me at the capital," Prince Shayn said, his gaze locked on hers. "If this is the beginning of a new chimerae war, we'll need to relearn everything we've forgotten about them. Promise me you'll come."

She found herself saying impatiently, "I promise," even as N'Rah leaped into the air, and then they were skyborne.

CHAPTER SIX

KIE MADE N'RAH HALT BRIEFLY at the Mrai oasis to drink, even though she hated every moment of delay. N'Rah wanted to keep flying, but he was already dehydrated from their fight under the blazing desert sun against the chimerae.

"We'll reach Durwen Town faster and be in better shape to help Uncle Dugs if we stop and let you drink now," she told her impatient skysteed.

While N'Rah drank thirstily from the skysteed trough and Kie dumped the cool water over her sweaty head, a woman came to fill her jars. Her eyes grew wide with terror as Kie warned her about the massacre at Terkann and the chimerae scourges, and asked her to have their healer ready in case the prince brought Commander Meem here for treatment.

Then she and N'Rah leaped into the sky again. As she hunched low against his neck and kept an eye out for more chimerae, N'Rah asked her anxiously, *Have you heard any more from the old one and your uncle?*

"I haven't, and I don't want to distract him in case they're fighting chimerae right now," she replied. She knew her uncle would try to fight the monsters attacking Durwen, and she was horribly afraid that his brave but weak heart might fail him. Eventually, though, she did reach out to the old skysteed, but her mind touched only silence.

She didn't need to urge N'Rah to hurry. His golden wings flashed up and down in the bright sunlight as he flew faster than she'd ever seen him fly before. A strong tailwind helped them along, and white lather formed on his neck and shoulders as slowly, oh so slowly, the desert sands and alai plants below gave way to the yellow grass of the plains. At last, the first wooden houses and shacks of Durwen Town appeared beneath them. Her heart heavy with dread, she saw the dusty streets were deserted.

Even as she called to N'Tor, she spotted a dead chimera sprawled in the ruin of a house near the center of town. The monster must have fallen from the sky and smashed the home to bits.

I see N'Tor, N'Rah said. *He's . . . lying on the ground near the shelter caves. Your uncle lies beside him.*

Icy fingers traced down her backbone. Skysteeds only lay down when they were very sick or terribly injured. She spotted another dead chimera not far from the massive iron doors to the shelter caves, a long spear shaft protruding from its chest.

"I—I see them now," she said, unable to keep a tremor from her voice. The old skysteed lay stretched out on his side in the yellow dirt, his eyes closed and his chest heaving as he struggled to breathe. Her uncle lay frighteningly still near N'Tor's head.

Mistress Vena, the town's healer, knelt beside Uncle Dugs, and Riken treated a deep gash on N'Tor's flank. Kie's panic eased a little when Uncle Dugs reached out to stroke N'Tor's muzzle. They both were still alive!

N'Rah landed a few feet away from the old skysteed. Sheri, along with Tyle Hoff, the town's balding mayor, hurried to meet her. The rest of the townsfolk stood inside the shelter doors, watching them with white, anxious faces.

"We wanted to take your uncle into the caves with us, but he wouldn't leave his skysteed," Sheri explained.

"Wh-what happened to them?" Kie asked, her eyes burning with tears. Uncle Dugs looked so small lying there.

"He saved us," Sheri replied wonderingly. "He fought both of the chimerae and held them off long enough for most of the townsfolk to make it to the shelters."

"He killed one, and we brought down the other with a spear from the old catapult," the mayor said. "Now I'm glad Duggan badgered us into practicing with that thing every year."

"How badly hurt are they?" Kie asked, her chest aching.

Mistress Vena met Kie's gaze, her expression worried. "I think your uncle must have caught a direct blow from the chimera's tail. He has several broken ribs, and he may have internal injuries. With his heart issues, it's important we keep him as still and quiet as possible."

"N'Tor has that gash on his flank," Riken added, "but I'm more worried by the sand dragon bite on his shoulder. Only time will tell if the brave old fellow will survive the venom. Are there more chimerae on the way?"

"All I know is that several scourges attacked Terkann yesterday," Kie said, fighting back tears she refused to shed in front of so many townsfolk. She just *couldn't* lose Uncle Dugs and N'Tor. "Topar and I helped that Imperial delegation you mentioned kill five chimerae south of Mrai, but I haven't seen more since."

"Kie, is that you?" Uncle Dugs said.

"Yes, Uncle, I'm here." Kie hurried to his side and took his hand.

"Brought one down, anyway," he said as his pain-filled gaze fastened on her face. "Girl, I know there were times you thought I was senile or a fool, but I was right."

"Uncle Dugs, I never thought that you were senile or a fool."

"Wouldn't blame you if you did." Uncle Dugs's lips lifted in a semblance of a smile. "Thought I might be crazy myself. But now the chimerae are back, you've got to take the manual to the Emperor's commanders . . . before his Skyforce launches."

"But you're hurt." She didn't want to say *You might be dying*, even though she was terrified it might be true. Hot tears streamed down her cheeks. "I want to stay with you. Someone else can take it."

"H-has to be you. Taught you how to fight the old way. You and N'Rah can show them."

"But my place is here with you."

"No, it isn't," he wheezed, and tried to raise himself up on his elbows. "O-only a Torsun can make them under—" His breath caught as he jerked and fell backward, and his face started to turn gray. The healer pushed Kie aside and placed one of Uncle Dugs's heart pills on his tongue. Then she held a cup of water to his mouth.

"I know your uncle," Mistress Vena said in an undertone to Kie as he drank. "That stubborn old cuss is *not* going to let this go. You best tell him you'll take that manual to one of our moons if that's what he wants."

Kie dashed away her tears and straightened her shoulders. Uncle Dugs had given her so much. If this was truly what he wanted, she would do it for him, even though she'd never been to a town larger than Terkann, and Pedarth, the greatest city in the Empire, was almost six hundred miles from here.

"I swear I'll take the manual to the capital, and I will give it to someone important," she pledged, thinking of the young prince she'd met. If he was still alive, he might listen to her. And then she could hurry back here and take care of Uncle Dugs.

"N-not just take it," he gasped. "Swear you won't come back until you've convinced them to use it."

"All right. I'll convince them," she promised recklessly, even as she wondered how on earth a thirteen-year-old girl could possibly convince anyone in the Imperial government to implement skyfighting tactics outlined in a handwritten manual hundreds of years old.

"You must reach Pedarth before the Skyforce launches," her uncle added as he relaxed back against the ground and his eyes closed.

"We'll hurry. You better stay alive until we get home. Your cooking is way better than mine."

"At last, she admits the truth," he whispered with a pained smile. A moment later, his eyes flickered open. "Find Hiren

Trishop. He's my friend and head groom in the Imperial Stables now. He'll help you." He closed his eyes again and lay quiet.

She leaned forward and kissed his forehead. Then she turned to N'Tor. *Old friend, please stay with us. Please, stay with my uncle. He needs you, and N'Rah and I need you,* she said as she stroked his white jaw, but he made no reply. She choked back a sob. The old sky-steed was beyond her mental reach.

A painful lump tightening her throat, she rose to her feet. "I'm sorry to leave you shorthanded at the station," she said to Riken.

"We'll miss you on the mountain route," Riken replied matter-of-factly.

She read sympathy in his gaze, but she was glad his manner was all business. Focusing on his words helped her keep from dissolving into tears again.

"For once, I agree with Duggan," Riken added. "He knows more than anyone alive about chimerae, and the Emperor's commanders need to read what's in that manual. I promise we'll send you word about your uncle. You're a sky courier, and sky couriers look after their own."

At least Riken didn't think she was flying off on a fool's errand. That helped a little. After taking one last look at Uncle Dugs, she vaulted onto N'Rah's back. He galloped down the empty street and flung himself into the air.

They flew straight to the house so she could gather her overnight kit, food, sweet oats, and Uncle Dugs's manual. She found it in the trunk at the foot of his bed, wrapped in layers of waterproof oilcloth. As she headed for the front door, she glanced up at the chimerae trophies. The sand dragon and the lion seemed to glare at her out of their empty eye sockets, but they no longer made her shiver. Living chimerae were so much more terrifying.

After she closed up the house, she strode to a nearby dayan tree and picked a leaf. Carefully, she pressed it between the pages of the manual, and then she placed the manual in the bottom of her weatherproof mail pouch. This way, a little bit of her father would come with her. She asked N'Rah to fly her to Uncle Dugs's equipment shed, where she grabbed every triwire packet she could find. She hoped with all her heart that she and N'Rah wouldn't need to use them.

Too weary to vault into the saddle, she climbed into it instead. "Tell me when you're too tired to fly anymore, and we'll camp. In the meantime, let's both keep a sharp eye out for more chimerae."

All right. I hope the old one and your uncle will live, N'Rah said, sounding as forlorn and shaken as she felt right now.

She leaned forward and hugged N'Rah's neck. "I hope so, too."

After sitting upright again and checking to make sure the sky was clear of chimerae, she squeezed her legs. N'Rah cantered forward, and they were airborne. As she peered back at her father's orchard slipping into the distance, she wondered with a sharp pain in her heart if she'd ever see it, or her uncle, again.

Chapter Seven

Late in the afternoon on the third day after leaving Durwen, Kie and N'Rah raced across the outskirts of the great city of Pedarth. They had seen no more chimerae along the way, but the relay stations where Kie slept were abuzz with rumors of sightings.

Each night of their trip, Kie had found herself briefing worried stationmasters on the chimerae she'd seen and fought out west. After flying long and hard these past three days, she and N'Rah were about to find out if they'd made it to Pedarth before the Skyforce left for the Western Desert.

"Now we have to find this Hiren Trishop and hope he listens to us," Kie said to N'Rah, anxiety twisting her gut.

Uncle Dugs had described Pedarth many times, but the sheer size of the city still shocked her. Hundreds of Durwen towns could fit within its sprawling boundaries. The homes and shops on the outskirts weren't too imposing, but soon they were passing over avenues lined with grand houses built of white, red, and yellow marble. She was glad no one could see her jaw drop when they flew over a temple crowned with a golden dome.

I think your uncle's friend will be happy to see us, N'Rah said as he, too, peered curiously at the great city stretched out beneath them.

"I just wish he knew we were coming," Kie said, feeling smaller by the minute.

At least finding the Imperial stables wasn't hard. She and N'Rah followed a stream of skysteeds flying toward Tavalier Park, a rolling expanse of trees, grass, and lakes. The first Emperor had wanted to create a space within his city where his skysteed allies could wander and graze and feel at home. At the closer end of the park lay a series of large open-air stadiums, where the skyfighters and cadets trained. At the far end of the park rose a shining white marble castle crowned with silver-colored amartine turrets that sparkled in the late afternoon sun.

"It's hard to imagine Prince Shayn grew up in that place," Kie murmured, remembering the skinny boy she'd met in the desert and his sunburned nose. "I really hope he and his skysteed survived and made it home."

There are hundreds of skysteeds milling about in the park, N'Rah said worriedly. *The Skyforce might be mustering.*

"But they can't go off to fight until their commanders have read Uncle Dugs's manual," Kie cried, her stomach twisting even tighter. "We've got to find Trishop before it's too late!"

The Imperial stables, a series of several long, low wooden buildings, stretched along the north side of the park. N'Rah landed in the courtyard of the largest one.

A dozen grooms in green shirts hurried about, leading skysteeds. They were magnificent animals, all as big as N'Tor or bigger. After she unclipped from her flight harness, she jumped from the saddle. She was trying to decide whom to ask about Trishop when a Rosari cadet with a stubborn jaw and thick dark red eyebrows walked up to her.

"This isn't a courier station. We fly *real* skysteeds here," he said with a scornful look at N'Rah. Two of the boys standing behind him snickered.

She longed to blurt that her *real* skysteed had fought *real* chimerae, but she didn't want to waste a moment. Instead she said, "I'm looking for Hiren Trishop. I need to speak with him immediately."

A third boy with their group, a blond cadet from the Northern Isles, jerked his thumb toward the closest arched doorway. "Try in there," he told her.

"Thank you." The kindness in his blue eyes gave her the courage to ask, "Has Prince Shayn made it back to Pedarth yet?"

The mean cadet grinned. "You mean, has the Royal Runt made it back yet?"

"I mean Prince Shayn, the brave boy I watched lead a fight against five chimerae in the Western Desert four days ago," Kie said angrily. "I'd like to know if he and Jann Mackson made it back here alive."

"The prince returned yesterday morning," the blond cadet said, "but Jann didn't. We heard his skysteed was injured and had to travel more slowly." The other cadets stared at her in growing surprise.

"Poor N'Tal. I hope his wing will heal all right." Kie shook her head and started to turn away.

The sneering boy blocked her path. "Wait, you were with them? You've seen a chimera?"

"I've seen five of the monsters and fought them alongside

Prince Shayn, but since I'm *just* a courier, I won't take up any more of your precious time."

It gave her great satisfaction to step around the boy and leave him gaping.

She marched toward the arched doorway, but then she noticed a fountain along the wall of the courtyard and led N'Rah there first. He was still drinking his fill when a deep voice with a western accent addressed her.

"A cadet said there was a junior courier looking for me. I assume that would be you."

Kie looked up. An older Mosai man stood several feet away. He had a long nose and short grizzled gray hair, and he frowned at her impatiently.

"Yes, sir." Kie struggled to gather her thoughts together. "My name is Kiesandra Torsun, and my uncle Duggan said I should find you when we arrived in Pedarth. He asked me to bring his great-grandfather's manual on skyfighting chimerae to the Emperor's commanders. And Prince Shayn asked me to come to the capital as well."

The man's lips quirked in a smile, and suddenly he looked more approachable. "Duggan Torsun, eh? Now there's a name I haven't heard in a long time. I'm surprised the old devil didn't bring that manual himself."

"He c-couldn't, sir. He fought two chimerae and saved most everyone in Durwen Town, but he and N'Tor were both badly injured. He made me leave right after they were hurt, and I d-don't even know if they're still alive." Kie couldn't keep her voice from trembling.

His keen brown eyes softened, and he strode forward and placed a hand on her shoulder. "If anyone can survive a fight with chimerae, it's your uncle. We'll find you some food and a place to sleep after the Skyforce launches. You two must be worn out." Trishop turned away.

"But Uncle Dugs said I had to show that manual to the Emperor's commanders right away!"

Trishop turned back to face her. "I'm afraid that's not possible. An advance guard already left yesterday afternoon for the Western Desert, and the bulk of the Skyforce leaves for the Telawa Valley within the hour. It's going to be impossible to get anyone to look at that manual right now."

"But it might be too late by then." She had to find the right words to make him understand! "Th-those commanders should be reading that manual now, *before* they fight the chimerae. Uncle Dugs says tournament tactics and weapons won't work against them."

"I'll pray to the gods for all our sakes that your uncle's wrong," Trishop said grimly.

Kie fought to keep from bursting into tears as he turned away again. She and N'Rah had flown so hard and so long, and now they'd come too late. The head groom brought a tall, thin Mosai youth over. Like Trishop, he was dressed in a simple green shirt and brown pants. "This is Terry Goodrow, one of my assistants.

He'll look after you both." Trishop strode off before her weary brain could think of some way to convince him that they *had* to stop the Skyforce from launching.

Terry had a good-natured face and big ears. "Your skysteed is a fine fellow," he said as he glanced at N'Rah. "He's wildborn, I take it?"

"Yes, sir."

"You don't need to 'sir' me." Terry smiled. "I'm just an assistant groom, but I'd give anything to be a skyrider. Maybe tomorrow you could tell me how you found a wildborn and convinced him to bind with you. The boss said you just flew over six hundred miles."

"My skysteed did the difficult part," Kie murmured, her tired mind reeling as she followed him into a feed room. She *had* to make someone understand before it was too late. She pulled the manual from her mailbag and tugged on Terry's sleeve.

"Look, I came here to deliver this manual to the Emperor's commanders. It describes the skyfighting tactics used during the Chimera Wars. My uncle, Duggan Torsun, is convinced that skyfighters who fly right at chimerae with their lances will get themselves killed. I fought chimerae with Prince Shayn in the Western Desert, and I'm afraid my uncle may be right."

Terry stared at her in growing dismay and astonishment.

"Those monsters are fierce and incredibly fast," Kie hurried on. "Our Skyforce could be flying into a slaughter. Can you think of any way I can contact Prince Shayn?"

"I suppose your skysteed could try to find his—" Terry started to say, when outside the stables, trumpets pealed.

"That means the Skyforce is fully mustered and about to take off. Come on." Terry ran for the door. Kie followed hard on his heels, her disappointment and despair rising in a choking wave.

Terry led her to a good perch on a hay wagon where several grooms stood looking toward the park. After she climbed onto the wagon seat, Kie blinked in amazement. Hundreds of skysteeds and their riders were lined up in rows, making a living column that stretched as far as she could see up and down the green park. The afternoon sunlight shone on the skysteeds' beautiful coats— chestnut, black, brown, gray, and white—and danced on their riders' amartine mail and swords. The skysteeds stamped impatiently while they and their riders listened to a man talking at the front of the great host.

"As long as I live, this is a sight I will never forget," Terry breathed.

"They are glorious," Kie agreed. She blinked back burning tears and tried not to think about the cruel monsters that might be waiting for them out west. Thousands of people were gathered around the edges of the host. Along this side of the park, hundreds of skyfighter cadets in their maroon uniforms stood watching. The ones closest to Kie looked envious.

A man on a platform with a regal black skysteed beside him addressed the host in a deep voice that carried well over the multitude. He encouraged the skysteeds and their riders to fight bravely.

The golden circlet on his head flashed in the sun when he moved.

"Is that the Emperor?" she whispered to Terry.

"That's Emperor Chiren, all right. Two of his sons, Prince Rupen and Prince Duren, will be fighting with the Skyforce."

"May all the gods of Prekalt protect you and bring you victory!" the Emperor shouted. Beside him, the black skysteed reared up and fanned his wings.

The onlookers broke into a cheer so deafening that Kie's ears rang. She cheered along with the rest, even though she felt like she had a boulder weighing on her heart. When the clarion trumpets pealed again, the skyfighters mounted. After a second trumpet peal, the first row of skysteeds surged into a gallop, the ground shook, and they were airborne. Then the next row galloped forward, and the next, until the western sky filled with waves and waves of skysteeds.

Kie sighed as the last rows of skyfighting pairs galloped past her and leaped into the air. Surely such a great host would triumph over an army of chimerae. But the creatures she'd fought had been so agile and ferocious. A shiver went down her back, even though the afternoon sun was warm. She climbed off the wagon and went to hug N'Rah.

I tried to get us here in time for them to read your uncle's manual, N'Rah said, hanging his head.

I know you did. Kie stroked his neck sadly. *We couldn't have flown here any faster.* But maybe if she had talked faster or found the right words, she could have convinced Trishop that disaster loomed for the Imperial Skyforce. But words had never been her friends, and now, like the head groom, all she could do was pray and hope that Uncle Dugs was wrong.

CHAPTER EIGHT

WITH A HEAVY HEART, KIE followed Terry back into the stables after the Skyforce took flight. The young groom studied her for a moment and said, "You look all in. We can talk more tomorrow. Right now, let's get you settled."

He helped her bring a bucket of sweet oats sprinkled with salt to N'Rah and showed her where to stash her flight gear.

"The mess hall is that way." He pointed to a big door at the end of the corridor. "And the dorm for female grooms and sky-steed healers is at the top of those stairs. Now I'm off to see to my own chores. It's been a wild day around here."

Trying not to feel abandoned, Kie gave N'Rah a thorough rubdown in a quiet corner of the courtyard. After he finished eating his sweet oats, he wandered off to graze in the park. N'Rah looked quite at home with a dozen skysteeds he'd never met, and he didn't seem the least bit concerned that they were all a third bigger than he was.

The dinner gong rang inside. Too weary to face more strangers and their questions, she washed up in the dormitory, ate two strips of jerky from her saddlebags, and crawled under the covers of an empty bed.

Tired to the marrow of her bones, she still couldn't fall asleep. Instead, she stared up at the unfamiliar dormitory rafters over her head, her eyes dry from days of flying. She missed her home and Uncle Dugs so much her chest ached. Was he still alive? Had she come all this way for nothing? What would happen to all those beautiful skysteeds she saw today?

She often spent the night in relay station dorms, but she'd never, ever felt this alone. At last, fighting tears and irritated with herself, she dressed and grabbed her bedroll.

Dear N'Rah? Where are you?

His mind roused at her touch. *I was sleeping out in the park under a pretty bawa tree that smells like your uncle's cookies. Are you all right?*

I'm fine, but the dorm is hot and stuffy. I'd rather sleep outside tonight, by you.

It is nice and cool out here, and if you come, I would not feel quite so far from home, he admitted. *I miss the old one.*

I miss Uncle Dugs and N'Tor, too. N'Rah met her at the entrance to the park off the main courtyard, and together they walked to his pretty bawa tree that grew in a quiet green glade.

The setting sun painted the clouds overhead shades of pink and scarlet as she spread out her bedroll and climbed into it. N'Rah lipped her hair, and soon he stood hipshot beside her, sound asleep. Listening to the twilight breeze rustle the bawa needles overhead, Kie stopped worrying about what they should do on the morrow. Instead, she closed her eyes and fell into an exhausted slumber.

The next morning, Kie woke with her belly empty as a drum and her hair damp from dew. As she rolled up her bedroll, she decided that making plans should definitely wait until after she'd eaten. She left N'Rah devouring mouthfuls of grass and went to find breakfast for herself. She sat alone in a corner of the mess hall and plowed through a small mountain of scrambled eggs topped with a rich yellow cheese and some sweet fried biscuits.

She'd just finished when Terry hurried over to her. "There you are," he said, looking relieved. "The boss wants to see you in his office right away."

He turned and led her down a light, airy corridor, wide enough to accommodate two skysteeds with their wings out-stretched, and showed her into an office that smelled of hay and well-oiled leather. As she stepped inside, she couldn't help won-dering uneasily why her uncle's old friend wanted to see her.

Hiren Trishop sat at a desk piled with papers, appearing even more tired than he had last night. He took off his glasses and motioned for her to take a chair.

"Terry, you stay, too," the head groom said, and Terry sat in a worn chair next to Kie's. "When I should have been sleeping, I spent a lot of time last night thinking about you and your uncle's manual," Trishop said abruptly. "Terry told me you fought chi-merae out in the Western Desert with Prince Shayn."

"Yes, sir."

"I'd like you to tell me what happened out there. I want to know what our skyfighters and their skysteeds are about to face."

"All right, sir." Intimidated by his steady gaze, she did her best to describe what she'd seen and experienced during that brief, terrifying fight. Whenever she faltered, he prompted her, until she had told him everything.

By the end of her account, she felt comfortable enough to add, "Sir, I love N'Tor, but N'Rah can fly circles around him when we practice skyfighting drills with Uncle Dugs, and as fast as N'Rah is, we barely survived that fight."

Trishop sighed, his face grim. "Your account squares with what Captain Nerone said at a briefing I attended. I respect our current skysteeds, but over the years, we've bred them to become stronger, not faster, and that may prove to have been a terrible mistake."

"Now that the Skyforce has launched," Kie said, looking down at her hands in her lap, "I'm thinking I should just head home and take care of my uncle and N'Tor. That is, if they're even still alive." Just saying that terrible possibility aloud made her tremble.

"But you promised your uncle that you'd stay in Pedarth until you made people understand how important that manual is," he reminded her sternly.

"Who is going to listen to a courier girl from nowhere?" Kie looked up from her hands. "I promised I'd try to make them listen, but now that I've seen Pedarth, I realize how stupid I was. I matter even less here than I did back in Durwen Town."

"By your own account, you are a junior courier who killed two chimerae, you're Duggan Torsun's niece, and you are a skyrider. All of those mean you matter wherever you go."

"But it's too late for me or that old manual to make any difference."

"I'm afraid this war isn't going to be won in a single battle," he said heavily. "The first one lasted almost a generation. If your uncle is right, and the Skyforce does take serious losses, we are going to need to know what's in that manual more than ever, and we're going to need young skyfighters like you"—he pointed a finger at her—"who can demonstrate the tactics we used three hundred years ago to beat these monsters."

Kie drew in a deep breath. She wasn't a skyfighter, and she *so* wanted to go home and take care of her uncle and her orchard. But a promise was a promise. She sat up straighter in her chair.

"Then can *you* think of a way I can get my uncle's manual to the Emperor's commanders?" she asked the head groom.

Trishop got to his feet and began to pace. "Right now, I'm not sure they'd read it or listen to you. They're an arrogant bunch, and from what I heard at that briefing, they're convinced they can whip an army of chimerae in a few days."

"But what if they're wrong and my uncle is right? Couldn't you show his manual to somebody important?"

Trishop shook his head. "It wouldn't do any good. I may be the head of these stables, but I'm still just a Mosai groom to them, and noble Rosari only listen to other noble Rosari."

Kie blinked at the anger and bitterness in his tone.

The head groom stopped in his tracks. "But didn't you say Prince Shayn told you to come to Pedarth and find him?"

"He did, and I think he meant it."

"Then the prince is your best bet," Trishop said, returning to his seat. "He's a bit flighty, but the boy looks after his skysteed properly."

Trishop paused and stared at her for so long, Kie blushed and wished she'd taken time to re-braid her hair this morning. "We're going to be shorthanded with so many healers and grooms gone off to support the Skyforce. If you can prove you're useful, you may stay here until you've had a chance to talk with Prince Shayn."

Still wishing he would just take the manual off her hands, Kie struggled to hide her disappointment. "Thank you, sir. Sometime today, may I fly to Central Relay and check if they've any news of my uncle and N'Tor?"

"You can go on your noon break, and let me know if you find out how they're doing. Terry, show Kie how we do things around here."

Terry got to his feet. Kie tried not to feel wistful as she followed him out the door. It would have been nice to talk more to someone who knew Uncle Dugs. All at once, she missed him and N'Tor and her quiet house and her dayan trees so much, her chest tightened up again.

Terry sent her an apologetic glance as they walked down the corridor. "He's not usually that abrupt, but he loves every skysteed in this city, and he's worried. We're all worried right now."

Kie forced herself to smile. "Right. So what are we supposed to do this morning?"

"Most mornings, I treat the skysteeds who are too old for skyfighting. We call them the senior herd. Much like their riders, the seniors can be cranky and particular, but they seem to like me well enough."

That didn't surprise her. Terry had a nice, quiet way about him. She followed him to another room that smelled like a healer's shop, where he loaded up a basket with liniments and bandages. He gave her a basket full of grooming implements and led her outside to the park. Two groups of older skysteeds waited patiently in two long lines.

Terry set his basket down near the closer line. "The skysteeds go to the real healers over there if they're truly sick. They come to my station when something hurts but isn't too serious. The trick is figuring out what's wrong with them."

"Why don't they tell their riders, and their riders tell you?" Kie asked.

"Because their riders are busy being nobles and going off to balls and banquets," Terry replied, "and even if they were here, some of them can't communicate with their skysteeds that well."

"Really? I understand everything N'Rah wants, sometimes almost too well," she said with chagrin, thinking of all the times he'd encouraged her to be friendlier and more outgoing.

"Then in my experience, you would be the exception," Terry said. He touched his right hand to his left shoulder and bowed to the first skysteed in line. "So, N'Sorle, what is bothering you today, sir?"

The old brown skysteed nosed his right leg.

"Ah, I see the cut," Terry said. "We will get that cleaned up and put some salve on it right away."

Determined to prove she could be useful, Kie approached the second skysteed in line, a plump old chestnut mare with feathery white stockings. Kie bowed and then said aloud, "May I help you?"

The old mare tossed her head up and down, which Kie fervently hoped meant yes.

"Well, then, could you please show me what hurts?"

The mare looked at her left hind leg and lifted her hoof.

"All right," Kie said, starting to appreciate her bond with N'Rah, which made it so easy for them to understand each other. "So, I'm guessing you might have a stone in your hoof?"

Kie grabbed a hoof pick from the grooming basket and reached for the mare's leg. The moment she picked up the hoof, Kie felt a strange tingle flow from her hand throughout her entire body to the base of her neck. The next instant, she heard someone saying crossly, *I do not have a stone in my hoof. I wish this new girl would hurry up and get those sharp burrs out of my fetlock hair.*

Startled, Kie dropped the mare's hind leg.

Oh dear, the voice came again, *she may be polite, but I am afraid this one is going to be terribly clumsy.* The old mare let go of a gusty sigh.

She had to be hearing the mare's thoughts, Kie realized with amazement.

I'm not usually clumsy, Kie thought back at her indignantly. *You startled me, is all. I would be happy to pick the burrs out of your fetlock feathers for you. Your feathers are quite pretty, by the way.*

The old mare snorted and turned her head to peer at her.

Thank you for the compliment, but by the High Valley, what are you doing in my head, young one?

I'm not sure. I've only ever been able to talk to my own skysteed, and my uncle's skysteed.

But this is remarkable. I can understand you as well as my own human. How is this possible?

I don't know. Kie glanced over and saw Terry was watching her and looking concerned. *Please, ma'am, may I clean your feathers for you now?*

Yes, yes, get on with it. But I have never heard of a skyrider being able to mindspeak with more than one skysteed. You are a very odd girl.

I've heard that before, Kie said bitterly, thinking of her disastrous years at Durwen's school. She picked up the mare's hoof and began plucking the burrs from her fetlock feathers.

Now, now, I did not mean to offend, the old mare said. Kie heard nothing more from her until she put the skysteed's foot down again.

Thank you, the chestnut said. *You do have gentle hands. My name is N'Talley, by the way.*

My name is Kiesandra, Kie said and bowed to the old mare again. N'Talley trotted away, but Kie felt the mare's gaze on her as she approached the next skysteed in line. A very old appaloosa stallion with gold spots scattered across his rump, he had brown circles about his eyes that looked like spectacles.

She bowed and asked if he could show her what hurt. In reply, the old skysteed opened his mouth. Gently, she cupped his muzzle, intending to get a better look at his teeth. The moment she touched him, though, that strange tingling sensation raced through her body again.

When it vanished, she heard someone say clear as anything, *I hope this youngling figures out I need my teeth filed. Those two molars cutting into my gums hurt.*

Kie dropped her hands and stepped back, her heart racing. It was happening again! She could understand this skysteed, too!

Excuse me, sir, but did I hear you correctly? Would you like your teeth filed?

The appaloosa snorted and backed up a step. *Is that you in my mind, youngling?*

Yes, sir. I'm sorry to startle you.

You did it again! N'Talley trotted back over, swishing her tail with her ears pricked.

Please, don't make a fuss, Kie told her. *I really don't want the other humans to know that I can talk to you.*

Moments later, N'Rah landed beside her and nuzzled her shoulder. *Something is upsetting you.*

"Is everything all right over there?" Terry called to her.

Kie's cheeks heated. It had to look very peculiar, two old skysteeds and her own young one peering at her so intently. "Um, everything's fine. I'm pretty sure this gentleman needs his back molars floated."

N'Rah, I can mindspeak with both N'Talley and this appaloosa here, she told her friend quickly. Then she turned to the old skysteed. *I'm sorry, sir. My name is Kie, but I don't know your name yet.*

My name is N'Rile, the old appaloosa introduced himself. *But this is a wondrous thing, a human who can mindspeak with more than one skysteed.*

I think it must have something to do with my touching you, Kie admitted. *I've never touched any skysteed except my own and my uncle's before.*

I have heard of this, N'Rile said thoughtfully. *My human used to share all the best stories his grandmother told him when he was young. Sian, the young mage who helped Prince Isen create the Great Alliance, could talk to every skysteed. She gained that ability as a result of the Great Binding magic she worked that made it possible for skysteeds and humans to understand each other.*

Well, I've never heard of such a thing, Kie said to all three skysteeds, trying to hide her growing consternation as Terry walked up with a file, *and I'm sure I'm nothing like that mage, because I can't do magic and I'm not anyone special.* Because she'd been considered different and odd most of her life, she did *not* need another reason for people to see her that way.

"Our seniors have never been so fascinated with a new groom before," Terry said, looking puzzled as he set to work filing N'Rile's teeth.

"Maybe I smell different, like the frontier, to them," Kie said weakly and hurried to treat the third skysteed in the line. Much younger than the others, she was a beautiful golden chestnut mare with a long flaxen mane and sad eyes. With her head, she indicated she had a sore front hoof. Kie touched her and introduced herself to the surprised skysteed, who said her name was N'Seella. Then Kie cleaned her hoof, but she couldn't find any stones in it.

Oh, it feels much better now, N'Seella assured her. *But my right hind leg is a little sore today. Perhaps some liniment would help it.*

Kie examined the sore leg but couldn't find any heat or swelling.

"I don't think there's anything wrong with that young mare," she whispered to Terry when she went to fetch some liniment from his basket.

"There isn't, except neglect. Her skyrider hardly ever visits her, and N'Seella's lonely. She often comes to sick call just to get some attention."

"That's so sad." Shaking her head, Kie hurried back to the young mare and rubbed liniment into the hind leg, which she suspected wasn't sore at all.

If you come back when I've finished my work tonight, Kie said casually to N'Seella, *I would be happy to plait blue ribbons into your mane. I saw some of the other young mares wearing them, and I think that color would look very pretty on you.*

It has been ages since I had my mane braided. I will come back tonight. Looking happier, N'Seella trotted off, her limp miraculously healed.

By midmorning, Terry and Kie had finished treating all the skysteeds in their line. Kie wiped her sweaty forehead as they walked to the stable well. Green Pedarth was just as hot as the frontier, but way more humid.

"That went faster than usual," the young groom said as they took turns drinking from the well bucket. "You have a knack for this. I was sure that last senior had a bad tooth, but you were right. He did have a cyst on the underside of his jaw."

It certainly made it easier when the skysteeds could tell her what was wrong with them. Kie smiled at Terry, relieved that he was pleased with her work. Still, what could it mean that she could talk to so many skysteeds?

As she glanced toward the park, she noticed many of the senior herd had gathered under a massive bawa tree, with N'Rile and N'Talley at their center. Kie couldn't shake the uneasy feeling they were talking about her. When she saw a flash of gold and cedar, she realized N'Rah must be there, too.

N'Rah, PLEASE ask them not to tell their riders that I can communicate with their skysteeds. One's bond with one's skysteed is a very personal thing. Some skyriders might resent me.

And I know you do not like people talking about you, he replied. *I will do my best, but the old ones say it is amazing and important that you can speak to so many skysteeds, and I think it is amazing, too.*

But I don't want to be amazing, or important, she thought to herself. *I just want to go home and look after Uncle Dugs and N'Tor.* If she still had an uncle, and his skysteed was still alive. She swallowed past the sudden tightness in her throat. The rest of the morning seemed to crawl by as she helped Terry tidy several tack rooms left in disarray by the departing Skyforce riders.

As they worked, Terry asked her how she had come to bind with N'Rah. Glad to be distracted from worrying about Uncle Dugs, she told Terry all about the summer she'd spent camping out in the Torgaresh, trying to find a skysteed willing to bind with her. She'd spent day after day climbing the grassy shoulders of the high peaks where she saw skysteeds frisking and grazing. Every time she drew close, the shy creatures flew away. Just when she was going to give up and go home, N'Rah had landed by her campsite.

"He was young, and he looked so curious as he watched me. I talked myself hoarse telling him all the reasons why I'd make him a fine skyrider. Then, he walked up and rubbed his head against my shoulder, and all at once I could hear his words in my mind, saying he thought we should recite the Binding Oath together. We did," she said, her voice growing husky at the memory, "and we've been together ever since."

"That does it," Terry said, his homely face ablaze with determination. "As soon as I save up enough money to pay my way, I'm going to the Torgaresh. I've always wanted to be a skyrider, but there's no way I can afford one of the big skysteeds they auction off here. I figure I'm skinny enough," he said with a wry look down at his lanky frame. "A smaller skysteed should be able to carry me."

"The wildborn may be small, but they're also incredibly strong," Kie reassured him.

When they finished that tack room, Terry headed toward the mess hall, declaring it was lunchtime.

"Then I'm off to see if there's any news from home for me at Central Relay," Kie said.

"You can't go without eating something." Terry hurried into the busy mess hall and came back with a sausage roll wrapped in a napkin. "Here, take this, and I hope you get good news. Be back in an hour if you can."

"Thanks," she called over her shoulder as she ran to find her flight harness.

Soon she and N'Rah were flying toward the eastern end of the park and the sprawling complex of offices, stables, and dormitories that comprised Central Relay. The heart and brain of Prekalt's great courier system, Central Relay was surrounded by four large green landing fields. A big blue windsock embroidered with a golden skysteed in flight—the sigil of all couriers—flew from a tall post in the center of each field.

A rush of pride briefly distracted Kie from her concern for Uncle Dugs when she saw dozens of couriers and their skysteeds making precise landings and takeoffs into the wind on those fields. Other couriers hurried in and out of the building with their precious mailbags while more synced mail handoffs a thousand feet above the huge station.

"You know, it was incredible to see the Skyforce take flight, but watching this is even more wonderful," Kie said to N'Rah.

Yes, but there are so many courier pairs coming and going, he said, sounding a little intimidated.

She leaned forward to give him a reassuring pat. "Maybe there's more mail than usual with everyone so scared about the chimerae." Now, if only a courier coming east from Durwen had brought her news.

N'Rah landed in a quiet spot close to a big building sided with elegant light yellow marble. She smiled when she spotted the motto of the Courier Service chiseled into the stone arch over its massive door. *Through storm and heat, and the darkness of the night, we fly and bind the empire together.*

Inside, she found a huge room with a high wooden counter dividing the public from the couriers and clerks hurrying about behind it. Customers stood in several lines before that counter. Kie had learned about this place during her training. Letters from all corners of the Empire were sorted here in Pedarth, rerouted, and sent out again. In this room alone, hundreds of sorting racks lined the walls.

It took her a bit to puzzle out the signs, but eventually Kie found the right line for individuals who wanted to pick up letters coming in from the west. Her innards wound tighter and tighter as she waited. The people waiting all around her looked worried, too.

When she reached the front of the line, her mouth was so dry that she had to cough before she managed to croak, "Do you have any letters or messages for Junior Courier Kiesandra Torsun?"

"Let me check," the middle-aged Mosai woman said briskly.

Behind her, an apprentice courier with a mail pouch slung over her shoulder stopped dead in her tracks. "Did you say Kie-sandra Torsun?" she asked in a carrying voice. "Are you *the* Kie Torsun of Durwen Town?"

An abrupt silence fell over the bustling sorting room. Most of the courier staff behind the counter were staring at her! Kie's heart skipped a beat. Had they heard bad news about Uncle Dugs and his valiant N'Tor?

CHAPTER NINE

HER FACE ON FIRE, KIE stared back at the girl. Why were they all looking at her? Had she done something wrong? If there was bad news about Uncle Dugs, how could these people possibly know it? Letters were supposed to be private, but maybe Riken had passed along a verbal message through his fellow stationmasters.

Desperately hoping she wasn't about to hear something terrible about her uncle and his skysteed, Kie lifted her chin. "Yes, I'm Kiesandra Torsun. Is there a problem?" she asked the apprentice courier.

"There's no problem," the girl replied with a grin. "We just want to thank you for giving us something to boast about to sky-fighters. They lord it over us something awful here in Pedarth." She raised her hands and began to clap, and the rest of the staff joined her.

"I d-don't understand," Kie said to the older clerk, who beamed at her now. "Why are they all cheering?"

"Because, according to Prince Shayn and Junior Courier Topar Singu, you and your skysteed managed to kill two chimerae all by yourself out in the Western Desert."

"But Junior Courier Singu killed a chimera, too. He saved my life out there, and the life of my skysteed."

"Yes, and in doing so, you've both brought honor to our service, dear. We're proud that our couriers have already struck a blow against those awful monsters. Now, here's your letter. I see it came with this note summarizing a message relayed through the stationmasters along the route. They said your uncle is holding steady so far, and his skysteed is a little better."

"Thank you. Oh, thank you so much!" Her eyes brimmed with tears she was *not* going to shed in front of all these strangers. Kie almost snatched the letter from the clerk's hand. Ignoring people who were calling to her, she fled outside.

Then she heard a voice behind her with a lilting Ledari accent that she couldn't ignore.

"Hey, Kie, wait up!"

She spun about, amazed to see Topar striding toward her. It was wonderful to see a familiar face after encountering so many unfamiliar ones over the past few days. She wanted to hug him, but her father and uncle weren't huggers. The Ledari were affectionate people, though, and he quickly embraced her and smiled.

"Whatever are you doing in Pedarth?" she asked.

"Prince Shayn got me transferred here so I could teach the Emperor's commanders how to use a botan and show them how desert couriers fight grytocs. So far, though, I haven't heard a word from him."

"But what about your mother and your little brothers and sisters? Are they all right? I'm so sorry I didn't have a chance to ask about them before I flew off that day." Topar's home station was Terkann Relay, and she knew his mother lived in the town.

"Lucky for us, our house is close to the old shelters. She got all the littles under cover in time. After the attack was over, my uncle came and fetched them out to the desert. Our clan is staying near caves where they can hide if the chimerae come. But I know you want to find out about your uncle. Let's sit in the shade, read your letter, and then we'll talk."

"All right." As they sat under an ewa tree with massive fronds, Kie opened the letter and pretended to skim it. Although she longed to know exactly what it said, she would take her time deciphering it later. Reading a printed book was hard enough because individual letters always seemed to trick her eyes and mix themselves up. Reading a letter like this, written in cursive, was ten times harder. Riken knew about her challenges with reading, which is why he must have insisted that a verbal message be sent to her along with the written one, bless his heart.

N'Meary is here, N'Rah said to her joyfully. *It is very good to see her.*

Kie grinned to herself. She'd always guessed N'Rah might be sweet on Topar's pretty mare. *Topar found me. I'm talking with him now,* she sent back.

"So what do they have you doing here?" she asked Topar.

"Today I've been sorting letters, which is *the* most boring job ever," Topar said, making a face that made her laugh. "But I'm glad to be doing something to help the service. It seems like everyone in the Empire is making sure their families are safe with the threat of a chimerae invasion looming."

"Have you heard anything? Are the chimerae coming?"

"No one knows for sure," Topar replied soberly. "After that

first attack on Terkann and Durwen, there've been no credible sightings."

"There weren't supposed to be any chimerae left. Some horrible mage must be creating them again." Central Relay had been built on the highest ground in the city, which meant Kie could see out over houses and shops that stretched to the horizon in every direction. "Can you imagine if the chimerae get past the Skyforce? There are so many people here." She rubbed her arms against a sudden chill.

"I know," Topar said. "I want to be a part of the fight if they do reach Pedarth. After my shift, I'm going to watch how real skyfighters train, and maybe you and I could practice together. I'd like to learn how to throw a triwire."

Kie stared at him in surprise. Topar had always seemed so carefree. Now he looked stern and resolute, and years older. It must have been terrible, what he saw that day in Terkann.

"And you could teach me how to use a botan," she said slowly.

He nodded. "I'll bring one and come find you at the stables later. I better get back to sorting letters."

"And I have to get back to sorting tack."

After Topar strode away, Kie pulled her own letter out again. Fortunately, Mistress Vena, Durwen's healer, had neat handwriting. There were still several words Kie couldn't puzzle out quickly, but the gist of the letter was clear enough. Uncle Dugs wasn't out of danger, but he wasn't getting worse, and N'Tor appeared to be holding his own.

As they flew back to the stables, Kie told N'Rah about the message and the letter. Her afternoon work went more swiftly. Just knowing Uncle Dugs had survived that first night after he'd been injured was a relief, and she prayed that he and N'Tor would keep fighting to stay alive.

An hour before supper, her stable shift ended. Topar and N'Meary showed up soon after that, and together they flew to the Skyforce Academy's practice grounds.

Leaving their skysteeds talking under a tree, they climbed up into a big open-air stadium, where two cadets in padded jackets and their skysteeds flew at each other in mock combat. Several of their classmates and a man in a maroon-and-gray Skyforce uniform watched them. A big cheer went up when the cadet on a charcoal-colored skysteed succeeded in knocking the other off with a long lance.

"That's fun to watch, but I'm not sure what it has to do with fighting chimerae," Topar said with a frown. "If you tried to charge the creatures we fought, they'd just swipe a spear away with their claws."

"And then they'd bite you with their poisonous fangs or crush you with their tail," Kie said, thinking of Uncle Dugs and N'Tor again.

When the cadets and their instructor left, Topar boldly walked down the stadium steps, jumped over a low railing, and made straight for the covered racks where the cadets had stored their practice gear.

This area is probably reserved for skyfighters and skyfighter cadets. I hope no one sees us, Kie said to N'Rah. Right after she climbed over the railing, the skysteeds landed nearby and trotted after Topar, their ears pricked.

We want to see the skyfighing equipment, too, N'Rah told her.

Thanks to their bright coats and wings, N'Meary and N'Rah were hardly inconspicuous. With a sigh, Kie walked over to where Topar and their skysteeds were studying the practice gear.

Topar picked up one of the wooden shields the cadets had been using. "This thing must weigh ten pounds," he said, shaking his head.

"These practice spears are awfully heavy, too," Kie said as she struggled to lift one from the rack.

"Imagine how much more weight their skysteeds have to carry when a skyfighter wears amartine mail," Topar said. "Amartine may be the lightest, strongest metal we have, but I wager a full suit of the stuff weighs a good fifteen pounds."

"Twenty pounds, actually, which is why only true skysteeds are big and strong enough to carry true skyfighters," a snide male voice broke in on their conversation.

Kie stiffened. She recognized that voice. When she turned around, sure enough, the same Rosari cadet who had been so rude to her yesterday stood there with three of his friends at his back.

"We meet again, courier girl who claims to be a friend of the Royal Runt. My name is Ruden Mirsar, and you have a knack for turning up in places you aren't wanted." He turned to one of his friends. "Go fetch the captain of the watch and tell him we caught two trespassers."

With a sinking heart, she watched the boy sprint away. She and Topar were in big trouble now.

Kie lifted her chin. "I never claimed to be Prince Shayn's friend. But I did meet him five days ago out in the Western Desert, and I did help him fight chimerae. Junior Courier Topar here and his skysteed killed one with a botan."

Ruden put his hands on his hips. "I think you're lying about fighting those chimerae, too."

"She isn't." Topar's eyes narrowed. "She killed two all by herself. The prince saw her do it."

"Now I know you both are liars. There's no way you and your scrawny little skysteeds could have killed three chimerae."

Topar tensed.

"You'd better apologize," Kie said quickly, anger pumping through her veins. "Claiming he's lying is one of the greatest insults you can deal a Ledari, plus you disrespected our skysteeds."

"Apologize to a lying Ledari courier?" Ruden sneered. "I don't think so."

Topar launched himself at the cadet, and the two boys went down in tangle of arms and legs. N'Meary neighed in distress and pawed the ground.

"He'll be all right," Kie tried to reassure the upset mare. She'd seen Topar fight at Terkann Relay when some Ledari kids had taunted him about his green eyes. He was fast and quick, and his clan were excellent wrestlers. Sure enough, shortly Topar had Ruden pinned.

"Apologize to Kie, to me, and most of all, to our skysteeds," Topar said coldly.

"A little help here?" Ruden gasped to his friends. The two remaining cadets jumped on top of Topar and started punching him. Three against one wasn't fair! Kie darted forward and grabbed the closest boy by his hair and his belt. Even though she was small, working in the orchard had strengthened her muscles, and she managed to drag the surprised cadet off Topar.

His face beet red, the boy rolled to his feet and started toward her. Kie gulped and raised her fists. This cadet was *way* bigger than she was. An instant later, N'Rah reared beside her, neighing in anger.

"WHAT is going on here?" a woman in a Skyforce uniform bellowed as she strode across the stadium. "Cadets, you will cease fighting this instant!"

Kie sucked in a breath. She and Topar were in even bigger trouble now. The cadets all froze, and the boy advancing on Kie snapped to attention. The other boy climbed off Topar and joined him. Reluctantly, Topar let Ruden go. The cadet got to his feet and stood at attention beside his friends.

"What is the meaning of this?" the Rosari captain asked, glaring at her cadets. "Our Empire is about to be at war, and I find cadets fighting couriers right here on our practice grounds. Explain yourselves."

"We found them messing around with the practice gear, Captain," Ruden said with righteous indignation. "We thought it our duty to stop them."

"And what do you have to say for your—" The captain turned to face Kie and Topar, and for the first time, she got a good look at them both. Her angry expression changed to surprised amusement. "Well, hello again, Topar Singu and Kiesandra Torsun. I knew your skysteeds looked familiar. I'm glad to see you both."

Kie blinked in astonishment. It was Captain Nerone! "Captain, it's good to see you, too," she said fervently. "D-did your commander make it?"

"I'm afraid he died from that sand dragon bite before we reached the Mrai oasis."

"I'm so sorry."

"I am, too," the captain said, her voice husky. "He was a good man. So, what are you doing in Pedarth?"

"Prince Shayn asked me to come"—Kie couldn't resist shooting Ruden a triumphant look—"and I've brought my uncle's manual on skyfighting with me. My uncle is . . . passionate about the ancient ways of fighting chimerae. That's why I had triwires with me that day out in the Western Desert."

"I thank the gods that you did. You and your triwires," she said to Kie, then turned to Topar, "and you and your botan saved our hides that day."

Kie grinned at Topar. Ruden and his friends were looking more and more uncomfortable by the moment.

"I'm here," Topar said, "because the prince asked me to come to Pedarth and show Skyforce commanders how to use a botan, but so far, no one except Kie here has shown any interest."

"Then we have something in common," the captain said.

"Prince Shayn had me transferred here to brief Skyforce commanders on our fight with the chimerae. I did give one short briefing on how fast and fierce the creatures were, but our officers seem quite sure they already know how to fight them."

"I'm sorry if we trespassed," Kie said, "but we thought that we should keep practicing fighting chimerae. If any of them get past the Skyforce, we want to be ready to help defend Pedarth."

"That's a good idea," Captain Nerone said, and relief flowed through Kie. She and Topar weren't in such terrible trouble after all.

"As of right now," the woman continued briskly, "you both have my permission to come early or late in the day and practice all you wish. You can use the old stadium next to this one. I'm afraid the time could be coming when we'll need every skyrider who can fly to defend the Empire."

She turned back to face her cadets. "So, who started this fight?"

The cadets stared straight ahead and didn't say a word. The captain sighed and looked at Kie and Topar. "Would you two care to tell me what happened?"

Kie crossed her arms and didn't speak, and Topar didn't either. This was between them and the cadets. Looking bored, the captain examined her fingernails.

"You know, I have all night, and the Academy cook and I go way back. I'll get a good, hot meal whenever I leave here. You all, however, are going to miss your dinners if we stay out here much longer."

Kie's stomach rumbled. It seemed like *ages* since she'd eaten that one sausage roll. "Ruden can say what he likes about us," she blurted, "but he insulted our skysteeds."

The captain turned on Ruden. "Is this true?" she asked him tightly. The cadet nodded once, his face pale.

"Then you will receive three demerits for breaking one of the fundamental rules of the Great Alliance we made with the skysteeds three hundred years ago—to treat them all, young and old, with courtesy. You will apologize to both Kie and Topar here and their skysteeds."

"I apologize for calling you liars and for calling your skysteeds small and scrawny." Somehow, the way Ruden said it, his apology still sounded like an insult.

"We will accept your apology in the spirit it was offered," Topar said, his green eyes flashing.

"Cadets, these two skysteeds may be small compared to your own," Captain Nerone said, "but the way they flew out in the Western Desert that day was a marvel. All right, the three of you are dismissed." Then she turned to greet N'Rah and N'Meary.

Ruden sent Kie and Topar a furious glare before he stalked away.

"Your wildborn skysteeds do have beautiful conformation," the captain said. "It's a shame they can't carry more weight, but they certainly were effective against those chimerae." She turned away from the skysteeds to look at Kie and Topar.

"I want you both to keep practicing with your triwires and botans, and hopefully I can get someone higher in rank to pay attention to what you can do with those weapons."

They thanked the captain, and she strode off across the stadium.

Kie turned to Topar. "Are you all right?" she asked worriedly. "Those boys looked like they were punching you *hard.*"

"I'll be a little sore tomorrow, but they don't hit nearly as hard as my Ledari cousins do when we fight for fun. Thanks for helping me out, by the way." Topar smiled at her, his green eyes warm.

Kie smiled back, suddenly breathless. Many of the courier girls at Durwen Relay flirted with Topar and sighed over his looks. For the first time, she noticed that his eyes were the same deep green as bawa tree needles. But why on earth was she noticing the color of his eyes? Maybe it was the strangeness of being here in Pedarth. It kept throwing her off balance.

Since it was too late to practice, Topar suggested they meet at the old stadium tomorrow after supper. N'Rah flew her back to the stables, and Kie slipped into the mess hall in time to get a bowl of lamb stew that tasted like heaven. She had just started on her dinner and was dreaming about falling into her blankets when N'Rah reached out to her.

I am talking to a nice mare out here in the park, named N'Seella, who is very excited about you braiding her mane tonight.

Kie sighed. So much for falling into bed.

Please tell her to meet me in the central courtyard in a few minutes. Kie downed her stew and put a roll in her pocket for later. She stopped by one of the grooming rooms and picked up some combs and blue ribbons.

N'Rah and N'Seella were waiting for her in the courtyard. As the twilight sky turned dusky lavender and the relentless heat of the day began to ease, she untangled the mare's beautiful mane. While Kie worked, N'Rah kept N'Seella entertained with stories of their more exciting courier runs.

Your work sounds wonderful. I would so like to be useful, but all I do is wander around gossiping with the other young mares. N'Seella stamped her foot.

"Can't you train for skyfighting?" Kie asked her.

My human does not want to train to skyfight anymore. Sometimes, I do not think she even likes me, N'Seella admitted, her dark eyes so sad that an ache built in Kie's chest.

Then she is a very stupid, selfish girl, Kie longed to tell her, but instead she said only, "I am sure she loves you."

Kie proceeded to plait blue ribbons into N'Seella's mane, working around the green-and-gold braid the mare already had. She was almost done when a shrill voice behind her demanded, "*Who* are you, and who said you could touch *my* skysteed?"

CHAPTER TEN

STARTLED, KIE WHIRLED AROUND. A Rosari girl stood there wearing a shining emerald-green dress embroidered with gold flowers. Kie had never seen anything like that gown, but she guessed it probably cost more than a year of her wages. With her long auburn hair and arching dark eyebrows, the girl would have been very pretty, except for the angry, petulant set to her mouth.

"I'm braiding N'Seella's mane because I thought she'd enjoy it," Kie replied. "She seemed so sad when she came to senior sick call this morning."

"What was she doing at sick call? No one told me she was sick," the girl said imperiously.

"The groom I worked with said N'Seella often comes to sick call, just to get some attention."

"That's ridiculous. N'Seella gets plenty of attention. She has her own personal groom to look after her."

Kie remembered what Terry had said this morning about the nobility and the way they spent their time. Her anger began to kindle. This sweet, lonely skysteed deserved so much better.

"I'm not sure where her groom is," Kie retorted, "but what N'Seella really needs is for you go to a few less balls and parties and spend more time with her."

The girl's eyes widened and her cheeks flushed. Many Rosari

had freckles on their cheeks, and hers stood out like angry red spots now. "How *dare* you talk to me that way! Do you have any idea who I am?"

"Actually, I don't," Kie retorted, fury burning through her, "and I don't care. I just know that you are a skyrider and your first duty is to the skysteed who agreed to bind with you."

"I am *so* going to get you fired. What is your name, groom?"

"Kiesandra Torsun," Kie said defiantly, but her stomach churned. What if this girl could get her dismissed? She needed work and a place to stay until she found some way to convince the Emperor's commanders to read Uncle Dugs's manual. If she lost her job here, she could only pray they would take her on at Central Relay.

"I'm going to find the head groom and make sure he fires you this very night." The girl turned on her heel and stalked away. Neighing angrily, N'Seella blocked her path.

The two stared at each other, obviously using mindspeech, but since N'Seella wasn't aiming her thoughts at Kie, she couldn't pick up the mare's words. It must have been something the girl didn't want to hear, though, because moments later, she burst into tears and went storming from the courtyard.

Kie let go of a shaky sigh. N'Rah trotted over and nuzzled her comfortingly.

"And I thought I had a temper," she said aloud to both skysteeds.

"So you do take after your uncle," a deep voice commented.

Startled, Kie glanced around. Trishop stood in a nearby doorway, watching her, his arms crossed. "You've been so quiet, I was starting to wonder if you truly were related to the Duggan Torsun I know."

"D-did you hear all that?"

"Enough of it," he replied. He uncrossed his arms and came to stand beside her.

"C-can she make you fire me?" Anxiously, she searched Trishop's impassive face. How angry was he?

"Well, that was Princess Halla, the Emperor's one and only daughter. She can make trouble for you, but I'm certainly not going to dismiss you unless his Supreme Highness orders me to. I've been meaning to take the princess to task for neglecting N'Seella, but you saved me the effort."

"Oh dear," Kie said. That awful, spoiled girl was Prince Shayn's sister? He'd seemed so nice and unpretentious. Wearily, she focused her attention back on the head groom.

"I talked with Terry," Trishop was saying. "He's pleased with your work, and I'm glad to hear your uncle is holding on. Now, finish up N'Seella's mane and get some sleep. We've plenty more for you to do around here tomorrow."

"Yes, sir," Kie said. At least for now, she still had a job and a place to stay. Relieved, she finished the last few braids and told N'Seella when she was done.

The mare looked at her solemnly. *Thank you for braiding my mane. I apologize for my human's actions. I told her she should not get you in trouble.*

"Oh, N'Seella, you aren't responsible for your human."

I love her very much, but she can be difficult. She is so unhappy these days and so frightened for her brothers.

Kie remembered that Terry had said two of the Emperor's sons were with the Skyforce that soon might be fighting an army of chimerae.

"I'm sure I will be fine," she said to the mare, careful to hide her worry over what Princess Halla might say to her father. "Please come see me whenever you want."

After saying good night to the skysteeds, Kie headed for the girls' dormitory. Worn out from the eventful day, she took a shower and fell into her bed.

At breakfast, she sat by herself again. Terry came to find her just as she finished up. "The boss wants you to work over in the Academy stables today."

"All right," Kie replied, trying to swallow her disappointment. She had been looking forward to helping him with the senior herd again.

Terry tugged at one of his ears, and for once he wasn't smiling. "Kie, you should know that some of those cadets can be pretty arrogant. Most of us grooms are used to them, but couriers are accustomed to being treated with more respect. Just . . . keep your head down, okay?"

"And keep my mouth shut?"

"Yeah, something like that."

"Shouldn't be a problem. I don't talk much anyway."

"I noticed." Terry grinned at her. "Well, good luck. Dessie here is going to walk you over."

For the first time, she noticed the Mosai girl standing at Terry's elbow. A tall, strong-looking girl with beautiful dark brown eyes and a long, thick braid, Dessie smiled at her warmly. Like Terry, she appeared be a few years older than Kie. As they strode toward the Academy end of the stables, Dessie asked her where she was from.

"From near Durwen Town, on the western frontier."

"Never heard of it, but I'm from a flyspeck of a settlement east of nowhere that no one's ever heard of, either."

"How did you come to be working here?" Kie asked.

"Well, when I was little, I dreamed of binding with a wildborn skysteed, but I kept growing and growing, and it became clear that the only skysteed that could carry me would be the large domesticated type, and there was no way my family could afford one of those. So, I packed up my things and came to the capital, and here I am. At least I get to take care of skysteeds every day."

"Why don't the cadets groom their own skysteeds?" Kie asked.

"Their instructors keep them too busy with classes and training."

"No wonder they can't understand their skysteeds very well," Kie said with exasperation. "Couriers groom and feed their own skysteeds and spend hours flying together. I know how N'Rah is going to react before he does, and that helps keep us alive on our route. I'd think it would be just as important for skyfighters to understand their skysteeds perfectly."

"Make sense to me," Dessie said with a shrug, "but it's obvious some cadets don't mindspeak with their skysteeds well, and it costs them in the tournaments they care about so much."

As she spoke, Dessie led her into a big storage room and handed Kie a wooden box full of grooming gear. "What tournaments?" Kie asked curiously.

"The cadets fly in aerial competitions, much like the Imperial Tournaments. In them, they earn points that affect their ranking in their classes, and to this bunch, rank means everything. There's one in a few days they're fretting about. And now, we better get to work."

Dessie led her to a large covered paddock, where a dozen grooms were already busy currying skysteeds. Because she didn't want the cadets' skysteeds talking about her, she was careful not to talk to them. But every time she touched another one, the strange tingle went through her, and she could hear that animal's thoughts if she concentrated.

Kie had just finished brushing a lovely dappled gray mare when a familiar voice drawled, "Well, look who's here. Our heroic courier girl seems to be stuck working as a groom now. I wonder . . . did your courier service fire you?"

"That's none of your business," Kie shot back at him.

Ruden's eyes narrowed. "Well, it's just your luck that I'm the cadet stable manager this week, and that means you'll have to do your fair share of work today, and you better do it well. Now that I think about it, that pile of manure over there is stinking up our grooming paddock."

Kie's heart sank when he pointed to a small mountain of manure.

"It needs to be shoveled up and moved out to one of the big piles where the farmers can come collect it. Then all the tack of the skyrider squadron I command needs cleaning."

"Grooms don't move big manure piles," Dessie told him angrily. "City laborers do that."

"You *will* move that pile, or I'll report you both to the Academy's commandant for defying my orders." Looking very pleased with himself, Ruden strolled away.

Kie took a deep breath. She *so* wanted to tackle him into the manure pile. "I'm sorry about that," she said to Dessie. "Yesterday Ruden picked a fight with me and a friend from home. Ruden ended up with three demerits, and now it's payback time."

"If it's any consolation, Ruden the Rude is horrible to everyone. We all hate him. But why did he call you heroic just now?"

"It's a long story," Kie said as she trudged over to pick up a shovel.

"I've nothing but a large pile of skysteed poop and time on my hands. Besides, I need to keep my mind busy." Dessie's humorous tone changed as she looked to the west. "I'm so worried for the Skyforce."

Kie looked to the west, too, and a chill traced down her spine, despite the fact that the morning was growing hotter. Today or tomorrow, skysteeds in the Advance Guard could be facing remorseless, hungry chimerae. And Uncle Dugs's tired heart could be failing him. Her eyes welled with tears, but she blinked them away. She needed to keep her mind busy, too.

"All right. I'll tell you why Ruden called me heroic, but first, tell me why these skysteeds do their business so close to their stables. Courier mounts would never foul their own area like this."

"I don't think anyone's ever told them not to," Dessie said, her eyebrows raised. "Certainly their partners don't care that their skysteeds are making more work for us."

"Well, now that the stable staff is so shorthanded, it's stupid that the skysteeds are doing this."

As the girls set to work on shoveling the stinking pile into a wooden cart, Kie told her all about the afternoon she'd fought the chimerae and met Prince Shayn. Dessie's eyes grew wider and wider as Kie talked.

"So, why in N'Rin's mane is one of the few people who has seen and killed chimerae shoveling road apples with me?"

"Because I need to eat, and I need a place to stay until I can find someone important to read that manual. This cart's pretty full now. What happens next?"

"Next we get to drag it out to the big manure pile," Dessie said unenthusiastically as she waved off flies.

They dragged the cart out to a huge smelly pile, dumped it, and dragged it back. They were about to dump their second stinky load when N'Rah and N'Seella landed beside them.

Kie made the introductions, happy for an excuse to step back from the cart and wipe the sweat from her face.

"I know who N'Seella is," Dessie said in a choked voice. "More importantly, I know who her skyrider is."

So is this your work today? N'Rah asked, flaring his nostrils in distaste.

'Fraid so, pal, Kie replied. *That dimtwad of a cadet we met assigned me this job.*

It is not right that he gave you disagreeable work because he is angry with you. Let me pull this cart like horses do. I can get it where it needs to go much faster than you can.

"I'm not going to harness you to a manure cart," she said aloud for Dessie's benefit. "You are a skysteed."

That is skysteed manure. You are my courier partner, and I should help you.

I want to help as well, N'Seella said, tossing her lovely mane.

"What's going on?" Dessie asked.

"They both want to help us pull the cart."

"We can't let Princess Halla's skysteed pull a manure cart," Dessie hissed.

"I know, but do you want to be the one to tell her she can't do something?"

"No, I just want to keep my job." Dessie moaned. "Why ever did I tell Terry I wouldn't mind helping the new girl?"

While they were talking, N'Rah had backed himself between the cart shafts. Dessie ran and fetched two harnesses. With the skysteeds' help, taking the carts out to the big pile went much faster. They were shoveling the last load when the plump chestnut senior with pretty white feathers landed beside Kie.

There you are. I have been looking for you everywhere.

Kie put her shovel down and bowed respectfully to N'Talley. "Is there some way I can help you, ma'am?"

I have more burrs in my feathers, and my groom is still sick.

"I would be happy to comb your feathers, but my hands are dirty. If you wouldn't mind waiting, I'm almost done here."

Oh, very well. Having spent half a morning looking for you, I suppose a few more minutes will not matter.

Just then, N'Seella came trotting up, looking very pleased with herself as she dragged the other empty cart behind her.

N'Seella, whatever are you doing? the old mare asked.

I am being useful, the young mare declared, and proceeded to explain earnestly to the older mare how and why the manure needed to be moved.

"Why is *she* here?" Dessie whispered as she stared at N'Talley.

"N'Rah says that she wants me to comb out her feathers, but I told him to tell her we needed to finish this last load first."

"B-but that's the Dowager Empress's skysteed," Dessie stuttered. "If N'Talley wants you to comb her feathers, you better do it this very instant!"

CHAPTER ELEVEN

KIE STARED AT DESSIE IN disbelief. "Are you sure N'Talley's bound to the *Emperor's mother*? She seems like such a sweet, down-to-earth senior skysteed to me."

"Didn't you notice the green-and-gold ribbon in her mane? All the skysteeds partnered with members of the Imperial family wear them."

"I did see her braid, but lots of skysteeds wear colorful braids around here," Kie replied irritably. She took another look at the manure pile. "You're certain you don't mind me leaving you to finish this up?"

"No, but I do mind you making one of the most powerful skysteeds in the Empire wait. She once had a groom thrown in the dungeon for combing her tail too roughly."

Actually, N'Talley said dryly to Kie, *I had him thrown in the dungeon because he had been stealing sweet oats and selling them. But the story that he pulled my tail has ensured that I receive excellent service from grooms since then. You might as well come comb my feathers. Your friend might expire from anxiety if you do not.*

Yes, ma'am. Kie dashed into the stables, washed her hands in a bucket, and grabbed a grooming box. She'd hurried halfway to where N'Talley waited for her in the shade of a tall yora tree with shimmering green leaves when Ruden stepped into her path.

"Just what do you think you're doing?" he challenged her. "I ordered you to move that pile of manure, and you're not done yet."

"You did, but this senior skysteed wants me to remove the burrs in her feathers. I thought I should help her first."

"You just wanted to get out of doing the work I assigned you, and you're using some senile old skysteed as an excuse."

A heartbeat later, Ruden found himself lying on the ground with an angry senior skysteed standing over him.

Tell this young fool that he should speak about his elders with more respect, N'Talley ordered Kie, suddenly sounding very much like royalty.

"Um, my skysteed says that N'Talley here, the Dowager Empress's skysteed, would like you to speak about skysteeds more politely."

"Sh-she's the Dowager's skysteed?" Ruden stammered, looking ill.

"So they tell me," Kie said. She could almost feel sorry for him, except that she had blisters on her hands from shoveling skysteed manure for the past two hours.

"Your Highness, I am so very sorry that I implied your . . . wits might not be as sharp as they once were."

Tell him his commander will be hearing about his rudeness. And he will also be hearing that it is a poor use of a skilled groom's time to have you shoveling manure. You are both to cease with that unpleasant chore at once.

Grinning, Kie relayed N'Talley's words to Ruden and to

Dessie, who had hurried over to watch all the excitement. Again, Kie pretended that N'Rah was telling her what N'Talley had said. The old mare stepped back, and Ruden scrambled to his feet. His Rosari freckles stood out like red bug bites on his cheeks now. He bowed to the old mare repeatedly and then made a quick escape.

After Kie picked up the grooming box, she followed N'Talley to the shade.

I cannot believe that boy said I was senile within my hearing, which, unfortunately for him, is as keen as it ever was, the old mare said. *These cadets should show skysteeds more respect.*

"Yes, ma'am, but, well, you could argue that the skysteeds could show humans more respect, too."

The mare put her ears back and stared at Kie. *I would not argue any such thing, but evidently you would like to.*

Cursing her unruly tongue, Kie straightened her shoulders and explained how the young Academy skysteeds were so careless about where they did their business, causing the humans who cared for them hours of extra work. "And now that we're at war, ma'am, it seems to me that everyone should be pitching in and making less work for each other."

N'Talley snorted. *It is obvious you have not spent much time at court, youngling, or you would not be so free with your opinions. But I will think about what you said. I fear both our species have come to take each other for granted, at a dangerous time when our alliance should be stronger than ever. Now, would you please groom me?* she finished, putting ironic emphasis on the word "please."

Yes, ma'am, Kie replied, and she was relieved when the old mare said little to her after that. She groomed N'Talley carefully, and even massaged the muscles at the base of her wingsprouts, which N'Tor had liked as he grew older.

That was very nice, N'Talley said when Kie had finished. *Thank you. Come along, N'Seella, it is time we had a chat with the cadets' skysteeds about their personal habits.*

Her head high in the air, the old mare trotted off with N'Seella and N'Rah at her heels.

"She's quite a regal old lady, isn't she?" Dessie said, looking after her. "By the way, I had no idea that spending a shift working with you would be such an adventure."

"The good news is, we're going to be spending a lot less time shoveling road apples around here," Kie said, and proceeded to fill her in on what N'Talley had promised to do.

"That's the best news I've gotten in years," Dessie crowed. "But now we'll have to hurry if we want lunch."

They washed their hands in the fountain, dashed into the mess hall, and got plates of food. As they approached a table full of Dessie's friends, Kie plucked at her sleeve. "*Please* don't tell the other grooms what I told you today about fighting those chimerae."

Dessie stopped in her tracks and stared at her. "You don't want me tell them the best story I've heard in ages?"

"I'm new and different enough as it is," Kie explained anxiously.

Dessie contemplated her for a moment. "All right. I guess not everyone loves being the center of attention. But I have to tell them what N'Talley's doing right now. That's going to make you a hero to my friends, anyway."

The group made space for them both at the crowded table, Dessie introduced her to everyone, and soon the Mosai girl had them in stitches telling them about the morning's events. Kie's cheeks burned when they all toasted her, but she felt embarrassed in a nice way.

After lunch, the girls returned to the Academy stables and set to work in a tack room, cleaning the flight harnesses for Ruden's squadron. Kie was rubbing oil into a chest piece when she noticed one of the boys who had been with Ruden last night stride by. A short, sturdy Rosari boy with curly auburn hair and dark green eyes, the cadet stopped for a moment to stare at her. Did he think she wouldn't clean his gear carefully enough? She scowled at him, and he had the grace to blush and hurried on his way.

But he came back a few minutes later with a second boy in tow, and the two stood awkwardly in the doorway. The second boy was a tall, slim Northern Islander with light blue eyes and short, straight blond hair. It was, she realized, the same boy who had helped her that first afternoon when she'd been so desperate to find Trishop before the Skyforce launched.

"Please, miss," the Rosari cadet said, "could you tell us about the chimerae you fought? Our instructors are saying the Emperor may have to call us up to help the Skyforce, and we know very little about the beasts."

"Are you sure I'll tell you the truth?" Kie asked. "You didn't seem too interested in believing me yesterday."

The two cadets exchanged sheepish glances. "Yeah, well," the first boy said, "I'm sorry about that. It's just hard to believe, you know, that a courier on such a little skysteed could kill one chimera, let alone two."

The taller boy elbowed the shorter one in the ribs. "Nice work, Gunge. She's never going to tell us about chimerae now."

From the tight set to their faces, Kie guessed they were truly worried. Uncle Dugs always said the unknown is often more frightening than the known. "Look, I have to work right now, but I guess I can work and talk at the same time."

Eagerly, the two boys came in and found seats on tack trunks, and introduced themselves. The first cadet's name was Gunger, but he said everyone called him Gunge, and the tall boy's name was Kelton. For the second time this day, Kie found herself describing the fight against the chimerae in the Western Desert.

"I told you Captain Nerone was tough," Gunge said to Kelton when she'd finished her account. "Imagine killing one of those monsters with just a sword."

Kelton looked at her earnestly. "Do you suppose we could see one of your triwires?"

"They're with my gear in the girl grooms' dorm, and I can't go anywhere until my work's done."

"If we take over cleaning our tack," Gunge suggested, "you could fetch one."

Kie considered the two cadets. Her first instinct was to say no, to teach these two a lesson. But somehow she *had* to get more folks talking about the old ways of fighting chimerae. It couldn't hurt if she could convince these cadets that triwires were effective weapons. "All right, but your friend Ruden may not be too happy if he finds out."

"Don't worry about ole Rudy," Gunge assured her. "He'll want to know all about your triwires as badly as we do."

"I want to see your triwires, too," Dessie said, "and I'll make sure these two do a good job while you're gone."

Dreading the steamy heat outside, Kie was happy to discover it was raining. She jogged to the dorm, caught up a triwire packet, and jogged back.

"So that's what they look like." Gunge pored over the triwire after she'd spread it out on the tack room floor.

"These wires *are* wicked sharp," Kelton said, sucking a finger he'd cut on one, despite Kie's warnings.

"I was going to teach my friend Topar how to use triwires this evening," Kie admitted, "but it's not safe to practice with the real thing, not at the start. It'd be too easy to miss your toss and slice an ear off your skysteed. My uncle taught me how to throw one with a set of weighted cords."

"I could make you something like that," Dessie said, studying the triwires. "With the cord we use to tie up bales of hay."

"And you could use some of the weights we use to make sure tournament gear is exactly balanced," Kelton said and loped off to find some.

To Kie's amusement, the two cadets, with lots of advice from

Dessie, were soon making mock-ups of triwires. She asked them to make one for her and Topar, too. She'd been afraid the boys would start whirling the practice triwires around right here in the tack room, but they were careful with the weighted cords. As they worked, she found out a bit about them both. Gunge was from an old noble house in Pedarth, and Kelton was from a big noble family from the Northern Islands, and both were surprisingly loyal to Ruden.

"He's not so bad, once you get to know him," Gunge said. "He's been a good friend, and he's a terrific skyfighter."

"He's horribly rude to grooms," Dessie said. "We all hate him."

"Rudy shouldn't act that way, but his father is always on him to maintain their family's proper position and rank," Kelton explained. "Since his older brother cratered in the last few tournament seasons, the pressure's on Rudy to do well in the Academy tournaments and even better after he graduates."

"I don't understand why you all care so much about tournaments," Kie said. "Uncle Dugs tried to explain it to me, but aren't they still just games?"

"They're games where our families can win and lose fortunes overnight," Kelton replied, looking somber. "That's why many noble families go into debt buying skysteeds for their children."

"Pedarth is all about keeping up appearances," Gunge said bitterly, "and it takes lots of prize purses and lucky bets to keep noble houses afloat. We've both had friends withdraw from the

Academy when their parents couldn't afford the fees anymore."

"Why aren't there more girl cadets?" Kie asked another question she'd been wondering about. "My uncle said a quarter of his class was female, and now it seems like only a handful of cadets are girls."

"To win tournaments today, you need to be big and strong," Kelton said. "The girls easily beat us in the archery contests, where skill, finesse, and practice make a difference, but they rarely take home the really rich prizes in jousting matches, where strength and size are such a huge advantage."

"It feels all wrong," Kie said, more to herself than to the boys. She was starting to understand why Uncle Dugs had left the capital. "People shouldn't be betting on how well skysteeds and their riders can fight. That wasn't what the Great Alliance was about."

"Right or wrong," Dessie said soberly, "that's how Pedarth works these days."

By the time she and Dessie had finished cleaning the squadron's harnesses, the cadets had created three decent practice triwires. Kie took one outside to test it. After whirling it over her head, she sent it spinning through the air to wrap about a nearby fence post.

"By the Warrior's Sword, you're good with that thing," Gunge said. "Would you mind if we came and watched your practice tonight?"

"I guess not," Kie said, "but I don't know how my friend Topar is going to feel about having you there."

Gunge grinned. "Bet he won't mind too much, particularly if we give him one of these practice triwires."

"And if the chimerae are coming," Kelton said seriously, "we all need to learn the best ways to fight them, and learn them fast."

CHAPTER TWELVE

GUNGE AND KELTON WERE RIGHT, Kie reflected later that night at the old stadium. Topar didn't seem to mind that the two cadets had come to watch their session. He was too excited to have the practice triwire they'd made that afternoon.

"I wish we had something like Uncle Dugs's target tree here," Kie said with a sigh. They would have to settle for throwing their triwires and botans at the crossbars on the tall posts the skyfighters had used for jousting practice.

Relieved that it was cooler after the rain, Kie showed Topar and the cadets how to throw the mock-up triwires, and Topar showed her how to hurl the botan. Then Kie and Topar traded weapons and spent an hour on their skysteeds diving at the crossbars.

On a quick rest break, she asked him, "Did any news come in today from the Western Desert?"

"No, but even though I'm sure our military couriers will fly day and night to bring the Emperor news of the fighting, they still wouldn't reach Pedarth until late tomorrow at the very earliest."

Kie looked to the west and hoped with all her heart that the Emperor's Advance Guard had been victorious.

That night in the dorm felt very different as Kie washed up

and got ready for bed. Many of the grooms and healers smiled and said good night to her. Dessie even offered to move over to Kie's corner.

"Um, thanks," Kie said, "but you really don't need to. I like some quiet at the end of the day."

"Well, would it be all right if I looked at your uncle's manual?" Dessie asked a bit stiffly.

Hoping she hadn't just offended the older girl, Kie reached for her saddlebags. "I'm glad someone around here is interested in this thing," she said after removing the dayan leaf from between its pages.

Dessie took the manual back to her bed and carefully skimmed through its pages, which were brown and brittle with age. In the meantime, Kie traced the veins on the dayan leaf gently with her fingertips. Already the green leaf was drying out. A wave of home-sickness washed over her, so strong it made her chest hurt. She hoped her trees back home weren't drying out, too, and even more she hoped that Uncle Dugs and N'Tor were getting better.

Resolutely, she pulled one of the small writing kits all couriers carried from her saddlebags. Smoothing out the thin, light paper, Kie set to work on a labor of love—writing a letter. And it *was* hard work, choosing her words and shaping each letter correctly. She told Uncle Dugs she was well, and that Trishop had given her a job, and that she was teaching some cadets how to use triwires. She wished she could tell him that she'd been successful at getting the entire Skyforce to change their tactics, but she couldn't lie to him. She closed by telling him and N'Tor to get better soon.

As she signed her letter, a tear from her brimming eyes fell onto the page, but luckily, it didn't smear any ink. Her letter was homely looking, but she knew Uncle Dugs would realize how much love and effort had gone into writing it. Tomorrow she would post it at Central Relay.

She'd put the writing kit away and was just dozing off when Dessie said suddenly, "Kie, did you see there's a whole section of notes for healers near the back of this manual? The writer listed the ingredients for two different antidotes for sand dragon venom. One's for skysteeds and a different one is for humans."

"I forgot that was there," Kie admitted, very glad to be across the room where Dessie couldn't see her blushing. She didn't want to admit that she'd read very little of her uncle's manual. His great-grandfather's old-fashioned cursive was almost impossible for her to decipher. But Uncle Dugs had read the manual to her so many times, she knew most of the fighting parts by heart.

"I wish we'd had these a few days ago," Dessie said as she brought the manual back, "when the healers were packing medicines for the Skyforce. If these antidotes work, someone important needs to know."

"Yeah, but I can't get anyone important interested in that manual," Kie said with a sigh of frustration. After carefully placing her dayan leaf back between its pages, she packed the manual away again.

"What about Prince Shayn?" Dessie asked. "You said he

seemed to know all about triwires. Surely he'd be interested in this manual."

"N'Rah's been watching for his skysteed since we first arrived in Pedarth, but so far he's seen neither hair nor feather of him."

As she drifted off to sleep, Kie wondered: where *was* the prince who had made her promise to come to Pedarth?

The next morning, Kie was assigned to help Terry with the senior herd. She'd just finished cleaning the hooves of a very chatty old buckskin stallion when N'Seella and N'Rah came galloping up.

Please, you must come talk to my human, N'Seella declared. *She is so upset, I am afraid she will hurt herself if she cries any harder.*

N'Seella, I don't think Princess Halla wants anything to do with me, Kie replied.

No one ever really talks to her. That is why she is so lonely. They are all too scared. You are not scared of her, nor of the old one, N'Talley.

That's not true. I'm plenty scared of them both now that I know who they are.

N'Seella tossed her head. *Halla is just a girl, and she is my human, and she hurts right now.*

All right, I'll come, Kie thought at the mare. *She better not threaten to fire me again,* she said privately to N'Rah, *or I'll probably say something to her that will make me lose my job.*

She explained to Terry what N'Rah had told her about Princess Halla.

"And N'Seella wants you to try to help her? You know this

isn't a good idea," he said, his brows coming together in a frown.

"Yes, but N'Seella's truly worried about her."

"And now I'll be truly worried about you," Terry said, looking glum. "I don't want my new helper tossed in the dungeon her first week on the job. Good luck with Her Highness."

Wondering if he'd been kidding her about the dungeon, Kie vaulted up onto N'Rah's bare back. They galloped after N'Seella to a secluded grotto where the princess lay sobbing on the grass. Kie slipped from N'Rah's back and stood there for a moment, watching her. The girl wore another spectacular dress, a white filmy gown embroidered with violets, and its skirt was going to have spectacular grass stains. Kie didn't envy the poor maid who would have to spend hours washing them out.

That thought made Kie say more sharply than she meant, "Whatever's wrong, crying like this isn't going to solve it."

Startled, Princess Halla sat up, her eyes red and swollen. "Oh, it's you again," she said. "G-go away before I have you thrown in a dungeon."

"I'd be happy to go away, but I promised N'Seella I'd come. She's worried about you."

"I'm g-glad someone is," Princess Halla wailed. "All my father does is go to war councils and pace in his chambers, and my big brothers are gone, and you were right, I am a terrible skyrider, and N'Seella should have bound with somebody braver than I am, and now it looks like Shaynie's so sick, he's going to die, and then I won't have anyone but N'Seella left who loves me."

Kie had gotten confused by the princess's ramblings, but then a name she recognized caught her attention. "Are you saying that Prince Shayn is seriously ill?"

"Yes," the princess said, more tears coursing down her cheeks. "One of those horrible chimera creatures bit him on his way back from the Western Desert, but he didn't tell anyone at first, and now the healers are saying they can't save him. Our grandmother just sits by his bed all day, and I can tell from her face that she thinks he's going to die."

Kie drew in a deep breath, her mind racing. "No, he's not," she said. "I have the recipe for an antidote that might save his life."

"But the healers all s-said it's too late." Princess Halla collapsed back onto the ground and dissolved into another wave of sobs.

Kie bit her lip as she watched the princess. Clearly, it would take too long to get the girl to listen to her. She needed someone with more sense. Taking another deep breath, she concentrated and reached for N'Talley's mind.

N'Talley, I need you to meet me at the central courtyard in the main stables as soon as you can.

She sensed the mare's surprise and then anger at the abrupt summons.

Youngling, just because you can talk to me does not mean you can—

Please, just listen, Kie interrupted her. *We may not have much time. I have an old recipe for an antidote to sand dragon venom. It might be able to save your human's grandson. You have to help me get it to the healers who are treating Prince Shayn.*

I will come right away, the old mare promised.

N'Rah raced back to the central stable courtyard, and Kie pounded up the stairs to the dorm and grabbed the manual. Even though she didn't want to make the Dowager's skysteed wait, she did take the time to find her dayan leaf and place it on the small table beside her bed.

Oh, Da, she thought as she stared at the leaf and a lump rose in her throat, *I miss you and our quiet orchard so much. Pedarth is too busy and noisy, and I'm so worried about that young prince I met. I don't want him to die.*

She turned and hurried from the dorm room. When she returned to the courtyard, N'Talley was already there, pacing back and forth. Her heart pounding, Kie held the manual out so that the old mare could see it. "This contains information from the Chimera Wars. It belonged to the great-grandfather of my uncle, Duggan Torsun."

You are Duggan Torsun's niece? Why did you not tell me this before?

"I guess it didn't come up," Kie said, fighting to hide her impatience. "Please, can you take this to the healers treating Prince Shayn before it's too late?"

Since I do not have hands or a harness on me right now, the old mare said in her dry way, *you are going to have to come with me, and you best ride on my back. The palace sentries are so jittery, they might shoot at a skysteed and rider they do not know.*

"All right, ma'am," Kie said, swallowing hard. Now didn't seem the right time to point out couriers were taught *never* to fly without a harness.

After stuffing the manual inside her shirt, she grabbed a piece of N'Talley's mane. The mare bent her front leg to make it easier for her to mount, and Kie vaulted onto her back. She shifted forward until her legs were tucked snugly under N'Talley's wing-sprouts. The mare's body was much wider than N'Rah's, and it felt odd to be sitting another whole foot above the ground.

"Kiesandra Torsun, what in Great N'Rin's name are you doing up on Her Highness's back?" Trishop thundered from the nearest doorway.

"I'll explain later. Really, it's all right," Kie called back to him as N'Talley galloped out of the courtyard, surprised grooms dodging out of her way and N'Rah hard on her heels. Seconds later, they were airborne and speeding toward the Emperor's palace.

That old mare could move when she wanted to. Tavalier Park flashed past beneath them in a blur of green, and soon they were sailing over the imposing battlements that guarded the Imperial Palace. The walls below them were indeed manned with hundreds of archers. Now Kie was very glad they had an Imperial escort. She had to squint when they flew by an amartine turret shining brilliantly in the morning sun.

Instead of spiraling down, N'Talley dove straight for a garden at the base of one of those turrets. The dive was so steep, Kie grabbed another handful of mane and hoped the mare remembered her rider wasn't wearing a harness. The moment N'Talley landed and cantered to a stop, a stout old woman hurried up to them. Her lined face looked weary, and her long pale orange hair was falling out of its bun, but her emerald green eyes were still bright and shrewd as she examined Kie.

"So you're the courier groom my skysteed's so taken with, and now she tells me that you're Duggan Torsun's niece."

Kie slipped from N'Talley's back, pulled the manual from her shirt, and performed a quick bow. "Yes, ma'am, and this is the manual he inherited from his great-grandfather. There's a recipe in the back for an antidote for sand dragon venom. I can't promise that it will work, but I thought it couldn't hurt to try it. H-how is Prince Shayn?"

The Dowager Empress almost snatched the manual from Kie's hands. "He's a very sick boy. We'd have already lost him, except he's such a fighter," the old woman said as she leafed through the manual. "Ah, here it is. It says to use yata powder and tarra root. I know our healers haven't tried those yet."

The old lady whirled around and headed for the base of the tower. "Thank you, girl," she called back over her shoulder, and then she vanished inside.

Kie walked over to N'Rah and leaned against him. Her legs were unsteady from the old mare's steep dive *and* meeting the Emperor's mother.

You did well, N'Talley told her, even as she gazed worriedly after her skyrider.

"That was some flying, ma'am," Kie said.

Yes, well, you youngsters are not the only ones who know how to fly, you know. Now let us pray that antidote saves the boy.

Hiding a smile, Kie bowed to the old mare and vaulted onto N'Rah. She noticed a pinto skysteed in the corner of the garden, peering forlornly through an open window. Kie trotted N'Rah over to where N'Laure stood. The small skysteed looked so gaunt, she guessed he wasn't eating or drinking properly.

Kie coughed, and the pinto swung his head around to look at them. The misery in his brown eyes made her own prickle with tears. "We just brought a recipe for an antidote to sand dragon venom. There's a good chance it could help your prince," she said. "But you must take care of yourself, so you are well when he is better."

The pinto pricked his ears and stared at her.

He remembers us from the desert that day, N'Rah told her, *and he wants to know if you are telling him the truth.*

"My uncle said those antidotes saved thousands of lives back in the old days," Kie said honestly enough. Uncle Dugs had claimed that. She just didn't know if his claims were true. "So, you see, there's a good chance Prince Shayn will be himself in no time, and I know he would be very upset to see you like this."

I could not have said it better myself, N'Talley chimed in. *As soon as I get back from escorting these two over the walls, I am going to make sure you have a good drink and feed.*

As N'Talley talked, Kie couldn't help looking past N'Laure through the window. She could just make out the prince, looking so small and still in a huge bed surrounded by healers. Remembering how brave he'd been that day in the desert, she hoped with all her heart that the old antidote would save him.

After N'Talley escorted them over the walls, N'Rah asked, *Where are we off to now? I like this city even though it smells. It never gets boring.*

"I wish it was a little more boring here," Kie said with a sigh. "We're going to try to have a real conversation with Princess Halla. I'm hoping she's worn herself out and can talk more sensibly now."

N'Rah craned his head around to peer at her slyly. *I promise I will come visit you if she has you thrown in her dungeon.*

"Ha, ha, ha. I doubt they let skysteeds visit Imperial prisoners."

By the Messenger's wings, she hoped they weren't about to discover whether or not that was true.

CHAPTER THIRTEEN

N'RAH FLEW KIE BACK TO the park, where they found Princess Halla sitting up, staring moodily into space while N'Seella grazed next to her. The morning was growing hotter, but here in the green grotto shaded by big bawa and yora trees, it was still blissfully cool.

"Oh, it's you again," the princess said without enthusiasm, grass stains on her dress and her beautiful auburn hair in a tangle.

"We just took a recipe for a sand dragon venom antidote to your grandmother. There's a good chance it will help your brother," Kie said with more confidence than she felt. "So hopefully that takes care of one of your problems. I think we should talk about some of the others."

"Well, I don't," the princess said, some color coming back into her cheeks. "I didn't mean for you to hear any of that."

"But I did hear it. I can't do anything about your brothers going off to fight, or your father being so worried, but you did say you were sorry that N'Seella didn't bind with someone braver than you. Are you scared of flying your skysteed?"

Princess Halla jumped to her feet, her bright green eyes spitting fire. "How dare you ask me that? I am a Rathskayan, a direct descendant of the first Emperor who forged the Great Alliance with all skysteeds."

"That's just wonderful," Kie said and crossed her arms, "but you didn't answer my question. So, I'm going to ask again. Are you scared of flying with N'Seella?"

The princess opened her mouth, and Kie braced herself to receive a scorching setdown. Then the girl closed her lips and buried her face in her hands. Her knees folded, and she started to sob as if her heart was breaking. N'Seella stopped grazing and looked at Kie crossly.

I did not ask you to come here to make her cry more.

Hey, we're finally getting somewhere. I think she's scared to fly with you.

N'Seella pricked her ears. *Truly? But I love her. I would never let her fall.*

I know that, and she probably knows that, too, but fear can make you forget what you know.

Kie let the princess cry for a few minutes longer before she asked quietly, "Have you always been afraid or is this something new?"

The princess was silent for so long, Kie feared she wouldn't answer. But then she began to speak, her voice low. "Ever since my brother Rodard died in that awful tournament, I've been afraid to fly. What kind of princess, what kind of skyrider is afraid to fly on the back of the sweetest, most wonderful skysteed in the world?"

Her expression was so woebegone that Kie's heart melted.

The princess looked down at her hands. "I was there that day, you know," she said tonelessly. "Shaynie was, too. Rodard had made it to the semifinals of the Imperial Tournament, and we were all so excited for him. Then, his opponent knocked him off his skysteed so hard, the harness snapped. Poor N'Tarin dove after him, but it was too late. My brother fell four hundred feet, and then he was dead. That's why Shaynie and I, we're never, ever going to skyfight. It's stupid and pointless, and the nicest p-people die doing it."

Kie's eyes filled with tears. She couldn't imagine seeing someone she loved fall to their death skyfighting, yet poor Princess Halla and Uncle Dugs had both suffered such a cruel and pointless loss.

"My uncle agrees with you," Kie said softly. "He was the first Mosai to win the Imperial Tournament, and the first person ever to win three in a row. But then the Rosari girl he loved died in a skyfighting tournament, and he left Pedarth and never came back here. So I believe you are very smart and brave not to participate in them."

"But I'm *not* brave. I'm too much of a coward to fly anywhere with N'Seella now."

"You're not the first skyrider to have this problem," Kie said, hoping she wouldn't be sorry for what she was going to say next. "We might be able to fix you."

"You could fix me?" The princess glanced up, looking so hopeful that Kie had to clear her throat. It would shatter her if she couldn't fly with N'Rah anymore.

"Maybe. Someone should have made you get up on N'Seella the day after your brother died."

"Everyone was too busy mourning Rodard," the princess said, plucking at her skirts. Kie could guess what had happened. There had been a big funeral, and everyone in her family had been mourning, and no one noticed that Princess Halla was too frightened to fly her own skysteed anymore.

"So how would you go about fixing me?"

Kie thought fast. There were one or two things they could try. "Could you meet me here at sunset?"

"But I couldn't possibly try flying here in the park," Princess Halla said, her eyes wide with horror. "People I know might see how scared I am."

"All right," Kie said, trying to be patient. "Could you meet me at the Academy's old stadium at sunset? I'll be there with some friends practicing skyfighting, but they'll all leave when it gets dark."

"It's all right if you or your friends see me. You don't matter."

"Thank you so very much," Kie said tartly.

The princess grimaced. "That came out wrong. You don't have to spend your days with the daughters of the upper nobility. If you make one mistake, those girls will devour you. They'd be thrilled to know I'm too scared to ride my sweet N'Seella anymore."

"But you're an Imperial princess. How can they be mean to you? Can't you ask your father to toss 'em all in the dungeon?"

"Being an Imperial princess doesn't work like that." Princess Halla shook her head regretfully. "Sometimes I wish it did."

"That's too bad. I've met a few Skyforce cadets that I'd love you to throw in the dungeon for me," Kie said, thinking of Ruden. "Well, I've got to get back to work. I'll see you tonight."

"I will come, but you won't get me flying," the princess said, an obstinate set to her mouth.

"You're right," Kie said, throwing up her hands. "We won't get you flying if you're determined not to fly. But if you want to be with N'Seella and make her happy again, you're going to try, for her sake."

Her obstinate look faded as the princess tilted her head and studied Kie. "Kiesandra Torsun, you are a very odd girl, but I think I like you," she declared. "No one ever dares to speak to me the way you do, except my grandmama and Shaynie. Thank you for trying to help me and my brother."

Trying to hide her hurt over someone else calling her odd, Kie nodded and vaulted onto N'Rah's back. She sent him cantering back to senior sick call. But when she reported to Terry, he told her that Trishop wanted to talk to her right away.

"Is it true you went flying off on N'Talley?" Terry asked, his eyes wide.

"It's a long story," Kie said with a sigh. "I'll tell you how that happened later."

She found Trishop reading through a sheaf of papers on his desk. After she closed his door and turned to face him, Trishop sent her a furious look.

"I don't know what they taught you in the courier service," he said tightly, "but no skyrider *ever* rides another's skysteed without that skyrider's permission. And you certainly don't go flying off on an Imperial skysteed. What were you thinking? The Dowager Empress is going to have your head, and mine as well."

Kie stared hard at her feet, stunned and sick that her uncle's old friend was so angry with her. But this wasn't fair. She hadn't done anything wrong! She forced herself to stand up straighter and meet Trishop's gaze.

"No, sir, the Dowager Empress won't want our heads. N'Talley ordered me to get on her back." She proceeded to tell tell him all about how N'Seella wanted her to talk to Princess Halla and how she'd found out that Prince Shayn was so ill.

"So you thought you'd just take that old manual to the Dowager Empress," Trishop said, running a hand through his gray hair and making it stand up on end.

"Well, yes, sir. Do you think it was a mistake to give it to her?"

"You're assuming that recipe isn't a useless piece of folklore. We're both going to pray that whatever's in that so-called antidote doesn't finish off Prince Shayn. Your uncle should have told you more about Pedarth before sending you here. It's dangerous for regular Mosai like us to deal with the nobility, much less members of the Imperial family. You meant well, but you'd be a great deal safer if you try to steer clear of them in the future."

Kie cleared her throat. "I know this probably isn't the best time to bring this up, sir, but is there a tandem flight harness around here that I could borrow?"

Trishop stared at her from under his dark brows. "Does this

have something to do with the fact Princess Halla hasn't been able to fly her skysteed since her brother died?"

"You don't want to know the answer to that, sir."

"You're right. I don't." The head groom stared down at his desk and rubbed his forehead as if he had a headache. "There's a tandem harness hanging on the wall in Tack Room Four. I'll make sure it's cleaned by this afternoon."

Trishop got to his feet and opened the door. "Obviously you didn't hear a word of my advice. I'm starting to think you're as stubborn as your uncle, but if you can help that poor girl and her skysteed, you would be doing us all a favor. Please don't get yourself or me clapped in irons while you're at it."

"I'll do my best, sir," Kie said, wondering if he was teasing her about that getting-clapped-in-irons part. Before she slipped out the door, she blurted out, "Has there been any word of the Advance Guard or the Skyforce?"

"Nothing yet," he replied, and the lines on his face seemed to deepen.

CHAPTER FOURTEEN

AFTER HER TALK WITH TRISHOP, Kie grabbed a sausage roll and a dayan apple from the mess hall. A couple of Dessie's friends stared at her so curiously, she feared the story of her flying off on N'Talley had already made the rounds. Desperate for some time to herself, she ate her lunch in the saddle while N'Rah flew her to Central Relay. The apple wasn't as tart and flavorful as the ones she grew, but it reminded her of home.

Central Relay was even busier than it had been during her last visit, and the atmosphere more strained. The same nice clerk who had helped her before relayed the message that her uncle was sitting up now and eating real food, and N'Tor was starting to eat a little, too. Kie posted her letter to Uncle Dugs for free, one of the perks of being a junior courier. When N'Rah dropped Kie off at the Academy stables, she ran into Dessie.

"I let you go off by yourself for one morning, and look at the trouble you get yourself into," the older girl said, shaking her head. "I'll forgive you only if you tell me why on earth you flew the Dowager Empress's skysteed."

Kie told her how that had happened as they both set to work grooming skysteeds who were waiting for their riders to appear for afternoon skyfighting practice.

"I wish I could have seen the boss's face," Dessie said,

laughing heartily when Kie had finished her account.

As the older cadets arrived to harness their skysteeds, they appeared even more focused and determined than they had the day before.

"What's up with the junior and senior cadets?" Kie asked Dessie.

"The Term's End Tournament is tomorrow. Nobles place bets on their own sons and daughters, and the winners take home purses rich enough to pay their Academy tuition."

"No wonder they look so worried," Kie said. Courier training had been intense, but nothing like this.

She glanced up to find a strong, arrogant-looking charcoal-gray skysteed with a silver mane and wings waiting next in her line.

"That's N'Saran, Ruden Mirsar's skysteed," Dessie told her quietly.

Kie set to work. She noticed the big skysteed shifted his weight when she rubbed a curry comb around the muscles at the base of his right wingsprout.

That muscle is still sore, she overheard N'Saran thinking. *Ruden will be so disappointed if we do not do well tomorrow, and his father will be furious. I must not tell him that it hurts.*

Kie bit her lip. She didn't want N'Saran to know she could hear his thoughts, but she also didn't want the skysteed to participate in a tournament if he was injured.

She'd just finished when Ruden showed up with his flight harness. "I hope you did a thorough job on him," the cadet said, thrusting his chin out and looking so much like his skysteed, she almost giggled. Uncle Dugs always claimed that like often found like when skyriders and skysteeds chose each other.

"I did," Kie said, glad Ruden had given her the perfect opening. "In fact, when I curried under his right wingsprout, he winced and shifted his weight. I'm pretty sure he has a strained muscle there."

The boy's face flushed in anger. "If you've hurt my skysteed, I swear I'll make you pay, no matter how many Imperial skysteeds like you."

Kie put her hands on her hips. "I would *never* hurt a skysteed," she retorted. "But did you have a rough practice session yesterday?"

His eyes narrowed, as if he'd just remembered something. "No," the cadet replied shortly. "Our practice went well yesterday, and N'Saran swears he's fine."

"Well, of course he'll say that. He knows how much doing well in the tournament means to you and your family. He'd cripple himself to make you happy."

Ruden took a step toward her, his eyes burning. "Haven't you cost us enough? I almost lost my position as squadron leader thanks to you. Just stay away from me, and stay away from my skysteed."

"I'll be happy to. But your skysteed is lying to you about that muscle, and either you can't tell or you don't care."

Kie stomped away from them both and counted to ten before she started to groom another skysteed.

That night after supper, Kelton, Gunge, Topar, and Dessie all showed up at the stadium. Topar brought a second botan he'd made over his lunch break, and Dessie had made a practice triwire for herself.

"I want to protect the city folk and our skysteeds if the chimerae attack Pedarth," Dessie declared, looking very fierce. She and the cadets practiced throwing triwires and the second botan on the ground while Kie worked on improving her botan toss in the air, and Topar got better and better with his practice triwire.

As the sun set, two riderless skysteeds landed at the far end of the stadium and watched them curiously. With tangled manes and muddy coats, they appeared scruffy compared to the beautifully groomed skysteeds she'd seen so far in Pedarth.

"What's up with those two skysteeds?" Kie asked the others.

"Oh, those are just a couple of the Unbound," Gunge said.

"They roam all over the city, getting into mischief," Kelton added. "They raid people's gardens and leave road apples in awkward places."

"Why aren't they bound to skyriders?" Topar asked.

"They got passed over at auction," Gunge replied, "because they didn't have perfect conformation, or they were too small, or they didn't have the right temperament for skyfighting."

"But that's so sad," Kie said. At that moment, the larger of the two skysteeds, a strong-looking strawberry roan with a spectacular roman nose, glared at her and snorted.

She can hear you, N'Rah told Kie, *and she wants you to know she does not want your pity.*

"What's truly a crime is that the breeders who own them are

so determined to keep prices up," Dessie said bitterly, "that they won't sell these skysteeds for cheaper or let them bind with Mosai like me who would do anything to have a skysteed. I think you're gorgeous, by the way," she called out to the roan and bowed to her.

In reply, the roan yawned rudely, and then she and her companion, a smaller bay stallion, thundered past them and flew off into the twilight.

It is wrong that they are not allowed to bind, Kie said to N'Rah.

I agree, N'Rah said. *The Great Alliance was not supposed to turn out like this.*

The more I see of this place, Kie said, thinking of Ruden and the pressure on him to win tournaments at any cost, *the more I understand why Uncle Dugs left and never came back.*

The cadets departed the stadium soon after that. As the dusk deepened and the second moon rose, Kie explained to Topar and Dessie whom she waited for, and why.

"I can't imagine anything more awful than being too scared to fly with N'Meary," Topar said. "I'd like to stay and help Princess Halla if I can."

"Me too," Dessie said, "although I might change my mind if she decides we all should be executed."

Princess Halla arrived at the southern entrance to the stadium a few minutes later, riding N'Seella. At least she had the sense to wear flight gear instead of a ball gown. After the princess trotted up, Kie introduced her to Dessie and Topar. The poor girl looked pale and tense. Kie longed to ask her how

Prince Shayn was, but she didn't want to start her crying again.

"First, we'll try using a tandem harness. Would you mind if I flew on N'Seella with you?" Kie asked, remembering Trishop's lecture earlier today.

"I wouldn't m-mind," she replied, and Kie realized the princess was trembling.

I will be glad to carry you, N'Seella chimed in, *if it means my human will be happy flying with me again.*

"Come on down here," Kie said briskly to the princess, "and Topar will introduce you to my skysteed, N'Rah, and to N'Meary, who is a sweetheart, and Dessie and I will get this tandem harness set up."

The princess slid from N'Seella's back. Crossing her arms as if she were cold, she walked over to Topar.

"Should you talk to an Imperial princess that way?" Dessie whispered as they fitted N'Seella with the tandem harness.

"I don't know how else to talk to her," Kie whispered back, "and she doesn't seem to mind."

"So, Your Highness," Kie said after they'd set up the harness, "we're going to fly around the stadium a few feet off the ground. If you were to fall, you'd only get a bruise or two."

"R-right. I should be able to handle that," the princess said.

N'Seella bent her foreleg, Princess Halla mounted, and Dessie and Kie made sure she was clipped into the tandem harness securely. Then Kie climbed up behind her and clipped in as well.

"Are you ready?" Kie asked. "You can close your eyes if that helps."

Princess Halla shook her head vehemently. "That d-doesn't help at all. Every time I close my eyes, I see my brother falling."

"Then don't close your eyes," Kie said quickly, her heart twisting for the princess. "Topar is going to fly in front of us, and you can watch N'Meary's pretty white tail and wings, and N'Rah will fly ride beside us. Should we try that?" Kie held her breath.

After a very long moment, the princess nodded. Impressed with her bravery, Kie squeezed her legs. N'Seella cantered them smoothly into the air. N'Meary tucked in right in front of her, her white wings almost glowing in the moonlight. The princess didn't say a word, but tremors still racked her. Kie bit her lip. Were they making a terrible mistake?

"Keep flying like this," Kie called out to Topar and N'Rah. Slowly, they made one full circuit of the stadium. The princess shook so hard, her teeth chattered, but she didn't ask to stop.

There had to be *some* way to make this easier for the terrified girl. Kie had an inspiration. "Topar, come fly beside us and tell us your wonderful Ledari story about the moons, and N'Rah, you can give us a lead now."

"All right," Topar agreed cheerfully, and when he was beside them, he started to speak in his storyteller voice.

"Once there was a Ledari woman who took great pride in making the most perfect and delicious balls of goat cheese. One day, she made the mistake of boasting that her cheese was even finer than that of Elenay, goddess of hearth and home. Koby, the trickster god, overheard her boast and hurried to tell Elenay about it. Furious, Elenay disguised herself as a mortal and took balls of her own cheese, created from the milk of her silver-haired goats, to a Ledari *kesali*. They're similar to one of your fairs," Topar paused to explain to the princess.

"But what happened to the woman?" Princess Halla asked impatiently, and Kie smiled to herself. It was hard not to get caught up in one of Topar's tales.

"Much to Elenay's astonishment, the judges liked the Ledari woman's cheese better and awarded her first place. Furious, the goddess revealed herself in all her immortal glory. Elenay wanted to strike the woman and the judges dead, but the Ledari woman begged so humbly for their lives that the goddess decided to be merciful. She threw one of her own goat cheeses into the night sky to remind all Ledari it is never wise to be boastful, and it became our larger moon, Cerken, and the Ledari woman's goat cheese became little Cira."

"But that doesn't make any sense," the princess protested. "I don't believe Cerken and Cira are made of goat cheese."

"Myths don't have to make sense." Topar's teeth flashed white in the moonlight as he smiled.

"Can we go a little higher now?" Kie asked Princess Halla.

She nodded, and Kie reached out to N'Seella. *Each lap, let's climb ten feet.*

I think this is working, N'Seella said. *She does not shake so much now.*

After another story from Topar, they had climbed above the stadium walls and could look out over the city. Streetlamps twinkled along the major avenues, and the palace's amartine turrets shone in the moonlight.

"I forgot how pretty the city looks at night," Princess Halla said in a choked voice. "Rodard used to help me sneak out and go night flying . . . but I'm never going to go night flying with him again. I've missed him so much, and I've missed you, N'Seella." She flung herself forward and sobbed into N'Seella's mane.

Kie's throat tightened. She'd never had a brother or sister, but surely it must be awful to lose one. She so hoped the princess wasn't about to lose Prince Shayn as well. When the princess's crying eased, Kie declared, "I think that's enough for tonight. Tomorrow, we'll do more of the same, if you'd like."

"Oh, I'd very much like." The princess sniffed and sat up. "I can't believe I'm flying again."

When N'Seella landed, Dessie and Kie took off the tandem harness. Princess Halla thanked them with surprising politeness and left with her skysteed.

Suddenly, Trishop stepped from the shadows by the gear sheds. Beside her, Dessie went pale and snapped to attention. Were she and Dessie about to get fired?

"That appears to have gone well," the head groom said.

"I think it did, sir," Kie replied, her heart racing. "But it wasn't easy for her." How she wished she could see his expression better in the dim light. If he was angry with them, she would make sure he knew that helping the princess was all her idea.

"The Emperor will be pleased," Trishop said. "We both knew she was too scared to fly, but our attempts to solve the problem failed miserably. We never thought to ask a stubborn frontier girl to help us. You have his Supreme Highness's permission to continue working with the princess."

Kie gulped. "He knew?"

"I had to tell him. She is his only daughter, and he loves her dearly. Now, you've all done good work today, and you should head back to your dorm and get some rest."

The approval she heard in his tone gave Kie the courage to ask, "Have you heard anything about the Advance Guard?"

Trishop looked toward the west and sighed. "There's still been no word."

CHAPTER FIFTEEN

THE NEXT MORNING, THE GROOMS at Kie's breakfast table were abuzz with the news that Ruden Mirsar had withdrawn from the Term's End Tournament.

"Rumor has it that his skysteed was too hurt to compete," Terry told them.

"I'm surprised he didn't fly him anyway," Dessie said darkly.

"I'm not," Kie surprised herself by saying. "He may be a bully and a buffletwit, but he loves his skysteed."

"Lord Mirsar can't be happy about this," Terry said. "Everyone thought Ruden and N'Saran would overpower the competition again. Now someone else is going to take home fifty gold dashins."

Happy that Ruden had listened to her, Kie smiled as she and Terry headed for senior sick call. They were just finishing up when N'Talley and N'Rah landed beside her.

Kie exchanged worried looks with Terry. Ever since she'd talked to Trishop yesterday, she'd been anxious that the antidote in Uncle Dugs's manual might have hurt poor Prince Shayn rather than helped him. Her stomach tightened like a vise as she copied Terry's formal bow. She prayed the prince had survived the night.

"I-is Prince Shayn better?" she asked the moment she had straightened up again.

My human wishes to see you right away, N'Talley informed Kie. *Her grandson is sitting up and eating a big breakfast even as we speak.*

Kie let out a big sigh of relief. The prince was going to live!

Now, I know you are new to Pedarth, youngling, the old mare said, *but it is never a good idea to keep a Rathskayan waiting.*

Kie looked down at her britches and brushed away some dirt. *Yes, ma'am. It's just that, well, I don't have any formal clothes.*

My human actually has sense, you know. She does not expect a courier or groom to visit her wearing court clothes.

All right, then. Quickly, Kie explained to Terry that she was to have an audience with the Dowager Empress. Then she swung up on N'Rah to fetch her flying harness.

You did well enough without one yesterday, the old mare protested with a gleam in her eye.

Ma'am, Kie replied firmly, *I was trained by the courier service never to fly without one.*

Oh, very well, the old mare agreed, and soon Kie and N'Rah were flying with her to the palace. After descending a great deal more sedately than they had yesterday, they landed in the same pretty green garden. The Dowager Empress walked out to meet them, looking much less frantic and more regal. This morning, her pale red hair was dressed neatly in a bun threaded through with a strand of pearls.

"So, you're Kiesandra Torsun, Duggan Torsun's niece," the Dowager said as Kie slipped from N'Rah's back.

"Yes, ma'am," she replied and bowed. It took all her willpower not to fidget as the old woman inspected her.

"We'll chat about your uncle in a bit, but first I must tell you that you've done the Imperial family a great favor. Thanks to that recipe you brought, Prince Shayn is much better this morning. In fact, it worked so well, we sent a military courier with the recipes for skysteed and human antidotes to the front last night."

"I'm truly glad to hear your grandson is better," Kie said, and something tight inside her unwound a little more.

"He claims you've saved his life twice now, by bringing that recipe and by downing two chimerae all by yourself out in the Western Desert."

"But I didn't down them by myself, ma'am. I have one of the fastest, bravest skysteeds anywhere, and Captain Nerone killed one chimera with just a sword, and Prince Shayn brought one down with a triwire."

"That you gave me," a familiar voice called from inside. "Grandmama, when are you going to bring Kie in here? I want to talk to her."

"In a moment, you rude, impatient boy. Some formalities need to be observed first. Where was I? Oh, yes, by saving my grandson's life—"

"You forgot to add your 'favorite grandson,'" Prince Shayn interrupted her again. This time he popped his head through the doorway and grinned at Kie. His skin was pale for a Rosari, and his face skinnier than ever, but he looked remarkably lively for someone who had just been on his deathbed.

"I won't let you see her at all if you don't get back in bed and finish your breakfast," the old woman snapped. The prince must have heard the steel in her voice this time, because he vanished. "By saving the life of *one* of my favorite grandchildren," the Dowager continued quickly, "I owe you a debt, and I will be happy to repay you with a favor or a reward."

"Um, thank you." Kie's heart began to race. Should she ask the Dowager Empress to tell her son about Uncle Dugs's manual? Surely the Emperor would listen to his mother.

"Now, let's go see that rascal before he gets out of bed again," the old woman said. She led Kie into a bedchamber bigger than her entire house. The walls were covered with royal-blue silk panels that matched the hangings on the massive four-poster bed. Leaning against a small mountain of pillows, the prince plowed his way through a breakfast served on gold-rimmed china.

Are you all right in there? N'Rah asked Kie. *I can sense you feel frightened.*

Intimidated, more like. Prince Shayn's bed is probably worth all the money in Durwen Town put together.

And the sunburned boy from the desert looked much more like a real prince this morning in his white silk pajamas. The Dowager motioned for Kie to take a seat on an elegant high-backed chair by the prince's bed. Hoping she didn't have any dirt or manure on her backside, Kie sat, and the Dowager sat as well.

"Good morning, Your Highness," Kie said shyly. "I'm very glad you're feeling better."

"So am I," he said, flashing her a quick grin. "Although getting bitten by that chimera was a fascinating experience. I knew sand dragon venom contains a strong toxin that paralyzes their prey, but knowing something and experiencing it firsthand are completely different. I could think fine as I lay here, but I couldn't speak because I couldn't open my mouth. But within a few hours of my taking your antidote, my muscles started working again."

The Dowager frowned, and the prince shoveled down another mouthful. "Good thing you came when you did," he said to Kie through his partially chewed eggs. "I probably wasn't going to be able to swallow or breathe for much longer, and then I'd have been done for."

Kie shivered at the careless way he spoke of dying.

"Clearly there's nothing wrong with your tongue now," the Dowager said dryly, "but your manners are execrable. I imagine even children on the frontier know not to talk with their mouths full."

"Well, if you wouldn't keep insisting that I eat, Grandmama, I wouldn't risk offending our guest," the prince argued, and shoved the tray away. On soundless feet, a male servant in green-and-gold livery picked it up and bore it away.

With a sigh, the prince leaned back against his pillows, and she became the focus of his intense gaze. "So, Kiesandra Torsun, when you went flying off that afternoon we met in the desert, you were frightened for your family in Durwen Town. Did you get there in time?"

Touched that he remembered, she nodded. "My uncle is all the family I have left. He and his skysteed fought two chimerae and gave the townsfolk time to reach safety. They both were seriously injured in the fight, but they're doing better."

"I'm very glad to hear it. Now, please, you must tell me everything you know about this amazing manual you lent to my grandmother."

Kie was startled to see the old leather manual lying there on the prince's gold satin counterpane. "My eyes only started focusing an hour ago," he added hastily, "so I've just gotten a few pages into it, but it appears to be chock-full of useful information about chimerae and how to fight them."

"The manual belonged to my uncle's great-grandfather," Kie explained, "and his grandfather interviewed descendants of the first skyfighters to record everything he could about fighting chimerae before we forgot how we won the Chimera Wars. He believed that the creatures weren't gone forever."

"And now," Prince Shayn said, "we know he was right. With your permission, I'd like to take this manual straight to my father's commanders. They need to read it as soon as possible."

Yes! Kie resisted the urge to jump to her feet and cheer. "I would be so grateful if you would. That's why Uncle Duggan sent me here. He's very worried that the Skyforce's current tactics and our big modern skysteeds may not be effective in fighting the chimerae."

"What a fine figure your uncle cut when he was the reigning champion of the Imperial Tournament," the Dowager Empress interrupted with a dreamy look. "All the girls at court set our caps for Duggan Torsun. But once he met Sharilee Lasar, he only had eyes for her. After she died in that awful accident, he wanted nothing more to do with Pedarth."

"So," Kie said to the Dowager, trying to wrestle the conversation back where she needed it to go, "you know that my uncle understands skyfighting and the chimerae as well as anyone, and he's convinced you can't kill chimerae by flying straight at them with a lance."

"They'll bat the lances aside or bite them in half," the prince chimed in. "Those monsters are much faster than I expected."

The Dowager appeared to be listening carefully, her expression worried.

"Ma'am, I already know the favor I'd like to ask," Kie said, her heart drumming against her ribs.

"My dear girl," the old woman replied, "you would be wiser to wait a few days and make sure this request is something you truly want."

"I don't need to wait, because I'm very sure. The favor has two parts."

The Dowager's eyes narrowed, and suddenly Kie became more aware than ever that she was talking to the most powerful woman in all Prekalt. "Are you sure that you aren't about to ask me for two favors, then?" the old woman asked silkily.

"No, but if you decide they are two separate favors, you did say I saved Prince Shayn's life twice."

The Dowager rubbed her chin. "There must be some trader

blood in you, girl. All right. Let's hear them."

"The first is, I want you to go with your grandson when he takes my uncle's manual to the Emperor's Skyforce commanders. It's *vital* that they listen to him, and I'm afraid they might not because, well, because—"

"Because he's a boy, and a headstrong, heedless one at that?" the Dowager finished for her. "Your point is well taken. And the second part?"

"The second is, I want you to pay a skilled blacksmith to make a hundred triwires. I'm training some cadets in the evenings to use them, but they're using mock-ups right now, and they need to practice with real triwires before they face real chimerae."

"I'm praying those awful creatures never come near Pedarth," the old lady said with a shudder, "but very well. Get one of those triwires to me, and I shall order a hundred made just like it."

The Dowager paused for a moment and a sly gleam came into her eye that reminded Kie very much of N'Talley. "You know, you could have asked me for a hundred gold dashins, and you could have ordered the triwires yourself and had money left over."

"With all due respect, ma'am, I did think of that, but I don't have time to track down a blacksmith skilled enough to make a hundred triwires, and even if I did, a city craftsman might try to cheat a frontier girl. But he wouldn't dare cheat you."

The Dowager sat back in her chair. "You have thought this through," she said, looking impressed.

The prince climbed out of bed and went to rummage through gear piled in a corner of his room. "Here, Grandmama, you can have this triwire copied, but I want it back. That helped me take down another chimera after you left us," he said to Kie, "but I wasn't as fast as you, and the sand dragon head struck me as we flew past." The prince yawned as he returned to his bed.

"That's enough talk for now," the Dowager declared. "The two of you chimerae killers can catch up when my grandson is fully recovered."

Understanding a command when she heard it, Kie stood and followed the Dowager to the door.

"Kie, I promise I'll come to your practices as soon as I'm able," the prince called after her.

"Good luck with your father's commanders, Your Highness," Kie called back.

As she strode across the garden to N'Rah, Kie heard a whicker behind her. She turned, and the prince's pinto skysteed stood there, his ears pricked. He looked much better than he had yesterday. He walked over and sniffed at her hands. Although she was tempted to pat him, she knew what would happen if she touched his skin.

He wants you to touch him, N'Rah said. *He knows you can mindspeak with many skysteeds, and he would like to thank you directly.*

All right, Kie replied and stroked the pinto's silky neck. As the familiar tingling sensation shot through her arm to her brain, she noticed the green-and-gold ribbon braided into his mane. That was a useful reminder that she was meeting another member of the Imperial family.

Can you hear me now?

Kie nodded, very aware that the Dowager stood a few feet away watching them.

So it is true: you can speak to all skysteeds. The pinto eyed her with a keen intelligence that reminded her of the prince. *This is a strange and wonderful thing. Thank you for bringing the old book to my human's grandmother. N'Talley says it saved his life. I also owe you a favor.*

I'm just glad your human is better, Kie replied quickly, uncomfortable with all this talk of favors. *The only favor I would ask is that you not tell Prince Shayn that I can speak with you.*

Very well, but I think you will not be able to hide this ability much longer, N'Laure warned her. *Many of the older skysteeds talk of the girl who can mindspeak with us all, and they wonder what it could mean.*

I'm sure it doesn't mean anything, Kie said, her face beginning to warm. She bowed to N'Laure, and then to N'Talley and the Dowager. With a sigh of relief, she swung up onto N'Rah's back, and they were away.

CHAPTER SIXTEEN

WHEN KIE REPORTED FOR HER afternoon shift, the Academy stables were deserted. She heard a big cheer go up from the newer stadium. Everyone must have gone to watch the Term's End Tournament. While she tried to decide whether she should do the same, she heard a man's voice raised in fury.

When she hurried around a corner of the building, there stood a Rosari nobleman shouting at Ruden Mirsar and his skysteed. That man must be his father, she guessed, because he had thick, ruddy eyebrows and strong shoulders like Ruden's. The boy stared at the ground, his face pale, his freckles standing out like brands, and N'Saran hung his head while the man berated them both.

"True Mirsars and their skysteeds fly through their pain," Lord Mirsar yelled. "You two are gutless cowards, and you disgrace our family's name!" With that, he turned on his heel and stalked off.

Kie tried to back away before Ruden or his skysteed spotted her, but it was no use. The moment she moved, they both raised their heads and glared at her.

"I bet you're glad my skysteed's injured and we can't compete today," Ruden said resentfully.

She had been feeling sorry for Ruden, but his words made her burn with anger. "I'm *not* glad you can't compete today because of N'Saran's injury. I wouldn't want any skysteed hurt."

"I guess I should thank you for telling me about his sore muscle," Ruden said as if the words were being dragged out of him. "I can't believe N'Saran lied to me. I should be able to tell when my skysteed is hurt." His anger seemed to drain away as he stroked N'Saran's neck. "We fly and fight so well together, but sometimes I can't hear his mindspeech very well."

"If the Academy would let you cadets spend more time with your skysteeds," Kie declared, "I think you'd understand them better."

Ruden shot her an intent look. "Would it help if I could find ways to be around N'Saran more often?"

"I just know that we couriers spend days and nights flying with our skysteeds and caring for them ourselves, and every courier I've met understands their skysteed perfectly."

"I'm not sure where I'd find any more minutes in my day, but I'd gladly spend my nights in the park next to N'Saran if it would help us understand each other better."

The big skysteed leaned into him and nibbled at his shirt while Ruden scratched N'Saran behind his ears. Then the cadet turned to face Kie again and squared his shoulders.

"Kelton and Gunge told me about the practice sessions you've been holding in the old stadium. May I come? I'm going to make a practice triwire like theirs, and I'd like to learn how to throw it accurately while N'Saran's healing up. If the chimerae attack Pedarth, I want to know how to use every weapon that might be effective against them."

Trying to hide her dismay, Kie thought quickly. Ruden was the best skyfighter in his class, and other cadets would surely take note if he started to learn the old ways of fighting the chimerae. Besides, it must have cost him to ask her.

"You'd be welcome, but you better not insult our skysteeds again."

"I won't. I want to learn how such a small girl and your little skysteed managed to kill two chimerae."

Kie sighed. Plainly some of Ruden Mirsar's attitudes weren't going to change anytime soon. As she headed off to watch the Term's End Tournament, she wondered how Dessie and Topar were going to react if Ruden showed up at tonight's practice.

As it turned out, neither Topar nor Dessie were thrilled to learn they might have a new recruit, but Topar accepted the news more philosophically than Dessie did.

"As long as he doesn't call me a liar again, I can put up with him," Topar said.

"You haven't had to deal with him for years the way we grooms have," Dessie muttered. "If he speaks to me like I'm Mosai dirt tonight, I might just triwire him."

Kelton and Gunge arrived then, toting a big pile of lumber between them. With sheepish grins, they assembled what was evidently meant to be a chimera target, complete with three heads and a long tail.

"It's not much to look at, but we thought it would be more useful than throwing at a post," Kelton said.

"It's a good start," Kie said, not wanting to discourage the boys, "but those heads need to be bigger and spread out farther. And Topar, wouldn't you say their tails stretched back to here?"

Topar paced out the length of their new target and nodded.

"Whew, those monsters are even bigger than I expected," Ruden said, walking up with N'Saran at his back.

"We'll keep working on it until we get it right," Gunge promised, "and we're building a second target we can hang high up on that old jousting post."

Kie promoted Kelton and Gunge to throwing their practice triwires from the air. Ruden, she set to tossing his triwire at their new chimera target. Halfway through the practice, the big roan mare landed at the end of the stadium, and this time a half dozen Unbound skysteeds came with her, including a striking black with silver wings.

"N'Saran can drive this riffraff off for you," Ruden said, scowling at them.

"Don't you dare," Kie said.

"They aren't riffraff," Dessie added. "They are skysteeds, and each deserves our respect."

"Particularly that one. He's Prince Rodard's N'Tarin," Terry said, pointing to the black skysteed, a catch in his voice. "He disappeared after the prince died. I-I never thought we'd see him again."

Kie turned to the Unbound and bowed. "You are welcome to watch our practice whenever you wish," she called to them.

Princess Halla and N'Seella appeared early for their flight session and watched the practice, too. As soon as the cadets and the Unbound left, the black skysteed approached the princess. With a cry of delight, she threw her arms around his neck. When she let go, he flew off.

"I can't believe N'Tarin was here," the princess said, looking after the black skysteed. "Usually when skysteeds lose their riders, they disappear. I'm so glad to know he's all right, but I wonder why he came back now."

The princess looked away from the twilight sky and focused on Kie. "Shaynie said you were teaching a class on how to fight chimerae."

"How is he feeling?"

"Much better. He's desperate to get out of bed, but Grandmama won't let him until tomorrow. For helping to save his life, I owe you a favor."

Kie raised her hands in protest. "Thank you, Your Highness, but I don't want any more favors from anyone in your family."

"It's obvious you don't know how Pedarth works," Princess Halla said, her expression peeved, but then she brightened. "Tomorrow night, I'll bring my bow and join your practice. I'm a good shot, you know."

"But you said that you never wanted to skyfight again," Kie said.

"I never want to fight in a tournament, but if the chimerae come, of course I'll defend my people," the princess said, looking very determined.

Topar and Dessie stayed to help Princess Halla. This time, she hardly shook at all during their first trip around the stadium. Kie encouraged the princess to talk, to distract her as they climbed higher and higher into the twilight sky.

"So, are you older or is Prince Shayn?" Kie wondered aloud.

"I'm twenty minutes older, and I never let him forget it."

"You're twins?" Kie asked with surprise.

"You didn't know?" The princess looked back at Kie, equally surprised. "But I thought everyone in the Empire knew all about our family."

"Well, actually, out on the frontier we're a little too busy fighting hailstorms and trying to raise enough food to feed our families to keep up on capital gossip."

Princess Halla stiffened for a moment, and then she giggled. "You talk just like Grandmama sometimes. No wonder she and N'Talley like you so much."

"They do?" Warmth kindled inside Kie. She liked the Dowager and her plain-speaking skysteed, too.

"Grandmama says you have common sense, which she thinks is seriously lacking in me and most everyone in Pedarth."

Kie wasn't sure how to respond to that, but luckily the princess kept chattering. "Where was I? Oh yes, we were talking about Shaynie and me. People always say he got the brains and I got the beauty, which isn't fair because I'm smarter than I look, and Shaynie isn't ugly."

"No, he's not," Kie agreed. "Has your father heard from the Advance Guard yet?"

"No, and their courier is long overdue. I can't believe that's a good thing," the princess replied, her voice tight.

That night, Kie drifted off to sleep hoping with all her heart that the missing military courier would arrive in the night, bringing news of a victory instead of a disaster.

CHAPTER SEVENTEEN

THE NEXT DAY, KIE SLIPPED away from her stable chores at lunch. This time at Central Relay, there was a letter from Riken waiting for her. Her uncle was resting more comfortably, N'Tor was on his feet again, and there'd been no more chimerae sightings in their area.

Kie was eating and sharing this news with Topar under a shady bawa tree when N'Rah pricked his ears and stared at the sky.

The prince comes to see you, he warned her. Shortly, N'Laure landed beside them, and Prince Shayn jumped from his back. His bright red hair was windblown, and he had more color in his cheeks today.

"Kie, you've *got* to come with me straight away," he said as he strode toward her. "Oh, hullo, Topar, it's good to see you. You should come, too."

Kie drew in a breath. Would she ever get used to Prince Shayn's headlong ways?

"Where do you want us to go, and why, Your Highness?" she asked.

"Please, don't bother with my title when there's no one official around," Prince Shayn said with a careless wave. "It's so inefficient. Just call me Shayn. You need to come right away to a meeting of the Imperial War Council. I tried to get my father's commanders to look at your uncle's manual, but those arrogant old fools are sure our Skyforce is going to exterminate the chimerae within a few days."

"Did your grandmother try to talk to them?"

"They dismissed her, too, and she was steaming mad about it."

Kie could imagine the old woman's displeasure. "So if they wouldn't listen to her, why would they listen to two junior couriers?"

"Because you've actually fought chimerae, and we'll have Captain Nerone along for backup, in case they don't listen to you," he replied with a resolute look in his green eyes. "We're going to fetch her next."

Prince Shayn was marching back to his skysteed when Topar cleared his throat. "I am supposed to be back at work soon, and I'd really rather not get fired. My family depends on the dashins I send home."

"Mine, too," Kie chimed in.

Prince Shayn turned around, obviously surprised that they weren't hurrying to follow him. "All right," he said after a moment. "Trishop already knows I need Kie, but you best introduce me to your supervisor, and quickly," he told Topar.

Soon they were on their way to the Academy, where Prince Shayn hurried inside the main building to talk to the commandant.

"I guess people don't say no to Imperial princes very often,"

Kie said as she watched Captain Nerone appear. In no time, they were flying for the palace, but the captain looked like she was braced for battle.

Kie's belly tightened. "Is it going to be that bad, talking to the commanders?" she asked the captain.

"Shouldn't be so bad for you, but telling the most powerful men and women in the Skyforce that most everything they believe about skyfighting is wrong is not a good way to advance my career," Captain Nerone said with a grimace.

They landed in a grand courtyard dominated by a fountain crowned with two amartine sculptures of rearing skysteeds. The sun danced on the shining statues and the water, dazzling Kie. She blinked and looked away, her trepidation growing by the moment.

"Does Lord General Rennart still serve on the War Council?" she heard Topar ask the prince as they dismounted.

"He's one of the High Commander's most trusted officers," the prince replied absently.

Why had Topar asked about the Lord General? How had he even known that the Lord General had served on the Emperor's War Council? Kie longed to ask, but the tight set to Topar's jaw discouraged her. The prince led them up some marble steps and through a massive door guarded by two armed sentries wearing the green-and-gold of the Rathskayan dynasty.

Then they marched down a wide corridor inlaid with bright tiled scenes of skysteeds fighting chimerae. She would have spent more time gawking at the floor, but she was too busy worrying that the prince might actually expect her to say something to his father or his father's commanders.

At last they came to another imposing set of wooden doors, inlaid with intricate amartine scrollwork and guarded by two more tall sentries.

"Wait!" Kie caught at the prince's sleeve desperately. "Shouldn't we have a plan before we go in there?"

"We don't have time for that. You'll do fine. Just tell them what you saw in the desert and how effective smaller, faster sky-steeds and triwires and botans were that day."

"But Your Highness, Kie's right," Captain Nerone said. "We should pre—"

Before she could protest further, the prince nodded to the guards, and they threw open the great doors. Kie glanced down at herself. Was she really about to go before the Emperor wearing her second-best pair of courier trousers, which she'd mended countless times? She glanced over at Topar, but he stared straight ahead, his face as closed as she'd ever seen it.

Her guts twisting themselves into a painful knot, Kie followed Prince Shayn into a large chamber with a massive oval table at its center. Around the table sat a dozen men and women, most wearing maroon-and-gray Skyforce uniforms festooned with shining silver braids and medals.

The Dowager Empress sat at one end of the table looking like she had just eaten something sour, and a distinguished-looking man with a short gray beard sat at the other. The air left Kie's lungs, and her legs felt shaky. She was standing in the same room with the Emperor of all Prekalt!

N'Rah, His Supreme Highness looks just like he does on the silver dashin coin, only more tired, Kie told her friend, and that thought helped to steady her, a little.

The commanders at the table turned to stare at them. *These people do not look happy to see us,* she added. *I really hope the prince doesn't make me say something.*

"I beg your pardon, distinguished commanders," Prince Shayn said, not sounding the least bit apologetic. "I've brought some people to this meeting whom you *must* hear."

"Your Highness, you've already shared your opinions with our council," an older Rosari with a hawkish nose objected.

"But you didn't listen to me, and you wouldn't listen to my grandmother, and so now, I am hoping you will listen to the only three people besides me in all of Pedarth who have actually survived a fight with chimerae. This is Captain Nerone, who, as you know, killed one chimera with her sword, this is Junior Courier Kiesandra Torsun, who killed two chimerae using a bow and a triwire, and Junior Courier Topar Singu of the Lsari clan, who brought one down with a botan."

The moment the prince said Topar's name, one of the commanders twisted about and gazed at her Ledari friend. Kie glanced at Topar. His hands were clenched at his sides. What was going on here? Why was that Rosari officer so interested in Topar?

"Very well," the Emperor said, "I will admit that through their valor, these three all deserve a chance to share their views with us. Captain Nerone, tell us your thoughts on how effective our skysteeds and weapons were against the chimerae."

Captain Nerone squared her shoulders. "I regret to say, Your Supreme Highness, our weapons and tactics were not effective in Terkann."

"But by your own report, you were surprised and vastly outnumbered," the man with the hawk nose protested.

"That's Lord General Virsart," Prince Shayn whispered in Kie's ear. "He's the commander in charge of all our forces."

"That is true, sir," Captain Nerone replied, "but twelve well-trained skyfighters should have inflicted significant losses on the chimerae scourges we faced that day, and yet we only managed to bring down two of the monsters before we lost ten skyfighters of our own and had to retreat. The only weapons that proved at all effective during that engagement were bows."

"Yet you managed to kill one chimerae with a sword and survived," the High Commander said sharply.

"Only because I communicate well with my skysteed, and she's smaller and quicker than most domesticated skysteeds. And frankly, sir, we were incredibly lucky. Every skyfighter who tried to fly straight at the beasts with a lance died, including Garrison Commander Meem, as capable and brave a skyfighter as I've ever known."

The High Commander sat back in his chair, his cheeks red. Kie had an awful feeling that Captain Nerone had been right to worry about her career.

The Emperor looked at Topar next. "Topar Singu of the

Lsari clan, do you have any thoughts to contribute?"

"I arrived at the end of the fight near the Mrai oasis," Topar said. His voice shook a bit, but then it steadied. "I saw Junior Courier Torsun and her skysteed being attacked by a chimera. I threw my botan, and it brought the chimera down by binding its wing to its back leg. My skysteed barely dodged out of the way of a strike from its sand dragon head and a blow from its spiked tail. The monsters are much faster than I expected and a hundred times more dangerous than grytocs."

And then the Emperor looked at Kie, and once again she couldn't get enough air into her lungs. "Junior Courier Torsun, I must thank you for the life of my son, and the effort you made to bring your uncle's manual to us," he said gravely. "What would you add to our discussion?"

"You're welcome, Your Supreme Highness," was all she could manage before her throat closed up. Her cheeks burned as she tried to force words out, but they wouldn't come. She was just a frontier girl. She had no business being in this room, much less sharing her opinions.

But as the silence grew more awkward, she realized she would have to say *something*. Maybe she couldn't talk to the ruler of all Prekalt, but she could speak to his mother. She focused on the old woman's face, and her throat relaxed a bit.

"Ma'am, triwires and botans and our brave, quick skysteeds kept us alive that day." Kie stopped for a moment, struggling to find the right words. "What I truly want to say is that everything feels all wrong here in Pedarth. People shouldn't be betting on skyfighting tournaments, and cadets need to spend more time with their skysteeds, and the Unbound should be allowed to bind with humans if they want to." She hesitated for a moment, afraid she was rambling, and the next moment, the High Commander slapped a hand on the table.

"Your Supreme Highness, I've heard enough. I'm not sure what this girl's getting at, but it's ridiculous to think two junior couriers and a lowly captain know more about skyfighting tactics than the commanders assembled here."

"It's ridiculous that you hidebound idiots can't see what they are trying to tell you," Prince Shayn shot back.

"My dear boy," the Dowager said, getting to her feet, "in the future you must learn the value of tact, but today, I must agree with you."

She paused long enough to rake the commanders with a scathing glance. "You are foolish not to listen to these young people, who had considerably more success in fighting those awful beasts than your own Skyforce fighters. I'm reminded strongly of the old adage 'You can lead a skysteed to water, but you can't make him drink.' Clearly, this afternoon, none of us can make you open your ears or your minds. Courier Torsun, I've already commissioned a hundred of those triwires you asked for, and now I'm going to commission a thousand more and pray we don't have to use them." And with that, the old woman swept from the room.

"We will wait to hear how our Advance Guard fared," the

Emperor told his council, "and we will discuss the possibility of incorporating more old-time weapons and tactics into the Skyforce's training at that time."

When he stood, the commanders instantly stood as well. "My son," the Emperor said with a stern look at Prince Shayn, "you will see your guests out, and then I expect you in my private chambers, where we will review the proper protocol to be followed at Council meetings."

The prince bowed, his own cheeks flaming, and the Emperor left the room. Prince Shayn had started for the door when one of the Rosari commanders stepped forward. "Topar Singu, I would speak with you."

Topar stopped in his tracks. Reluctantly, he turned around to face the man who had been staring at him with such interest.

"Who's that man Topar's talking to?" Kie whispered to Captain Nerone.

"That's Lord General Rennart, one of the most powerful nobles in all Prekalt."

And the one Topar had asked the prince about before the meeting ever started. As Kie watched the noble speaking to Topar, the oddest notion occurred to her. They had the same dark green eyes, and the same wide shoulders and slim hips. Topar *never* mentioned his Rosari father, who had left Terkann and his mother years ago, but now Kie couldn't help wondering if Topar might be related to this man.

Suddenly, Topar shook his head, his face tight with anger.

"No! I don't want to hear anything else you have to say," he said vehemently, and turned away from the Lord General.

"Your Highness, I'm ready to leave now," he said to the prince. After sending him a curious glance, Prince Shayn nodded and led them back the way they'd come.

The moment they reached the fountain courtyard, the prince burst out, "By N'Rin's mane, why can't they see that smaller, fleeter skysteeds and triwires are the answer? Now I'll have to think of another way to convince them."

"Why can't your father just order his commanders to use tri-wires?" Kie asked. "He is the Emperor, after all, and he looked like he believed us."

Prince Shayn shrugged. "He may be the supreme ruler, but he rules with the support of the Rosari nobility, and some of the most powerful nobles in all Prekalt serve on the War Council. If he alienates them, they'll put one of his cousins on the throne."

She stared at the prince. The Emperor wasn't all-powerful? Since she'd come to Pedarth, so many of her assumptions had been turned upside down.

"I'll see you at your training session in a few hours," Prince Shayn promised Kie. "But first, I have to listen to a lecture on all the rules I broke just now. Thanks for coming."

The prince strode back up the stairs.

"He reminds me of a *tararr*, a desert whirlwind," Topar said, looking after the prince.

"If only he'd let us plan what we were going to say," Kie said.

"I know I blathered on in there." *And sounded like a stupid country girl.* Her cheeks burned again when she thought about how she'd frozen up before the Emperor, and then rambled on in front of his Council.

"I doubt our being better organized would have made a difference," Captain Nerone said. "They're quite sure the way they've been training skyfighters is right, and only a major defeat will convince them otherwise."

"I hope we don't find out soon that there's been one," Topar said soberly.

Chapter Eighteen

Kie and Topar headed straight back to their jobs after their appearance at the Imperial War Council. As they flew across green Tavalier Park side by side, his expression was so withdrawn that Kie decided not to ask him about his conversation with Lord General Rennart. Instead, she tried a sneakier way to find out how her friend was doing.

N'Rah, can you ask N'Meary if Topar's all right?

I will, N'Rah replied, and a few moments later, he reported back. *She says he is very angry at a man he talked with in that meeting, but he will not tell her why. She is worried because her human does not get like this very often.*

Please tell her I will try to talk to him later and find out why that man upset him so much.

That night, at their practice in the old stadium, Topar arrived shortly after she did. Before she could talk to Topar, though, Ruden, Kelton, and Gunge arrived with two more cadets in tow, and Terry and Dessie came with a couple of their groom friends, including a small, very enthusiastic boy named Hedly who had made a practice triwire almost as tall as he was. Even Princess Halla appeared, carrying a beautiful, lethal-looking bow and a quiver full of arrows.

"I think we should call ourselves Kie's Cadets," she declared gaily as she strung her bow.

"I don't," Kie said firmly. What would Trishop or the Academy's real instructors think if they heard that nickname? The others laughed, though, and the princess went to shoot at targets in the far corner of the stadium.

Kelton and Gunge showed off a new three-headed chimera target they'd built, and they proceeded to hoist it up the old jousting post. Kie allowed Kelton, Gunge, and Topar, now her most advanced students, to attack the target with their practice triwires from the air.

The only person who didn't come that night was the prince himself. Kie found herself looking for him several times throughout the practice session. On a quick break, Topar and Kie walked away from the others.

"Princess Halla wasn't exaggerating. She's a good shot with that bow," Topar said.

"Maybe there's a way we can use her archery to get her flying without the tandem harness," Kie mused. Then she noticed Topar's troubled expression. "Are you . . . all right?" she asked.

"Yeah. I'm better now."

"I'm here if you want to talk," she offered shyly. "Us frontier folk need to stick together."

"It's a long story, but I think I'd like you to hear it. Maybe we can talk after we help the princess and N'Seella."

Prince Shayn, on N'Laure, appeared after the cadets and the

grooms had left and Dessie, Topar, and Kie were getting ready for Princess Halla's flight session.

The prince dismounted stiffly, and for once he didn't seem to bounce as he walked. Instead, his face was pale and his eyes were red-rimmed. His serious expression caused them all to gather around him.

He started to speak, but he had to clear his throat first. "I didn't want us to be right, but we were. The Advance Guard was wiped out. A military courier just brought the news. Only five skyfighting pairs out of two hundred made it back to the rendez-vous point with the Skyforce in the Telawa Valley, along with a handful of individual skysteeds and fighters who also survived."

Kie drew in a breath in dismay. Skyriders were never quite whole again after they lost their skysteeds, and skysteeds likewise were terribly hurt by the death of their riders. Her heart ached for the skyriders and skysteeds who had just survived such terrible loss.

"Oh no," Princess Halla cried, her beautiful eyes filling with tears. "Some of our own palace skyfighters volunteered to serve in that advance guard."

"And the commanders are already saying it was routed because they faced such overwhelming numbers," Prince Shayn said bitterly, "not because flying straight at chimerae with lances on big, slow skysteeds is an incredibly stupid idea."

"We tried to tell them, and they wouldn't listen to us," Kie said, wanting to kick something, hard.

"There's only one thing left to do," the prince declared. "We three have to prove to the Skyforce commanders that our smaller, faster skysteeds and our bows, botans, and triwires are the answer. We have to go out to the Telawa Valley and show them by fighting chimerae again, successfully, ourselves."

Kie's heart skipped a beat. Was he serious? They'd barely survived their fight with one scourge of chimerae.

"But, Shaynie, that's going to be awfully dangerous," Princess Halla protested, "and you're still recovering from that horrible sand dragon bite."

"I'm better now, and this can't wait. If we don't go and show them a more effective way to fight these monsters, the Skyforce could get wiped out, and then there won't be anyone left to stop the chimerae from scourging the whole continent."

"What exactly are you suggesting we do?" Topar asked.

"We fly out to the area where the Skyforce is fighting, and we tackle the first scourges we come across, and then the Skyforce commanders in the field will have to admit that the older weapons and smaller, faster skysteeds are the answer."

"Father and Grandmama will never let you go," Princess Halla said.

"That's why I'm not going to tell them, and you can't, either."

The princess wrapped her arms around herself. "But what if you go off and get yourself killed?"

"I won't get myself killed. I learned a lot in that last fight, including to never take my eyes off the sand dragon head," he said with a wry glance at Kie and Topar. "Please," he said to his twin, "promise me you won't tell them. I *have* to do this."

She thought for a moment. "I promise I won't tell Grandmama or Father what you're planning to do."

"Thanks, sis," he said with relief.

Kie noticed the princess's careful phrasing, but she guessed the prince had not.

"Kie and Topar, I'll go out there by myself if I must," the prince forged on. "But we fought well together last time, and with a little planning, we can be even more effective this time."

"I have to talk to N'Rah about this," Kie said, tasting bile in the back of her throat. She couldn't believe she was even considering volunteering to fight those terrifying creatures again. She walked away with her skysteed, while Topar did the same with N'Meary.

Oh, dear N'Rah, what do you think we should do?

I do not want to fight more chimerae, he said with unusual seriousness, *but the prince is right. It is foolish to fly at our ancient enemies with a lance. If we can prove there is a better way to fight them, we should do it. I do not want more skysteeds to die.*

But I don't want you to die. I don't want us to die!

We will not die. I am very fast, and we also learned a lot the first time we fought them.

Kie closed her eyes and pictured the beautiful legions of skysteeds she'd seen flying into the western sky when the Skyforce launched, and she knew what her choice would be.

She walked to where Topar stood with his hand on N'Meary's neck. "What are you thinking?" she asked him.

"I hate putting N'Meary in such danger again, but I'm afraid we have to do this. As my granny used to say, 'To see is to believe,' and those commanders we met today are never, ever going to believe unless we show them these weapons work."

"All right, then," Kie said, dread settling low in her belly. "Let's tell the prince."

Prince Shayn was a good organizer. Within two hours, they were on their way, loaded up with all nine of Kie's real triwires, Topar's three botans, and some light travel rations. Kie, Topar, and the prince carried bows as well. Princess Halla had seen them off at the old practice stadium, her face pale and set as she hugged each of them and told them to take care of themselves.

Kie was glad she'd been able to pack while Dessie was at dinner. She had a hunch her new friend would have strongly disapproved of the prince's dangerous plan. Kie had considered leaving a note for Trishop, but she'd been afraid that he'd show it to the Emperor, and guards would be sent after them right away to haul the prince home.

Now they were flying swiftly west, into a warm moonlit night. Although she flew day shifts, Kie loved soaring with N'Rah through the night sky. Fields and forests, hills and lakes transformed into shades of black, gray, and silver while the clouds they passed glowed like pearl-white castles.

But tonight she couldn't enjoy flying. With fear a bitter taste in her mouth, all she could think about was their terrifying fight against the chimerae in the Western Desert. Until this evening, she'd slammed shut the door to her memories of that afternoon. Now she made herself review each moment, trying to remember how the chimerae had moved and reacted. N'Rah said he'd learned from that fight. She had learned, too, but had they both learned enough to stay alive if they fought chimerae again?

Talking little, they flew for hours over the rich, rolling farmlands of central Prekalt. Smaller Cira rose in the east, and bigger Cerken set in the west. When the sky started to lighten, the skysteeds asked for a quick rest.

They set down beside a quiet lake far from any farm. The skysteeds walked themselves cool and then began to drink. Too keyed up to sleep, Kie went to stretch her legs, leaving the prince by the lakeshore muttering to himself and drawing attack plans based on what he'd read in Uncle Dugs's manual.

She came around a bend in the lake, and there was Topar, frowning at the moonlit water. She hesitated. Did he want to be left alone? The only way to know was to ask. He looked up as she walked closer.

"Do you want to tell me what the Lord General wanted?"

"Not really, but it's better than thinking about fighting chimerae again," Topar replied.

As they stood side by side, staring out at the lake, the dawn breeze riffled its smooth surface. "I did hear you ask the prince about him before we went into that meeting. How did you know Lord General Rennart even existed? I'd never heard his name before."

Topar drew in a deep breath. "I knew his name because he's my father."

Kie snuck a peek at him. It had occurred to her that he might have been related to the Lord General. Everyone at Terkann station knew Topar must be part Rosari because of his green eyes. Few boys ever teased him about his missing parent, though, because Topar was well-liked and such a good fighter.

"How did your parents—" she started to ask, and then he interrupted her.

"How did they come to marry? Because they *were*, you know," he said defiantly, "no matter what you may have heard. My father was a young Skyforce captain stationed at the garrison in Terkann when they met at a dance and fell in love. He was a third son with little chance of inheriting his father's title, and so they married against the wishes of both families. But then his brothers died, and he was called home to be the new Lord Rennart."

"Did your mother go with him? If she did, it must have been hard for her," Kie said. Pedarth seemed so strange to her every day.

"She did. She gave up the desert and her clan to be with him, but within a year, she knew they'd made a terrible mistake. His mother and family seemed so ashamed of her, and she missed her home and her people, and . . . she knew she was going to have me."

Topar leaned over and picked up a small rock and hurled it

into the lake. "Afraid I'd be treated with scorn and veiled insults just as she had, she left one night and never returned to him. By Ledari custom, her leaving meant they were divorced, and eventually she remarried Thersi, my stepfather. He was a good man and kind to me and all my half brothers and sisters until he died last year."

"Did Lord Rennart ever remarry?"

"That's what he wanted to talk about today. He said he never married or had other children, and now," Topar said after taking another deep breath, "he wants me to be his heir."

Chapter Nineteen

Her thoughts in a tangle, Kie turned to study Topar, the lake a silver mirror behind him as the dawn breeze died. Topar was one of the nicest, most hardworking people she knew. She couldn't imagine him living the lazy life of a Rosari noble in Pedarth.

"Would you want to be his heir?" she asked him.

"Of course I don't want to be his heir!" he replied fiercely. "If he couldn't protect my mother from his family, I don't want anything to do with him."

"It might have been more complicated than that," Kie said, trying to imagine what life had been like for them in Pedarth. Mosai and Rosari classes were so far apart, maybe Topar's Ledari mother and aristocratic father never had a chance of being accepted. "They must have loved each other very much to marry against their families' wishes."

"If she was that important to him," Topar argued, "why didn't he try to bring her back to Pedarth to be with him? Why didn't he try to bring *us* back?"

Kie winced at the hurt in his voice. "Maybe," she said slowly, "he was trying to respect her choice. He must have cared about her very much if he didn't marry again."

"That's the bag of road apples he tried to hand to me at the

Council meeting this afternoon," Topar said, and flung another rock into the lake.

"Maybe you don't have to be his heir, but perhaps someday you should try to get to know him. It must have taken guts to go against his parents and marry your mother in the first place."

Topar slanted her a look. "Would *you* want to know your mother? She hasn't been a big part of your life, either."

Kie stiffened. "That's different. Your mother didn't *want* to leave your father. But my mother chose to leave Da and me when a fancy peddler man offered her an easier, more exciting life, so we were better off without her."

Sometimes, though, when Kie was waking up or falling asleep, her unruly mind would wander, and she could still remember the soft feel of Mama's lap, or the scent of the rose soap she used, or the awful day she left when Kie was six.

"I'm dying here, my little owl, trapped on this hillside with a bunch of boring dayan trees," Mama had said. "You're so clever, you'll be fine without me." Then she'd kissed Kie on the forehead and ridden away on the peddler's cart without a backward glance.

At first they hadn't been fine. She'd cried day and night, and poor Da looked like he'd never smile again. Then, when she'd gone off to school in Durwen, she found out she was anything but clever. In time, she and Da had both healed, but Kie had learned one very important lesson from her mother: There were very few people in this whole world she could trust.

"Well, I'm sure I've been better off without a father," Topar was saying, "and he doesn't have a right to become a part of my life now."

"He doesn't, not unless you want him to," Kie said firmly. "The sun's almost up. We better get back to the prince."

When they returned to the skysteeds, Prince Shayn handed them papers with arrows and X marks all over them.

"These are attack plans I've made based on your uncle's manual," he declared. "The X's represent chimerae, and the arrows represent our flight paths. As Kie already knows, in the olden days, skyfighters often worked together in groups of three they called triads when they fought chimerae. Study these plans while we fly, and we'll talk about them at our next rest break."

Trying not to look skeptical, Kie took the papers and tucked them into her flight jacket. The Skyforce had used fighting triads three hundred years ago to confuse and distract the three heads of a chimera, but those were well-trained teams composed of skyfighters who had spent months practicing together. The three of them had never once trained as a team.

When the sun had risen and set the eastern sky on fire, she brought the sheets out and tried to read them. Chewing her lip in frustration, she couldn't make sense out of the prince's scrawled handwriting and arrows pointing every which way. At their next rest stop, she asked the prince to explain his fight plans.

He launched into a detailed explanation of where each of them should be in the sky as they attacked a single chimera. "You two are better with your bows, triwires, and botans than I am, and

N'Laure is super quick, so we'll be the distraction, or the bait."

"But what happens if we end up fighting more than one chimera at the same time?" Topar asked with a frown.

"Then we need to communicate quickly with gestures and through our skysteeds."

As they reviewed the arm signals they'd use, Kie wondered if she should tell the prince that she could talk to N'Laure. It might help them communicate faster, but she doubted the prince could keep a secret like that. Plus, she couldn't bear it if Topar— perhaps her only human friend—thought she was peculiar and different like so many people back home did.

After the skysteeds had rested, they took off, heading west once again. They flew over a small mountain range and followed the Telawa River, which had forged the wide Telawa Valley ages ago. Now the air was hotter and the land more arid. Farms and towns below them were clustered along the green banks of the river. Beyond those banks, the land quickly turned to dry, grassy plains.

As the sun neared the western horizon, N'Rah woke Kie from an uneasy doze to warn her that he'd spotted a courier flying east. She jerked awake and told the others.

"We need to find out where the Skyforce is," the prince said, and sent N'Laure racing to intercept the courier.

"He won't want to stop to talk to us," Kie said after they caught up with Prince Shayn, "particularly if he's a military courier."

"Maybe, but N'Laure's green-and-gold braid should help. People often won't believe I'm a prince," Prince Shayn said, making a wry face, "but no skysteed except one bound to our family would dare to wear the Rathskayan colors."

"Let's spread out across his flight path," Topar said, "and give the courier a distress signal. Maybe that will get him to stop."

He waved both arms over his head, and the prince and Kie did the same. The courier arrowed straight at them and only slowed when he was a few wing lengths away. Young and Mosai, he wore a Skyforce uniform.

"Whatever trouble you're in, I can't help you," the courier said, his voice tight with strain. "I have to get my dispatches to relay as fast as I can."

"I'm Prince Shayn Rathskayan, Lord of Tirgaz and Duke of Torenth," the prince said in a commanding voice. "Tell us what's happening with the Skyforce, and you can be on your way." The prince patted N'Laure's neck, and the courier's eyes widened when he saw the skysteed's braid.

"Your Highness, the Skyforce is taking heavy losses as it engages hundreds of chimerae scourges where Telawa Valley opens onto the Western Desert. So far we're holding them, but at a terrible cost. Lord General Furen is afraid they're going to slip around our lines and start attacking settlements in this valley soon."

"Have the settlers taken shelter in caves?" the prince asked.

"I'm from these parts," the courier said, "and I can tell you most of the settlements out here have no caves."

"But by law, every settlement is to be built near sizable underground shelters," the prince said, looking horrified.

"Mosai settlers are so desperate for cheap land, they often build where there is no underground protection," Kie explained to him quietly.

"How far is it from here to the front lines?" the prince asked.

The courier glanced down at his timepiece. "I left the front lines seven hours ago, and we've been flying fast the entire time."

"Thank you," the prince said. "On you go."

"Fly safe, fly free," Kie and Topar called after him.

Sobered by the courier's news, they said little as they flew on. When the setting sun turned the long, thin clouds along the horizon into bloody gashes of scarlet, goose bumps rose on Kie's arms. *I hope those clouds aren't an omen for us,* she thought to herself.

After they traveled well into the night, the prince suggested they land and try to get some sleep. "We need to make sure the skysteeds, at least, are well rested. I'm not sure how much sleep I'll be getting," he confessed.

They made a tiny fire, ate some travel rations and, once more, Kie asked the prince to talk her through his complicated attack patterns. They made a bit more sense as he described them. *I just wish we had time to practice his plans before we use them in a fight,* she told N'Rah as she folded up the papers and placed them in her jacket. He snuffled her hair comfortingly and promptly fell asleep.

Jealous of her skysteed, Kie lay wide awake in her bedroll.

Both moons had set, and the black heavens were ablaze with stars. Eyes burning from lack of sleep, she gazed up at them.

Trying not to think about the chimerae she'd be fighting tomorrow, she concentrated on the stories Da had taught her about the constellations. There was Koby the prankster, spilling water onto the head of Elenay, goddess of hearth and home, and there were the great scales of Nimro, the stern god of justice.

Dominating the skies overhead were the bright silver stars in the wings and mane of fiery N'Rin with Prince Isen on his back, sword raised, challenging the first waves of chimerae attacking his father's kingdom. Prince Isen had forged the Great Alliance with the skysteeds with Mage Sian's help, and eventually he would unite all Prekalt and become the first Emperor.

What had Prince Isen been like, and had he been as terrified as she felt now, before he fought chimerae?

At one point in that endless night, she glanced across their camp and saw the shine of Topar's eyes in the starlight. He was wide awake, too.

It was almost a relief when the skies began to gray, and the prince sat up in his blankets. "It's time," he said, his voice cracking.

Despite the warm temperature, Kie shook with tremors she hoped the others didn't see. She tried to eat a biscuit, but her mouth was so dry, she almost choked. She tucked the rest of the biscuit back into her saddlebag. *I hope I'll still be alive to eat it later,* she thought numbly.

She handed three triwires to Topar, two to Prince Shayn, and kept four for herself. Then they all strung their bows, and she gave N'Rah a long hug.

I will do my best to protect you today, she promised him.

And I will do my best to keep us both alive, N'Rah pledged seriously in return.

After they took off, they flew in a tight triad formation with the prince in the lead and Topar and Kie covering his flanks. They all kept their eyes peeled for chimerae and the Skyforce.

They'd been in the air for two hours, and the sun was hot on Kie's back, when N'Rah pricked his ears and tensed.

There's a scourge ahead of us, he told her. *From the way they keep diving toward the ground, I think they attack a settlement.*

"Do you see any signs of the Skyforce?"

No, he replied worriedly, *I do not see skyfighters anywhere. If we try to help these settlers, we will fight alone.*

CHAPTER TWENTY

HER HEART POUNDING AGAINST HER ribs, Kie relayed the news to Topar and Prince Shayn that there were chimerae ahead but no skyfighters. As N'Rah's every wing stroke brought them closer to the monsters, she checked her triwires and made sure she could reach them easily. Then she slung her bow into fighting position across her shoulder and wiped her sweaty palms on her shirt.

"N'Meary sees the chimerae, too," Topar called out, "and she agrees they must be attacking something on the ground."

"Let's move higher so we can see, and so the chimerae don't see us," the prince suggested. N'Laure turned and sprinted up to a nearby cloud.

Soon they were hovering on the cloud's edge, above a settlement along the river, surrounded by dekkar trees. Kie clenched her hands as she watched six chimerae dive into the settlement again and again. From Uncle Dugs's manual, she knew they were probably using their tails to smash shacks apart and send their occupants fleeing into the streets, where they would be easy prey.

"I wanted the Skyforce to watch us fight," the prince said hoarsely, "but I can't go on and leave those settlers to be slaughtered."

Kie glanced over at Topar, and he nodded. "We agree," she said through dry lips. "We have to help them."

"All right, then," the prince said. "Remember, N'Laure and I will serve as bait. Because we're so outnumbered, we need to lure the chimerae away and kill them one by one. If there is a scourge master directing them this time, we need to eliminate him as quickly as possible."

"Kie and I can hide behind that tall dekkar tree," Topar said. "We can ambush them from there after you lead them to us."

The prince nodded, his face pale. "Good luck," he said, and N'Laure shot away. Topar and N'Meary dove for the tree, N'Rah hard on their tail.

They hovered side by side behind the thick treetop. Kie shuddered when the wind brought with it the deep roar of a lion and the frantic ringing of an alarm bell. She had to clear her throat before she could speak. "So, how do you want to tackle this first one?" she asked, proud that her voice barely trembled.

Topar glanced at her, his face tight. "I'll try to shoot the central heart, and you try to bring the chimera down with a triwire?"

"Works for me," she said, and unslung a triwire. With her other hand, she reached out and stroked N'Rah's neck.

How are you? she asked her friend.

I am glad the wait is almost over, he said. *I am ready to fight.*

His steadiness helped to steady her. But what if the entire scourge had spotted Prince Shayn, and six chimerae were charging their way instead of just one? Desperate to know what was happening, she reached out to N'Laure. *Are you two all right? Are you close?*

We are almost to you and have one chimera on our tail.

"N'Rah says they're almost here," she told Topar as N'Rah started to climb. "Come on!"

Moments later, N'Laure flashed over their heads, flying all out, the prince lying low against his neck. A hundred feet behind, a tan-and-black chimera raced after them, all three of its heads straining to reach the pinto skysteed and his rider.

Shivers traced down her back as N'Rah sped after the monster. This chimera seemed even bigger than the ones they'd fought in the Western Desert!

N'Rah caught up to the chimera, and Kie guided him into the blind spot below the chimera's right wing. She tried not to gag when she caught the familiar stench of rotting flesh.

White wings flashed as N'Meary took up position in the blind spot beneath the chimera's left wing. Topar waved to indicate he was ready. Kie twirled her triwire. N'Meary moved first, darting along the left side of the chimera. Topar shot one arrow into the beast, and then he and N'Meary disappeared behind the chimera's body. The lion head roared, and the bloodgoat head screeched in pain. The chimera halted midair and spun to attack N'Meary.

Seeing their chance, she squeezed N'Rah's sides hard, and he hurtled ahead and above the monster. As the chimera's right wing flashed down, she threw the triwire. The copper wires glinted in the sunlight as they spun through the air. Two caught the chimera's wing and sliced through leathery skin and cartilage to the bone, and the third bound the wing to the chimera's foreleg. Bellowing in pain, the chimera tilted to the right and crashed to the ground, hard. It staggered about down there, all three heads snapping at the triwire. Even if the beast worked itself free, that wing was so damaged, she doubted the chimera could fly again.

"Nice work," the prince called. "We'll bring you another one."

Kie turned N'Rah about and flew back to hide behind the tree. She leaned forward and patted N'Rah's neck, grateful for a moment to catch her breath, and very grateful they were still alive.

"You were brilliant," she told him.

That toss was brilliant, N'Rah said warmly, peering back at her.

When she sat up again, Topar and N'Meary were beside them.

"By the Huntsman's spear, that thing was big," Topar said, sounding as shaken as she felt. "This time you shoot, and I'll try a botan?" he suggested.

She nodded in reply because she didn't trust her voice.

We come, N'Laure warned her. *Be careful. This one is smaller and faster than the last.*

All at once, Kie realized it was stupid to try to hide that she could talk to other skysteeds. Keeping them all alive right now was *way* more important.

"They're almost here," she relayed to Topar, "and N'Laure says this one is faster than the last one."

She saw the question in Topar's eyes, but before he could ask, N'Laure contacted her again. *We are almost to the tree.*

"Now!" she yelled to Topar, and she and N'Rah sprinted upward. N'Laure shot over them, his wings slicing through the air, the chimera snapping at his tail. She flattened herself against N'Rah's neck. *We've got to catch that thing before it catches N'Laure and Prince Shayn!* she urged him.

Beside them, N'Meary flew all out, her wings a blur of white.

I hope it doesn't see us before we reach its blind spot, Kie thought to herself, her pulse drumming in her ears while N'Rah's sides heaved and his neck darkened with sweat.

A lifetime later, it seemed, they drew even with the chimera's tail and moved up behind its wing. Kie notched an arrow. She glanced over at Topar, and he nodded grimly. She squeezed her legs, and somehow N'Rah found the strength to fly even faster. She aimed for the lion's heart, located behind the right-front leg. Her shot went home, and the chimera jerked to a halt, the lion's head roaring in anguish as all three heads wound about angrily, trying to find her. Then the bloodgoat head spotted her and gave a triumphant screech.

N'Rah ducked forward and down while the chimera twisted in midair, and the sand dragon head struck at the space they'd been a heartbeat earlier. Now they were the bait, as N'Rah raced on and the chimera charged after them.

Where's Topar? This thing might actually catch us, Kie thought at N'Rah, even as she notched another arrow and fired back at the chimera's chest. There was a flash of white as N'Meary dove at the chimera from the side. Topar threw a botan as the beast's wings dipped downward. The botan caught its foreleg and curled up to wrap around the wing tip.

Biting at the botan and the arrow in its chest, the chimera

lurched sideways and began to spin in descending circles as it fought to stay aloft with one wing. It hit the ground hard, spasmed, and lay still.

"Sorry, I missed my first toss," Topar called to her.

"The second did the job just fine," Kie shouted back breathlessly.

"There's a third chimera coming toward us," the prince cried and pointed toward the village. "We've got to take it out before the others get here. I'll be bait again."

Kie grabbed for a triwire while Prince Shayn and N'Laure flew right at the charging chimera. It looked like they would crash into each other! At the last moment, N'Laure veered hard right and led the chimera away from the tree, and Kie and Topar. They dashed after the chimera, both twirling triwires.

With the other three chimerae likely on their way, she had no time to hide and attack from the chimera's blind spot. Instead, Kie told N'Rah: *Bring us up beside that right wing.*

As they drew even with the chimera, the lion head spotted them and roared so loudly, the sound rattled her brain. The chimera veered their way just as she hurled the triwire. It missed the foreleg but did wrap around the wing, cutting it deeply in three places. N'Rah ducked into a dive before the chimera's powerful tail whistled over their heads.

Moments later, Topar must have made a successful toss, because the chimera tilted his way, hissing, roaring, and screeching. The prince fired one arrow into the creature's chest, and then he gestured frantically that they all needed to climb.

"The other three come," he shouted as they left the stricken chimera behind them.

Kie glanced over her shoulder. Three chimerae flying in a triad formation of their own were heading straight for them. She shuddered when she spotted a man sitting on the back of the leading chimera. With a scourge master directing them, these three would be far more dangerous than the first.

"Remember my plan for attacking multiple chimerae," Prince Shayn yelled.

Kie bit her lip. That was the pattern that had made the least sense to her when she had tried to puzzle out the prince's handwriting. Was she supposed to attack the lead chimera from the attacker's right with a triwire, or was she supposed to kill the scourge master with her bow? She had no time to ask because the chimerae were so close, she could see their master wore a helmet, and his face and arms were covered with swirling scarlet tattoos.

What is our plan? N'Rah asked her, sounding rattled.

"Line us up for a bowshot at the scourge master," Kie replied, trying to hide her uncertainty.

The moment he was in range, she fired. The arrow hit his chest and bounced off. That dark vest he wore had to be some sort of chain mail! The sand dragon head hissed and struck at them, but N'Rah had already tucked in his wings and swooped under the lead chimera before the other two could react. Now they were behind the triad.

"Nice move. Now climb." Kie gasped, kneeing N'Rah into a

turn. "We need to get back to help the others." She unslung her third triwire and peered over her shoulder at the chimerae. The two outer beasts had split away from the scourge master. One chased N'Meary and the other N'Laure. The scourge master hovered in place, watching the other two, his back to her.

She'd never have a better shot at the scourge master's chimera. Twirling the triwire over her head, she dove N'Rah at the beast, but the bloodgoat head saw them coming and screeched shrilly.

With appalling swiftness, the chimera pivoted to meet their charge. She hurled the triwire, but it missed the wing and caught the creature's front foreleg. N'Rah fell away in a side dive as the bloodgoat head tried to spear them with its horns.

Kie drew in a shuddering breath.

"Thank the Messenger you're so fast," she said to N'Rah, and gave him a quick pat as he climbed above the fight. Now she only had one triwire left. How were the others doing? Sunlight flashed on metal. The prince twirled a triwire as a chimera dove toward him.

The scourge master shouted something in a harsh language and pointed toward N'Meary and Topar, who had confronted a chimera closer to the river. The chimera advancing on the prince broke off its attack and sped after the palomino mare. Topar was so focused on the chimera in front of him that Kie was terrified they didn't see the one menacing them from behind.

"Topar, look out!" she screamed, but he was too far away to hear her.

"N'Rah, warn her!"

I am trying, but I cannot reach her.

Between themselves, skysteeds' mindspeech range was very limited. If only she could warn N'Meary about the chimera on their tail, but she'd never established a link with Topar's mare.

We have to cut that chimera off! N'Rah cried and sprinted after the second monster.

All right. Numb with fear, she notched an arrow as her brave skysteed chased down the chimera and dove between it and N'Meary. Roaring and hissing in fury, it swerved to meet their attack. Kie fired an arrow into the beast's chest, but they were so close, its right foreclaw slashed N'Rah's flank. Trembling in pain, he still managed to swerve away and dive.

As they came out of the dive, Kie glanced back at his flank. It was already covered in blood.

How bad is it? she asked, trying not to panic.

I can still fly, he gasped, *but I hurt!*

She looked forward again, and her heart froze. The scourge master and his chimera must have followed her. The pair were so close, she could see his cruel grin. Kneeing N'Rah into a turn, she fired at his face, but her arrow flew wide. N'Rah did turn, but too slowly. The lion head bared its teeth, ready to tear at them, and the sand dragon head drew back to strike.

Just when Kie was sure she and her skysteed were both dead, there was a flash of gold and red, and a skyrider with a bow dove in front of the scourge master, firing at his chest. The skyrider's arrow bounced off his mail, and the chimera spun about and chased after the newcomer. Kie blinked. A long red braid trailed down the skyrider's back.

That was N'Seella! N'Rah declared in amazement.

Instantly, Kie reached for the young mare's mind. *N'Seella, tell the princess that the scourge master's mail is too strong. She'll have to shoot his face or his neck.*

I will tell her. She is no longer scared of flying with me, N'Seella replied, sounding remarkably proud and happy for a skysteed in the midst of a desperate fight.

I can see that, Kie said, *and I'm* very *glad you brought help.* A dozen skyfighters flew at the remaining three chimerae from all sides now.

As the scourge master turned to face a skyfighter flying straight at him with a lance, N'Seella dove at him from the side. This time the princess shot a perfectly aimed arrow at his face. The scourge master fell back, Princess Halla's arrow protruding from his eye. Disoriented by the death of its rider, the chimera hovered in place and, seconds later, the skyfighter plunged a lance deep into its chest.

Panting, Kie twisted around. Where were the other two chimerae? *There!* N'Laure raced away from one monster, which had a ripped wing. The prince must have thrown a triwire at it. A skyfighter rammed a lance into its belly, and the crippled chimera smashed to the ground. Roaring and screaming, the final beast lunged at a half dozen skyfighters who were riddling it with arrows. At last, someone must have scored a fatal shot, for the chimera stiffened and fell from the sky.

Panting hard, Topar appeared beside her on a sweaty N'Meary, and then the prince and N'Laure joined them as well. Kie was relieved to see they and their skysteeds appeared unhurt. But she was so worried for N'Rah.

"I g-guess it's over," the prince said shakily as his sister soared up beside him on N'Seella. She was grinning from ear to ear.

"I promised not to tell Father or Grandmama, but I didn't make any promises about alerting the Skyforce," she said to them all, "because I was afraid that *you*"—she shook a finger at her brother—"might get in over your head. So N'Seella and I followed you, snuck over your camp last night, and picked up a wing of skyfighters from the front lines, and here we are."

Princess Halla's grin vanished when she noticed N'Rah's bloody flank. "Oh no—brave N'Rah's hurt. That doesn't look good."

"I know. We have to land *now*," Kie told the others. N'Rah was starting to tremble, and she didn't want her courageous skysteed to stay in the air a moment longer. Just how severely injured was he?

Her eyes swimming with tears, Kie urged her friend to land near the same dekkar tree they'd hidden behind a lifetime ago, it seemed.

Please, oh, please, don't let dear N'Rah be too badly hurt, she prayed to whatever god might be listening. *I don't know what I would do if I lost him!*

CHAPTER TWENTY-ONE

THE SKYFIGHTER WING PRINCESS HALLA had brought had a healer with them. Since N'Rah had suffered the most grievous hurt of any of the humans or skysteeds involved in the fight, the healer offered to treat him first. A thin middle-aged Mosai woman with kind eyes, she let N'Rah drink from a water bucket brought by a grateful settler boy. Then she led the skysteed into the shade of the dekkar tree and set to work numbing and cleaning the bloody gash on his flank.

"It looks worse than it is," the healer tried to reassure Kie and N'Rah, and started to stitch it. "I don't believe there's any serious muscle damage. But flesh wounds bleed a lot, and they hurt."

When her needle pierced his torn skin, N'Rah flinched. *That does hurt!* he said to Kie.

"Please," Kie pleaded, "couldn't you put more numbsalve on that before you make another stitch?"

The healer sighed, but she did as Kie asked before she began stitching again.

"I'm sorry, I'm sorry, I'm sorry," Kie murmured to N'Rah through her tears as she stroked his neck. "I wish those claws had caught me instead."

"You'll have quite a scar to match the one on your haunch,"

the healer said to N'Rah. "I didn't realize courier skysteeds saw so much action."

"This one manages to," Kie said with feeling.

"Just think of all the mares you can impress now." The healer kept up a light banter as she worked, and at last, she finished stitching the long, jagged tear. She gave Kie some ointment to put on the stitches every day and a powder to put in his sweet oats to alleviate the pain.

"Your skysteed should rest tonight, but he should be able to fly by tomorrow, as long as you two don't take on any more chimerae in the meantime. Those stitches should be ready to come out in two weeks."

"Thank you *so* much," Kie said, too weary to be able to express her gratitude in fancier words.

"I'm glad I could help him. There have been too many skysteeds in the past few days I couldn't," the healer said, a haunted look in her eyes. After treating another skysteed, she and half the skyfighters left to return to the front lines.

The other half stayed in a circle around their little group, forming a guard of sorts. Topar and the prince tried to go retrieve the triwires and botans from the dead chimerae, but the skyfighters wouldn't let them pass.

"Best you stay here, Your Highness," a captain said stiffly, "until Lord General Stygurt has had a chance to talk you."

It almost felt like they were under arrest. At least some of the bravest settlers ventured out to bring them buckets of water from the nearby river for the thirsty skysteeds. Kie coaxed N'Rah into eating a handful of sweet oats with the healer's powder on it, and soon he dozed.

A short time later, an older man in a Skyforce uniform covered with shiny medals landed a large chestnut skysteed near their dekkar tree. With him came a half dozen skyfighters, many of them officers.

"That's Lord General Stygurt," Prince Shayn whispered in Kie's ear. "He's probably here to give me a lecture." A Rosari with a huge red handlebar mustache, the man was so stout, the silver buttons on his coat looked like they were about to pop off. Either his face was terribly sunburned or he was furious.

The Lord General began lecturing them even before he reached the spot where the prince, Princess Halla, Topar, and Kie were standing in the shade of the tree. "Your Highness, I regret to say this is your most reckless escapade yet. You could have gotten yourself, your sister, and these couriers all killed."

Prince Shayn lifted his chin. "For your information, Lord General, we didn't come out here on some reckless jaunt. We came out there to see if weapons and tactics from the time of the Chimera Wars would be effective against these monsters, and they were. Between the three of us, we brought down three chimerae."

"You and those couriers claim to have killed three of those monsters, and yet you stand before me unharmed? That's ridiculous. I don't see any dead chimerae except the ones my forces downed," the Lord General blustered.

"Excuse me, your Lordship." A Mosai man stepped forward from the crowd of curious settlers who had gathered. "My family and I were hiding in those rocks over there, and we saw the whole fight. You'll find two more dead chimerae beyond that bend in the river, and one more that's dying. These youngsters did bring down three, sir, and I'd wager they saved a good portion of our settlement by tackling them when they did."

"Well, then," the Lord General said, turning back to Prince Shayn, "you must be one of the luckiest boys in the history of this Empire. Now I'm going to have to detail ten fighters I can't spare to escort you and your sister safely back to Pedarth."

"Then don't send them with us!" the prince said, losing his temper at last. "We got here on our own, and we can get back on our own."

Princess Halla elbowed her brother in the side and smiled sweetly at the Lord General. "What my brother means to say, sir, is that we would be delighted to travel with any escort you choose to assign us, and we will be sure to tell our father how careful you were with our safety."

"Yes, well, you do that. And you two"—the Lord General pointed an accusing finger at Topar and Kie—"can be sure I will be notifying the Head Courier about your actions here. What is the world coming to when couriers think they can be skyfighters?"

While the disgruntled Lord General swung away to confer with his lieutenants, Kie fought to keep from bursting into tears. First she got N'Rah injured, and now she was going to be in serious trouble with the head of the Imperial Courier Service.

A lanky young skyfighter with bright red hair strode toward them. Princess Halla screamed "Duren!" in a very unprincess-like way and threw herself into his arms. After he gave her a big hug, he strode forward and clapped Prince Shayn on the shoulder.

"I should have known you'd find a way to be a part of the action, with or without Father's permission," the young man said to the prince with a rueful smile. "Is it true you three killed three chimerae?"

"It is, but then the fight got away from us. I'm not sure we'd still be here if Halla hadn't brought reinforcements," the prince replied. He turned and introduced Kie and Topar to his brother, Prince Duren.

"So how on earth did you manage to slay three chimerae on your little skysteeds?" Prince Duren asked them curiously.

"Because our skysteeds are smaller, they're faster in the air," Prince Shayn replied proudly, "and we used triwires, botans, and bows, but the triwires were the most effective."

"Triwires, eh? Like those ones on display in the Great Hall?"

"Just like them, but we shouldn't have them on display," Prince Shayn said. "You should be using them to fight these monsters. You'll find several wrapped around the dead chimerae out that way. So how's the fighting going?"

Prince Duren's smile faded. "It isn't going well. Our archers are the only ones who've had much luck with killing chimerae. Most of the skyfighters who fly straight at the beasts with a lance get massacred. We've been taking terrible losses."

"I knew it." The prince hit his palm with his fist. "We have to change our tactics."

"Old Styggy here, and our Supreme Commander, Lord General Shurr, are both slow to understand this," Prince Duren said in a lowered voice, "but our captains have grasped it now, and they've sent to Pedarth for more archers and more arrows. I'll tell my captain to look at the damage your triwires did before we leave here."

In the end, Lord General Stygurt left eight skyfighters to guard and accompany the twins back to Pedarth. He wanted them to begin their journey right away, but the prince refused to leave Kie and N'Rah.

Harumphing under his breath, the Lord General was boosted into the saddle by his orderlies, and at last he left. Prince Duren left, too, with a triwire Kie had given him tied to his saddle.

Despite the trouble they were in, the prince and his sister were quite cheerful that night. Their skysteeds drowsing nearby, the four of them sat around their own fire. They'd finally been allowed to retrieve their triwires and Topar's botans from the chimerae they'd killed. Worried another scourge might appear, Kie was glad to have her weapons back, and she was very glad that the adult skyfighters were taking turns patrolling the sky overhead.

Even though the settlers were busy tending their wounded and dead, they had brought a dinner of roasted wedda fowl and fresh nut bread to the young skyriders. Kie hadn't had much appetite for the meal, and she didn't feel like talking now. Topar said little, too.

"If you two are worried about your jobs," the prince said when he at last noticed how quiet his companions were, "I promise I'll tell the Head Courier that I ordered you both to come with me."

Kie exchanged a look with Topar. "Thanks for offering to help us, but I'm not sure you can fix this," she said.

"I'm supposed to be sorting mail at Central Relay today," Topar said, staring moodily into the fire, "and my new boss was probably furious when I didn't show up."

"And even though my courier boss gave me a leave of absence," Kie added, "the Lord General was right. Junior couriers aren't supposed to go around pretending to be skyfighters."

"You weren't pretending to be a skyfighter," the prince said indignantly. "You *are* one, having killed at least three chimerae now, which is three more than most Skyforce skyfighters have killed."

"And I almost crippled my skysteed doing it," Kie retorted.

"I'm so sorry about that," Princess Halla said. "I would just die if my darling N'Seella got hurt." She reached up to pat N'Seella's muzzle. Now that the princess had gotten over her fear of flying, the two were inseparable, and N'Seella almost glowed with happiness.

"The worst thing is, what we did today didn't make any difference," Kie said as she threw another stick on the fire, anger burning inside her. "You heard the Lord General. He's sure *luck* is the only reason we downed three chimerae."

"But a few of his captains know what we did and how we did it, and my brother does, too, and that's a good start," the prince said. "I'm going to hold on to that."

"What we did today made a big difference to these settlers," Topar added.

"And I'm not afraid to fly anymore," Princess Halla said, beaming at Kie. "That's best of all, and it never would have happened if you hadn't challenged me to start flying with N'Seella again."

"And N'Meary and I are still in one piece, thanks to you and N'Rah." Topar sent her a warm smile. "We had no idea that chimera was on our tail."

But I could have warned N'Meary if I'd told everyone that I can talk to every skysteed I touch, and then N'Rah wouldn't be hurt now, Kie thought miserably.

"I do have a question for you," Topar said, and her heart sank even farther. She was afraid she knew what he was going to ask. "When we were hiding behind the dekkar tree, I'm sure you said that N'Laure told you that second chimera was fast. But didn't you mean that Prince Shayn told you that through N'Rah?"

Kie sighed and looked up from the fire. It was time to share the truth with them. She thought the princess and the prince were her friends now, and Topar had long been one of the few people she truly trusted. Would they remain her friends when they found out how different she was? If only she could find the right words to make them understand. She was so exhausted, her head felt like it was full of river mud.

"I did mean to say that N'Laure told me . . . because I *can* talk directly to him and to N'Seella. I could mindspeak with N'Meary, too, if I touched her first."

The prince and princess looked at her blankly, but Topar was nodding as if she'd confirmed his guess.

Kie plunged on. "I—I began hearing N'Seella's thoughts my first day in Pedarth when I treated her at sick call," she said to the princess, and then she turned to Prince Shayn. "N'Laure asked me to touch him when you were feeling better after your sand dragon bite. He'd heard from other skysteeds that I could mind-speak with them, and he wanted to thank me for bringing that antidote recipe to your grandmother."

The prince frowned. "You mean our skysteeds already knew you could hear them, and you didn't think to tell me? Being able to communicate quickly would have been a huge help earlier today. We could have—"

"Kie understands that now," Topar cut him off. "It was her skysteed who was hurt, after all."

"Believe me," Kie said, her voice thick with pain, "every time I look at N'Rah, I wish like anything I had told you all and set up a mental link with N'Meary before the fight."

Princess Halla tilted her head in puzzlement. "But why didn't our skysteeds tell us that you could talk to them?"

"Because I asked them not to. When I first found I could

mindspeak with some of the senior skysteeds like N'Talley, I worried that if their skyriders found out, they might believe that I was interfering with their bonds with their skysteeds. I—I also didn't want people looking at me the way you are now, like I'm some sort of freak."

"Well, I do need a moment or two to get used to the idea you can talk to N'Seella," Princess Halla declared. "I've never heard of a skyrider being able to mindspeak with more than one skysteed."

"I have," Topar said. "We Ledari tell the old tales more often than you do. Sian, the young mage who helped Prince Isen create the Great Binding, became a skyrider, too, and one unexpected outcome of their spell was that she could communicate with every skysteed."

"An old skysteed told me something like that," Kie admitted, "but I still have problems believing that ability has been given to me now. It makes no sense."

"It makes perfect sense if you believe the magic of the Great Alliance still exists," Princess Halla said, her eyes alight with excitement, "and somehow it knew the chimerae were about to threaten Prekalt again."

"But it doesn't make perfect sense that the magic chose me," Kie burst out. "I'm just a junior courier."

"You're a courier who happens to know how to fight chimerae," Topar said, giving her a thoughtful look, "and within days of arriving in Pedarth, you gained the trust of three members of the Imperial family. Think about that. It's hard *not* to believe the magic is guiding your path, and you've some bigger role to play in all this."

Kie crossed her arms and tried to ignore the cold creeping down her back. A spell created three hundred years ago *couldn't* be guiding her actions. She just wanted to be home with her orchard and her uncle again.

"I agree. It must be some sort of sign that you were given this gift." Suddenly, Prince Shayn sat up straighter. "So is this how you knew your town was under attack that afternoon I first met you? Did your uncle's skysteed actually tell you?"

Kie nodded.

"And Durwen lies a hundred miles from where we were fighting chimerae that day. So your mental range for mindspeech is much farther than most skyriders' or skysteeds'," the prince said, frowning in concentration. "It would be a tremendous advantage in a battle, having a human who could talk to dozens or hundreds of skysteeds across large distances."

"But I don't know if I can talk to several skysteeds at once, and I'm too tired to try tonight." She held up a hand to forestall the prince, who looked eager to start testing her ability right away.

"So is there anything else you haven't been telling us?" Topar asked. "Can you talk to chimerae, too?"

He'd probably asked that question to lighten the mood, but there was more she had to tell them. "I can't talk to chimerae, but there is something else you should know, especially if we end up fighting more of those monsters together."

Her face burned as she turned to the prince. "I've always had problems reading. It took me years longer than my classmates just to learn my letters. In the end, the teachers gave up and sent me home. Uncle Dugs and my father wouldn't give up, though, and finally, they taught me. I can read, just slowly now, but your handwriting is almost impossible for me to understand. So if I didn't follow your battle plans, I'm sorry." Even though she longed to stare at the ground, she forced herself to meet their gazes instead.

They were all quiet as they digested her words.

"Well, no one can read Shaynie's handwriting except me," Princess Halla said at last. "And our brother Rodard, who was the smartest of any of us, had terrible problems learning how to read. Father went through a dozen tutors before he found one who could help him. Rodard used to complain that the letters in his books kept moving around on the page, and when he tried to write, his own letters sometimes came out backward and upside down."

"But that's exactly what happens to me, too!" Kie exclaimed. How could an Imperial prince have the same problems she had with reading and writing? For the longest time, she'd been certain she was stupid. The teachers and kids at Durwen's school had certainly thought her backward.

But Uncle Dugs and Da were both convinced the problem had more to do with her eyes and her brain, and they were both sure she was plenty smart. Every day, they pointed out the intelligent things she did, and eventually, they convinced her that she did have smarts enough. But she still *hated* the fact she had to struggle to read anything, from a sign to a letter.

"Well, now I know," Prince Shayn said, "and I promise I'll explain my plans to you tomorrow as we fly."

"We better go through them now," Kie said, stifling a yawn. "If one chimerae scourge made it this far behind our lines, we could encounter more at any moment. But this time, don't talk so quickly."

All four of them went through the prince's plans, incorporating the princess and her bow into their attacks. When Kie felt sure she had the patterns down, she checked on N'Rah. Glad he slept soundly, she crawled into her bedroll beside him.

She was so weary that her every bone ached, but her mind was spinning. If Lord General Stygurt sent an angry letter to the Head Courier, she might never get promoted to senior courier. Her petty pride and foolishness had gotten poor N'Rah hurt today, and she'd never forgive herself for that.

Worst of all, tomorrow more skysteeds and skyfighters would fight and die not far from here, and the Lord General hadn't been convinced that the old tactics and weapons could help kill chimerae. What if Topar was right? What if she did have some more important job to do in all this? If it was to make the Skyforce commanders believe in the weapons and strategies outlined in Uncle Dugs's manual, so far she was failing miserably.

Chapter Twenty-Two

THE NEXT MORNING, N'RAH INSISTED he could fly. When they left
their camp, he cantered gently into flight instead of leaping. He
flinched when he pushed off, and Kie flinched with him.

They circled over the settlement they had fought so hard to
save. A half dozen cabins and shacks had been smashed apart by
the chimerae, but many more still stood. Kie's heavy heart lifted a
little as the surviving settlers waved at them enthusiastically before
the captain led them east, toward the newly risen sun and Pedarth.

N'Rah assured her that his flank pained him less after they'd
been flying for an hour. Kie kept watching for more scourges, but
the prince spent a good part of the day asking the different members of their escort about the fighting they'd seen. His expression
grew grimmer and grimmer as he listened to their accounts.

In the afternoon, he insisted that Kie practice talking with all
three of their skysteeds. Topar and N'Meary were intrigued with
the experiment and happy to let Kie link with her.

It is odd to hear another human's words in my head, but I do not mind,
the mare said sweetly after Kie stroked her neck. *Now I can thank
you for what you and N'Rah did yesterday, and I am so sorry he was hurt.*

*And I can thank you for saving us out in the Western Desert that first day.
N'Rah and I wouldn't be here if it weren't for you two.*

Once Kie had established a mental link with N'Meary, the

prince asked her to send different messages to their skysteeds one at a time.

"N'Seella says you think the flaxen color of her mane is very pretty, and I agree," Princess Halla said with grin. "But you shouldn't say things like that to her. She's vain enough as it is."

"N'Laure says you are worried I'm going to get sunburned again." The prince smiled good-naturedly and reached for his hat.

"N'Meary says that you think the mean cook at Ruout Relay has a nose shaped like a potato." Topar chuckled. "And I agree."

With practice, she got faster at communicating with the other skysteeds, but pain began to pound at her temples. Although she rarely had headaches, right now she was building a whopper.

"Now," the prince said, "I want you to send a message to all three of our skysteeds at once. We will raise our hands the moment they relay your message to us."

Kie concentrated and tried to reach for the minds of all three skysteeds at the same time. *I'm hungry, my head hurts, and I'd like to stop practicing now*, she thought at them. The prince let out a whoop when he, Princess Halla, and Topar all raised their hands at almost the same instant.

"We will stop practicing for today," Prince Shayn promised her, "but now we know you can maintain mental links with three skysteeds plus your own with N'Rah. I wonder how many more skysteeds you can talk to at once." From the eager look in his eyes, Kie had a sinking feeling they'd be trying to figure that out in the coming days.

That night after they made camp, the young captain

commanding their escort asked if they could give his skyfighters a botan and triwire demonstration.

"We think it's incredible that the three of you on such small skysteeds managed to kill three chimerae," the captain explained. "Sometimes it takes four or five skyfighters just to bring one chimera down, and usually they take some of us with them."

"She's the real expert with the triwires," the prince said, nodding to Kie, "and he's the expert with botans." But Topar and the prince ended up conducting the demonstration because Kie didn't want to make N'Rah fly any more than he had to. The Skyforce fighters were so intrigued with the triwires, Topar gave them the practice triwire he'd brought along.

"I can see why you insist on practicing with a mock-up first," the captain said to Kie, nursing a cut on his finger from handling one of the real triwires. "Throw this thing wrong, and you could slice off your skysteed's wing."

They flew faster and longer the next day and, with help from a strong tailwind, reached Pedarth late in the afternoon. Topar and Kie thanked their escort and gave them Topar's spare botan and three of Kie's precious triwires. They also said goodbye to the prince and the princess and promised to resume their training sessions the following night. Prince Shayn wanted to accompany them to Central Relay to talk to the Head Courier, but they declined his offer. Courier business was courier business.

Before they tried to see the Head, Kie and Topar stood in line to pick up letters from home. "We can always hope the Lord

General didn't write to her," Kie said as they waited, her whole body tense with worry.

"You'd think the man would have more important matters on his mind than two junior couriers," Topar said, but from the way he tapped his fingers on his leg, she knew he was anxious, too.

When they picked up their letters from the same kind clerk who had served her before, each had a handwritten note clipped to them. Kie's was so short, it was easy enough to read. She was to report to the Head Courier at once.

When Kie looked up, the clerk was watching her with such sympathy, Kie's eyes prickled with tears. She'd always dreamed of meeting the Head Courier on the day she was promoted to senior courier. She'd never expected to meet the woman because she was in disgrace. Resolutely, Kie blinked her tears away. She was *not* going to cry before or during a meeting with the head of her service.

"Sully," the clerk called over a young man, "please show Junior Couriers Singu and Torsun to the Head's office."

He gave them such a curious glance, Kie wondered uneasily if the Central Relay staff had been talking about them again. They followed him down a long corridor and up a set of stairs. The young man announced their names importantly to a woman sitting at a desk.

She did not look impressed. "I'll let the Head know you're here," she said, and slipped through a door behind her. She returned after a few moments and motioned them inside.

The Head's office was a bright room with a wide window overlooking Central Relay's flight fields. The walls were covered with large maps of the various provinces of Prekalt. A slim Mosai woman with gray hair caught back in a bun sat reading at a wooden desk. She wore a courier blue uniform shirt, and the only sign of her station was the gold skysteed pinned to her collar.

At long last, she put down her spectacles and looked up to appraise them out of cool, dark eyes. "So, Kiesandra Torsun and Topar Singu, our two famous chimerae-fighting couriers, we meet at last," she said in a crisp voice.

Kie longed to glance at Topar. Was the Head being sarcastic? Her expression was so unreadable, it was hard to tell. Since she didn't invite them to sit in the two chairs facing the desk, they both remained standing.

"This morning I received this remarkable dispatch"—the Head tapped a paper on her desk—"from Lord General Stygurt, complaining that two of my couriers had dared to fight chimerae. He demands that I discipline or fire you both, even though you did manage to kill three of those monsters, which I understand is becoming something of a habit with you."

Anger flashed in the Head's eyes. *I really hope she's angrier at the Lord General than she is with us,* Kie thought.

"Relations are already strained between our services right now, and your actions didn't improve the situation. The Skyforce keeps conscripting our fastest and most reliable couriers. How Stygurt and his fellow officers in the Skyforce think we're going to deliver the mail to the rest of the Empire, I'm sure I don't know."

The Head Courier pushed her chair back. "So, tell me, what in the Messenger's name were you doing out in the Telawa Valley fighting chimerae when you"—she pointed at Kie—"were supposed to be on leave, and you"—she pointed at Topar—"were supposed to be working in our sorting room?"

Topar bravely launched into an explanation of why they both had come to Pedarth, and what the prince had asked them to do. Kie took over whenever he faltered. "In the end, ma'am, it seemed important that we help Prince Shayn with his mission," he finished.

"It seemed more important to you than sorting mail, or more exciting?" the Head asked sharply.

Topar stood up straighter. "Ma'am, with all due respect, facing those chimerae in the Western Desert that first time was the most terrifying experience of my life. I never would have gone with the prince to face them again if I didn't think what he was trying to do was important."

A treacherous lump began to form in the back of Kie's throat, but she forced herself to speak past it. She had an awful feeling she was about to lose her job, or at the very least, any chance of becoming a senior courier. "And all I've ever wanted is to be a good courier. I believe delivering the mail is the most important job in the Empire, and my skysteed and I are good at it. But my uncle asked me to convince officers in the Skyforce to look at his manual on skyfighting, and I have to stay here until I honor that promise."

The Head Courier linked her hands on her desk as she studied

Kie and Topar. "I'm not the least bit surprised to hear couriers can make fine chimerae fighters. My skyriders have to be fast and resourceful to survive their dangerous routes. When I was a junior courier, I fought grytocs in the Western Desert." Topar must have looked surprised, because for the first time, the Head smiled, and her whole face lit up. "And I've fought storms in your Torgaresh Mountains," she said to Kie.

"But to be honest," she continued, her expression turning stern again, "you two represent a very great threat to our service. If the Skyforce figures out how useful couriers could be in fighting this war, I'll never get the mail delivered, and our service is what ties this great Empire together."

She got to her feet, her face pensive, and stared out the window at the flight fields. "But I also understand that you were just trying to help, and there will be no Empire if we can't stop the chimerae. Some of our couriers conscripted by the military have shared reports of the appalling casualties the Skyforce is taking out west."

The Head turned away from the window. "Very well, Junior Courier Torsun, for now your leave is extended. And Junior Courier Singu, we'd rather use you in the air, but Prince Shayn was quite adamant that we keep you available to him here in Pedarth. So for now, you may have your job back in the sorting room."

The Head Courier walked toward her door, signaling their interview was over. Kie and Topar followed her.

She stopped at the threshold and turned to face them. "I'm

afraid the time may be coming when you two will have to choose between the Skyforce and us," she warned them, regret in her gaze. "A skysteed cannot serve two masters. I hope you choose us in the end. Your records indicate you both are fine couriers, and our service needs you desperately."

They walked out of her office, and she shut the door behind them. Kie exhaled the breath she'd been holding as they started down the corridor back to the sorting rooms.

"So I'm thinking that could have gone worse," Topar said.

"It could have gone better, too," Kie said wearily. What if the Head Courier was right? She never wanted to have to choose between helping the Skyforce win the war against the chimerae and her own career as a sky courier.

She said goodbye to Topar and walked N'Rah back to the main stables. Along the way, she deciphered Uncle Dugs's letter. It was a good sign he felt strong enough to write to her himself. His ribs were healing, Mistress Vena kept plaguing him to eat more, N'Tor was moving about better, and he hoped Kie was making progress "getting those stubborn, medal-laden dunderheads in the Skyforce to listen to you."

That sentence made her smile, but the last line of his letter chilled her to the bone. "Remember, the chimerae were created to purge this continent of humans. I fear for Pedarth."

When Kie walked into the mess hall the next morning, hair damp with dew from sleeping outside next to N'Rah, Dessie ran across the room and hugged her so hard, Kie thought her ribs might crack.

"You're all right! I'm so glad you're all right!" the young groom kept saying.

Kie couldn't help smiling over Dessie's enthusiasm. It was nice to have a friend who cared so much.

"I know you've been off doing something brave and stupid with Prince Shayn again," Dessie rushed on. She insisted on accompanying Kie through the food line and making sure she had heaping portions of everything. A sleepy-looking Terry woke up in a hurry when he spotted them. He joined them at the table, too.

"I'm very glad to have you back, and the senior herd will be, too," he told her, his face lighting with a warm smile.

"We're dying to know what you did," Dessie declared, "but you need to eat. So we'll talk first." She and Terry went on to explain that their practice group had kept meeting after work. Almost twenty cadets were now coming to their sessions, along with a dozen grooms, and Kie's original students were teaching the others how to throw their practice triwires.

"Oh, and that big roan mare and a half dozen other Unbound skysteeds, including N'Tarin, keep popping in to watch us," Terry added.

Kie had just finished her breakfast when Dessie's eyes widened. "Don't look now, but the boss is coming over here."

"He was worried when you disappeared like that," Terry said quietly.

Her appetite vanishing, Kie dropped her fork and rose to her feet as Trishop strode across the mess hall. He stopped in front of her table, his expression somber.

"I'm glad to see you're still in one piece. Have you been off fighting chimerae again with Prince Shayn?"

"Well, yes, sir. We just got back from the Telawa Valley."

Shaking his head, Trishop pulled out the bench across from her and sat down heavily. "I don't suppose it occurred to you to let me know where you were going, or to the prince and princess to let their father know?"

"I didn't know the princess was going to follow us, and we didn't think you'd let us go, sir," Kie replied.

"You're right about that," Trishop said, raking a hand through his hair. "Your uncle is one of the best friends I ever had. I know he'd like me to keep you safe, but I can't do that if you don't tell me what you're up to. Plus, my grooms are supposed to do their work and not go off skyfighting chimerae whenever they please."

"I-I'll understand if you feel like you need to fire me, sir," Kie said, even as she gripped her thighs under the table. Where would she go if he did fire her? She *really* didn't want to ask for a job and a place to stay at Central Relay right now, while the Head was so unhappy with her.

"I try not to fire grooms first thing in the morning," he replied sardonically, "especially when we're so shorthanded. First, tell me what happened out there. Dessie and Terry, you might as well stay and hear what she has to say. Maybe you can stop her from going off and doing something so reckless next time."

At least she still had a job and a place to sleep. Because she was more used to Trishop and his abrupt ways, she managed to launch into an account of their trip and fight. Her voice trembled when she admitted N'Rah had gotten hurt. "I'd like to take him to sick call soon," she said when she had finished recounting their adventures in the Telawa Valley.

"You're lucky those chimerae didn't tear all four of you apart," Trishop said grimly.

"But they didn't," Kie replied, trying to hide the shudder that ran through her. Trishop was right. They had been lucky. If the princess hadn't arrived with reinforcements, their fight with the chimerae might have ended very differently. "At least Princess Halla is over her fear of flying now."

"And the first thing she did, thanks to you and her brother, was go haring off to the front lines. His Supreme Highness is not going to be happy about this. He was frantic when he found out they'd both gone."

So now she had the Head Courier, the head groom, and the Emperor of all Prekalt mad at her. Kie fought the urge to burst into tears. If N'Rah wasn't so badly hurt, she'd fly straight home. But of course she couldn't, because the chimerae were coming, to Durwen and to Pedarth itself, if her uncle was right.

She told them of the warning in Uncle Dugs's letter. "Based on that scourge we encountered twenty miles behind our lines, sir, it's very possible more chimerae are going to slip past the Skyforce. And I'm horribly afraid Uncle Dugs is right. This is the place they'd want to attack more than anywhere else."

"Have you told this to the prince yet? He or the Dowager are likely the best way to get this warning to the Emperor himself."

"No, but I'm going to," she said. "There's something else you should know, sir, and I want you two to hear this as well," she said, looking at Terry and Dessie.

She paused to draw in a breath. "I can speak with other sky-steeds besides N'Rah. Every time I touch one, somehow that establishes a mindspeech link. That's why I can tell what's bothering the senior skysteeds."

"But is that even possible?" Dessie asked, her brown eyes wide.

"I've never heard of such a thing," Terry said slowly, "but that would explain how quickly you diagnose our senior friends, and their interest in you."

"Prove it to us," Trishop said, his dark brows drawn together as he frowned.

Kie thought for a moment. "I don't want to call N'Talley. That makes her grumpy. I know—I'll ask Topar's mare, N'Meary, to meet us in the courtyard. She won't mind."

Thanks to all the practicing the prince had made her do, she linked with N'Meary's mind swiftly. The mare agreed to come at once. By the time the four of them had left the mess hall and reached the courtyard, she was spiraling down out of the sky, the morning sun shining on her white wings. She landed near the fountain. Kie hurried forward and gave her an apple from the mess hall. After eating it delicately, N'Meary thanked her, reared up, and kicked off in an impressive standing launch.

"One forgets how agile courier skysteeds are," Trishop said to himself. "No wonder they do so well at skyfighting." He turned to face Kie. "Does your uncle know you have this ability?"

"He knows I can talk to N'Tor, but we both assumed that was because I spent so much time looking after him. We never thought it odd, or that I might be able to communicate with other skysteeds."

"For now, the four of us are going to keep this news to ourselves," Trishop said. "I'm afraid some of our noble Rosari skyriders might not like the idea that a Mosai courier can speak to their skysteeds. Dessie and Terry, off you go to your work. You"—he pointed to Kie—"get your uncle's warning about Pedarth to the prince as soon as you can, take your skysteed to sick call, and I'm going to search our old stable records and see if there is any precedent for what you can do and what it could mean."

Kie considered telling him what Topar had shared from his Ledari legends, but Trishop looked worried enough about her already. So she let him go while she hurried off to make sure a healer took a good look at N'Rah's stitches.

CHAPTER TWENTY-THREE

AFTER INSPECTING N'RAH'S INJURED FLANK, the healer declared that the skysteed's wound was healing well, much to Kie's relief. The man gave her some more salve, and Kie walked with N'Rah back into Tavalier Park. Pedarth almost felt cool after the scorching temperatures they'd endured out in the Telawa Valley.

"Please, tell me honestly, how do you feel?" she asked him.

Mostly I only hurt if I move suddenly. So today I am going to laze around the park and brag about fighting chimerae to pretty mares. What are you going to do?

"Right now I'm going to ask N'Laure if the prince can come and see us. He needs to know Pedarth's in danger."

It is proving very useful that you can speak to other skysteeds.

"You don't mind, do you?"

I do not mind at all. I am proud to be the skysteed who carries the Nexara.

Kie stopped in her tracks. "The *what?*"

The Nexara. It means you are the connector between our species. The old ones call you that now. N'Rile remembered the name from the stories his human's grandmother used to tell them.

"Our two species have been connected perfectly well for three hundred years. I don't know why we need a Nexara person now," Kie grumbled.

Perhaps that connection needs help if we are to defeat the chimerae and whoever creates them in our time.

Kie stared at N'Rah. Because he was so cheerful and funny, she forgot sometimes how smart he was. Who *was* creating the chimerae, and why? Could it be the scourge masters themselves? During the Chimera Wars, the evil Mage Yagarth had created the chimerae, and his most loyal students had commanded the monsters in battle. Could some of them, or some of Yagarth's descendants, have survived? Someone would have to answer that question soon, but for now, she was more concerned with making sure Pedarth was ready in case more scourges slipped past the Skyforce.

She reached out and found N'Laure's mind. *Can the prince come to see me in the park? My uncle is worried that the chimerae will try to attack this city,* she told him.

His father was very angry about what we did, N'Laure replied promptly. *So my human is under guard and not allowed to leave the palace or have visitors for a week. I will tell him about your uncle's warning.*

N'Laure broke off contact, and then his mind linked with hers again.

My human agrees that Pedarth is in terrible danger. He is rereading your uncle's manual right now. He and his sister will try to sneak out for the practice tonight, and you can talk then.

After she thanked N'Laure, she broke off their link. She shook her head as she left the park to report to work. Somehow she didn't doubt that the prince and princess would find a way to fool their guards and be there tonight.

N'Rah insisted on accompanying her to the practice session in the abandoned stadium. Several cadets and grooms were already there, enthusiastically throwing practice triwires at posts, and the roan mare and several other Unbound skysteeds watched them. Kelton and Gunge hurried over to introduce her to their friends. The new cadets almost seemed awed to meet Kie. What a difference a few weeks could make, she thought wryly.

Frowning as usual, Ruden showed up about the same time that Topar did. "How is N'Saran healing?" she asked Ruden.

"He's better," the cadet replied.

"I'm glad to hear it." She was saved from having to talk to Ruden further because the twins landed beside her on their skysteeds.

"After reading that manual again, I'm sure your uncle is right," Prince Shayn told her in an undertone. "The chimerae were created to kill as many people as possible, and that makes me think their scourge masters will direct them here—the most populated city in all Prekalt—if they can get past the Skyforce."

Before they could talk further, Kie and Topar were pelted by so many questions about where they'd been and what they'd done that Ruden finally bellowed at the top of his lungs, "All right, you lot be quiet and have a seat in those stands. NOW!"

The noisy group of grooms and cadets promptly obeyed him. "Guess you'll have to give a briefing before practice starts," Ruden said to Kie. "We know you've been off killing chimerae. Everyone wants to know what you did and how you did it."

"All right," she replied, feeling overwhelmed. There were just so many people and skysteeds here. Before Kie could address the group, Captain Nerone and several young Skyforce officers strode into the stadium. As the cadets in the stands jumped to their feet and stood at attention, Kie glanced at Topar and the twins in dismay. Was the Skyforce about to shut down their practice sessions? Her stomach did flip-flops as the captain approached them.

"The six of us just received our orders," Captain Nerone said, a steely look in her eyes. "We'll be leaving for the front lines in two days. Before I face chimerae again, I want to learn more about fighting with triwires and botans. Clearly, they can be effective. May we join your practice?"

"O-of course. We'd be honored," Kie managed to reply.

"As you were," the captain said to the relieved cadets. As she and her companions turned and marched to the stands, Princess Halla glanced up.

"Uh-oh. What's *she* doing here? We're in big trouble now."

Kie followed her gaze. N'Talley spiraled down out of the sky, the Dowager Empress dressed in flight gear on her back. N'Talley landed near them, and the old woman slipped nimbly from her saddle. The cadets, grooms, and officers all stood at attention again as she walked over to join Kie, Topar, and her grandchildren.

"I read your uncle's manual while you were off in the Telawa Valley," she said to Kie. "The manual makes it appallingly clear those monsters were created to kill the greatest number of people possible. That means they will try to attack Pedarth sooner rather than later. I tried to convince members of the War Council of this today, and they dismissed me once again. So I'm here to watch these training sessions of yours, and to learn how I can help you defend our city."

She nodded to her grandchildren. "I didn't see you two here, and you didn't see me," she said with a small smile, and went to sit in the stands with the rest.

Kie cleared her throat. "I shouldn't be the only one to tell them about what happened out in the Telawa Valley," she said to Prince Shayn, Princess Halla, and Topar. "We were all there."

And so they stood, four in a row, and took turns explaining their fight and the tactics they'd used to kill chimerae.

When they had finished, the princess took the archers in the group over to shoot at targets and talk more about the most vulnerable parts of the chimerae and the scourge masters' bodies. Topar worked with students who wanted to throw botans, and Kie and Prince Shayn took over triwire practice. She was amused that cadets like Kelton and Gunge, who had been coming to the practices the longest, ended up sharing their cord triwires with Captain Nerone and her fellow officers.

When it was twilight, Kie called a halt to the session, and Ruden relayed her orders in his deep, carrying voice. Captain Nerone, Ruden, and his friends lingered after the rest had left the stadium. When Kie drew closer, she heard the captain and the cadets arguing tactics with Prince Shayn while the Dowager listened with great interest.

"Your Highness, I know you're convinced that smaller, fleeter skysteeds are the best way to fight chimerae," the captain was saying with exasperation, "but our current Skyforce is made up of over two thousand big, powerful skysteeds. We should start creating *new* tactics that use the strength of our modern-day skysteeds combined with the fleetness of smaller ones."

At first the prince looked startled by her words and more than a little angry. But then, he got that abstracted look he had when he was thinking hard, and suddenly he slapped his forehead. "You're right. I've been a stubborn fool. We should find more effective ways to use our modern skysteeds since we can't just *make* smaller ones. Today's skysteeds were bred to carry the heavier load of armored skyfighters. What if their riders didn't wear armor, but carried bags of metal wing-shredders and dropped them on chimerae, or strong nets that would tangle the chimerae's wings?"

"I know there's a design for wing-shredders in that manual," the Dowager Empress said. "My blacksmiths are almost finished with the triwires we ordered. I'll get that wing-shredder design to them tonight, tell them to get every blacksmith in the city working on this, and hopefully we'll have thousands ready for you in a few days."

"Nets could work well, too," Topar said. "If you can get some of its heads tangled with its wings, a chimera will crash."

"I know how to make a strong net," Kelton spoke up, his pale skin flushing as everyone looked at him. "Just about everyone from the Northern Islands knows how to weave a fishing net. I could teach people if you can find me a lot of light, strong cord."

"I think weaving nets is about to become all the rage at court," the Dowager Empress said with a gleam in her eye. "I know a hundred noblewomen I can put to work making nets instead of embroidering useless handkerchiefs. Tonight, I'll send my household staff out to buy all the cord in the city. Young man, come find me in my chambers first thing tomorrow."

Kelton's eyes widened, but he had the presence of mind to nod and bow.

"Your Highness, may we take some of those triwires with us when we leave for the front lines?" Captain Nerone asked the Dowager Empress.

"Of course." The old woman nodded. "I'll send two dozen to your quarters tonight."

"We'd better get back," Princess Halla warned her brother. "Someone may check our rooms soon."

"I promise we'll be here tomorrow night if we can," the prince said to Kie before he and Princess Halla hurried off on their skysteeds along with the Dowager Empress.

Kie and Dessie walked back to their dorm together. As she lay in her bed that night, Kie's mind churned with worry. She'd been surprised and pleased that the cadets were finally treating her and Topar and their skysteeds with more respect, but the responsibility of what she was trying to accomplish seemed to weigh on her like a giant boulder. Was she right to push so hard for the others to learn the old tactics? Now even Skyforce officers like Captain Nerone were learning about them. What if those tactics didn't work, and those officers *died?* What if the cadets she was teaching hurt their skysteeds terribly when they finally practiced with real triwires?

Restlessly, Kie turned over and tried to punch her pillow

into a more comfortable shape. Then she remembered what had happened to the Skyforce's poor, doomed Advance Guard and the terrible casualties the Skyforce were taking now. It was obvious that modern skyfighting wasn't working against the chimerae. If Uncle Dugs was right, and the chimerae *were* coming, Pedarth desperately needed defenders who could fight the monsters effectively.

She had to keep teaching and sharing the knowledge in Uncle Dugs's manual, and pray that in the end, if the chimerae came, that knowledge *would* make a difference.

At last, Kie's exhausted body won out over her anxious mind, and she slipped into a restless sleep, plagued with bad dreams. In the worst of them, a nightmare that seemed frighteningly real, she and N'Rah and her new friends faced hundreds of chimerae scourges spread out across the pink blush of a dawn sky. Even as they charged forward to engage their enemies, deep in her heart, she knew they were about to be overwhelmed, and the city they wanted so desperately to protect, destroyed.

Late the next morning, N'Talley came to find Kie just as she and Terry had finished with senior sick call. *My human wishes you to come to her chambers at once. You may ride on my back again. I know your brave skysteed is injured.*

But N'Rah insisted on carrying Kie to the Imperial Palace. *I am not crippled,* he said a bit testily. *I feel much better today, and I do not want to miss out on anything important.*

N'Talley landed in the garden near the prince's quarters. N'Meary was already there, which meant the Dowager must have sent for Topar as well. A woman dressed in green-and-gold livery ushered Kie inside a large sitting room lined with lovely tapestries. Kie blinked when she spotted rolls of cord stacked along one wall of the chamber. The Dowager's staff had been busy.

The prince, princess, and Topar were already there, sitting at an ornate inlaid table with their grandmother. Their grave expressions sent shivers tracing down her back.

The Dowager motioned that she should take a seat at the table. The old woman's eyes were red, and the lines on her face seemed deeper than usual, but she still sat regally upright in her chair. "The War Council received a terrifying dispatch in the middle of the night. Almost half the force we sent west is now dead or too badly hurt to fight."

Kie gasped. Already half the Skyforce was gone? She fought back tears and clenched her hands under the table. She remembered how glorious those skyfighting pairs had looked as they charged into the sky that day the Skyforce left Pedarth. And now, so many of those beautiful skysteeds and their riders had been destroyed by the cruel chimerae. Disbelief warred with pain inside her.

"The commanders begged for reinforcements," the Dowager continued, "and so an additional seven hundred skyfighters are leaving for the front today, and my son feels it is his duty to go with them as the Emperor of all Prekalt."

"B-but how many skyfighters does that leave to defend Pedarth?" Kie blurted.

"Three hundred, with an additional five hundred bow and spearmen manning the city walls. That's the bad news. The good news is that my son has granted me emergency powers to rule in his stead, and the most hidebound Lord Generals on the War Council are going with him."

The Dowager paused to rub her eyes. "But the Emperor is very worried about the safety of Pedarth. The Lord General he put in charge of the defense of the city is a capable man and more open-minded than his colleagues. He has agreed to let the Lord Mayor and me stage drills and see how rapidly we can evacuate the population of Pedarth into the old caverns beneath the city. We've sent word out to every ward that we will start practicing those drills in a few hours."

"And," Prince Shayn added, plainly unable to keep quiet a moment longer, "the entire senior class of the Academy was called up, along with their instructors. This afternoon, Grandmama wants *us* to start training the remaining two hundred cadets in attack maneuvers with the tactics and weapons we've found to be effective."

"But Pedarth's so huge," Kie protested. "Even if we can train the cadets to drop wing-shredders and throw triwires and botans within a few days, five hundred skyfighters can't possibly defend a city of this size."

"It could make all the difference if we had some warning," the prince said, "and that way we'd know where to face them."

"And it would be much better if we could engage the chimerae outside the city walls," Topar added. "A grounded chimera can still kill a lot of people, and wing-shredders could go right through people's roofs."

Kie glanced at the door where N'Talley and the other skysteeds were listening intently. And then, an idea came to her! "Why don't we use the senior skysteeds in a sentry network? Those who are as fit and fast as N'Talley could be posted fifty miles outside the city. They can keep watch day and night, and they could warn us if the chimerae are coming, and from what direction."

N'Talley tossed her head and pawed at the ground. *The Nexara is right. We can keep watch, and we can relay our warnings through her. This is something we could do, and we want to help.*

The Dowager explained to the rest what her skysteed had just said.

"If we knew which direction the chimerae scourges were coming from, we could mass our forces to meet them," the prince said slowly. "It's an excellent idea, and it puts to good use our Nexara's amazing ability to talk to so many skysteeds."

Kie looked down at the table, her cheeks heating. Even though it was embarrassing to be called the Nexara, it gave her a warm curl of pleasure to know the prince thought that *her* idea was excellent.

I will summon the senior herd, and we will organize a sentry system right away, N'Talley said, and moments later, she was airborne. Kie smiled to herself. She had a hunch the Dowager and her skysteed would both prove to be good organizers.

Now the question was, could she and the twins and Topar train and organize two hundred cadets into an effective fighting force in the next few days? And what would happen if the chimerae reached the city before they were ready?

CHAPTER TWENTY-FOUR

AFTER TELLING THE TWINS THEY were no longer confined to their rooms, the Dowager hurried away and left Kie and the rest sitting in her chamber. Even though the prince wanted to go charging off to the Academy straight away, Topar, Princess Halla, and Kie convinced him to stay put a while longer. They had to figure out exactly how they would go about training two hundred cadets to use the old weapons, wing-shredders, and nets.

They had finished with their planning session, and Kie and N'Rah had just landed in the main stable courtyard to tell Trishop about her new assignment when a deep horn somewhere nearby blew and blew again. Then warning drums began to boom and thunder throughout the city.

Kie froze, her heart galloping in her chest. Was this it? Were the chimerae already here? Then she remembered what the Dowager had said.

"They must be practicing a citywide evacuation," she said to N'Rah. Curious, she sent him trotting out into the park, where streams of city folk hurried toward tall iron doors that led down into the caves. A line of senior skysteeds headed that way as well.

Kie winced when she saw a Mosai family rushing their children toward the doors. Their youngest daughter cried into her father's shoulder, and the oldest kept looking at the sky in terror.

"It's just a drill. The chimerae aren't here yet," the mother tried to reassure them, but her face was tight with fear, too.

Kie looked away from the family and swallowed hard. She hoped with all her heart these people would never have to face a real chimerae attack.

Where do you go now? N'Rah asked.

"I was going to talk to Trishop, but now I need to head to the Academy," Kie said, her stomach starting to churn. "I'd almost rather fight chimerae than try to convince two hundred arrogant Skyforce cadets to listen to me."

But they should respect a girl who has killed three chimerae. I will come with you. My stitches might help them understand what we have faced together.

Kie hugged his neck. "Thank you." It was a good idea, and right now she needed *all* the moral support she could get.

N'Rah insisted on carrying her into the old stadium where the twins, Ruden and his friends, and Topar had already gathered. After she slipped from his back, N'Rah made a point of standing proudly behind her, his injured flank toward the stands.

"D-do you think they'll listen to me?" she asked Gunge and Ruden. A wave of nausea washed over her and left her chilled and sweating as she watched hundreds of cadets file into the stadium, along with a handful of instructors too old to fight.

"Yeah. The fact most of the city just evacuated into the caverns shook us all up," Gunge said with unusual seriousness. "As if watching the whole senior class pack up and leave for the front didn't do that already."

"Besides, we've been telling our classmates their lives could depend on how well they listen to you," Ruden declared. "Every cadet in those stands wants to fight chimerae and live to boast about it, and they know you have way more experience at fighting those monsters than our teachers have."

Kie stared at Ruden in surprise. *Did you hear that, N'Rah?*

Yes. He wants to listen to you now, and the others do as well.

A spurt of warmth and pride thawed some of the freezing fear that gripped her. Shortly, all the cadets were seated, and an older Rosari instructor approached their group, looking like he'd just swallowed a very sour nura fruit. "I am Commandant Turine. Lord General Rennart has ordered us to turn over the cadets' training to you. I argued strongly against such a ridiculous and dangerous plan, but he insisted. So here they are."

"Thank you, Commandant Turine," Prince Shayn said. "We'll take it from here."

He waited until the commandant had stalked back to the stands, and then, facing all the cadets, he launched into a dramatic description of the day Kie and Topar had helped him fight chimerae in the Western Desert.

"All on their own, Kiesandra Torsun and her skysteed killed two of those monsters, and yet I heard a Skyforce captain say just days ago that it often takes four or five of their skyfighters to kill a single chimera." He went on to make Kie sound so heroic, her cheeks were burning with embarrassment by the time he finished.

"Now they'll listen to you," the prince told her with a wink.

Kie's guts turned somersaults. She looked around the old

stone stadium where her uncle had trained fifty years ago. For his sake, for these cadets' sake, and for the city's sake, somehow she *had* to find the right words. Straightening her shoulders, she stepped forward and tried not to notice how many faces were turned toward her right now.

"M-my uncle," she began, but her voice sounded too thin and frail. She took a deep breath, and started again.

"My uncle Duggan Torsun," she declared in a stronger voice, "is the only person to have ever won the Imperial Tournament three times. Throughout his life, he has studied the old ways our ancestors fought the chimerae. He trained me in those tactics, and now we want to teach them to you because we *know* they work. Pedarth may very well come under attack from these monsters soon, and we *must* help to protect the citizens of this city."

Kie placed her hand on N'Rah's neck, drawing strength from his presence beside her. "My skysteed and I have faced chimerae twice now. I won't lie to you. Fighting them was frightening and hard, and N'Rah was hurt, but the fact that we are still alive and here talking to you is proof the old tactics and weapons *are* effective."

She turned away from the cadets and nodded to her fellow instructors. "All right. Show them what you can do, and don't be afraid to impress them with some fancy flying."

Topar and N'Meary took off from a standing launch. When they were high over the stadium, they dropped into a spectacular dive, wrapping a botan around the lion neck and right wing of the wooden chimera target. Then, from a swift side pass, Prince

Shayn demonstrated how to use a triwire that tangled the goat head with the chimera's left wing. On three separate passes, Princess Halla demonstrated the most effective spots to shoot a chimera and a scourge master. The cadets burst into applause after each of her arrows struck home.

When all three of her fellow instructors and their skysteeds were standing next to her again, Kie addressed the cadets. "To fight chimerae effectively, you have to improve your flying skills. I'm alive today because my skysteed is incredibly agile in the air. You are going to practice turning, diving, and twisting until you and your skysteed are tired and sore."

She paused for a moment to look at them all. "But to be a better skyfighter, first and foremost, you need to be able to communicate with your skysteed clearly. To improve your mind-speaking abilities, as of today, you will be caring for your own skysteeds. You will feed them, water them, and groom them, just the way we couriers do. The more time you spend with your skysteeds, the stronger your bond will grow."

A murmur of surprise rose from the assembled cadets.

Ruden Mirsar raised his hand. Hoping she wasn't making a huge mistake, Kie motioned that he could speak. He stood and faced his fellow cadets.

"I hate that there are times I can't understand what N'Saran is trying to tell me, and I want to understand him perfectly. I've been sleeping out in the park next to him, and I've been feeding and grooming him for the past few days. Already I can understand his mindspeech better."

"So that's why you had grass in your hair at breakfast," Gunge said loudly, and many of the cadets laughed.

Kelton, who had just arrived from teaching the ladies of the Imperial court how to tie nets, raised his hand. Kie called on him next. "I'd like to spend more time with my skysteed," he admitted, "but our class schedules are too tight."

"As of this afternoon, we are altering your schedules so you will have time. Right now, you are dismissed to groom and harness up your skysteeds and report back here. Junior Courier Singu and Prince Shayn are going to run you through some flight drills. Tonight, you will make your own practice triwires and report to this stadium with them immediately after breakfast. Gunge, Kelton, and Ruden, I want to talk with you."

After the rest had left and those three had gathered around her, she asked if they would serve as both officers and instructors for each year level. "You know your classmates, and we need your input. Soon we'll have to decide which cadets and skysteeds can fly fast enough to fight in attack squads, and which ones are strong enough to carry bags of wing-shredders and nets."

Kie paused to clear her throat. "We're also asking you to do this because we know some of your Rosari classmates aren't going to want to take orders from a Mosai courier girl, but I'm hoping they will if those orders are relayed through you."

When all three promptly agreed, she put Kelton in charge of the first-years, Gunge the second-years, and Ruden the third-years. When the cadets returned with their skysteeds, Topar and Prince Shayn led them through a series of flight drills that emphasized quick midair turns, stops, and dives. They dismissed the cadets only after the sun set.

"I had no idea that couriers or princes could fly like that," she heard one of Ruden's classmates tell another as they left, and she smiled.

Toward the end of the practice, a half dozen Unbound sky-steeds landed in the stadium and watched the flight drills with great interest. Dessie and several of her groom friends had come as well and were practicing throwing their triwires on the ground. Kie ached at the envy on the grooms' faces each time they glanced up at the cadets flying overhead.

When most of the cadets had left, the big roan mare galloped straight at Kie. She forced herself to hold her ground when the skysteed came to a plunging stop a few feet away and stamped impatiently.

Her name is N'Forth, N'Rah said as he cantered to Kie's side, *and she has heard that the Nexara can speak with all skysteeds. She wants you to touch her so that she may talk with you directly. N'Forth is the lead mare of the Unbound, and she claims she has an important idea to share with us.*

CHAPTER TWENTY-FIVE

KIE SWALLOWED HARD AS SHE gazed up at the Unbound skysteed towering over her. She couldn't help noticing that the mare's hide was crisscrossed with scars. The Unbound must live rough here in the city.

She bowed and asked, "May I touch your neck?"

N'Forth tossed her head.

She says you do not to need to waste time being so polite with her, N'Rah relayed dryly.

"Some might say if you don't expect to be treated with respect, you won't be," Kie said aloud as she reached up and stroked the roan's warm neck.

A familiar tingle swept through her, and moments later, she heard a firm, clear mental voice say, *We Unbound long ago stopped waiting for humans to treat us with the respect we deserve. Do you understand my thoughts clearly?*

I do, Kie thought at her. *And my name is Kie.*

So it is true! It is strange to hear your words in my mind. The roan snorted and shook her mane. *We were sure it was a rumor put about by those silly, prissy court skysteeds. Do you believe the chimerae will attack the city?*

Prince Shayn, Dessie, Princess Halla, and Terry had gathered around and were watching their exchange. For their benefit, she said aloud, "The Skyforce's leaders don't believe the chimerae will attack the city, but we young ones think there is a good chance some will come here. The chimerae are driven to kill and gorge, and in this city, there are thousands of people and skysteeds they could prey on."

Yet more and more skyfighters leave the city. Who will defend it if the chimerae come?

Kie shrugged. "The skyfighters who remain will defend Pedarth, and many of the young humans in the Skyfighting Academy we train now. All we can do is our best."

You do not have enough skyfighters. The big mare stamped her foot. *Many of us wish to help. Even though we have not been allowed to bind, this is our city, too.*

"What is she saying?" Dessie asked.

"The Unbound want to help defend Pedarth if the chimerae come," Kie said bemusedly.

We can lift, we can carry. We can fight the Foul Ones with our hooves and teeth. Some of us are even willing to carry riders.

Kie relayed the mare's words to her friends. "But the penalty for an unauthorized binding is death for the skyrider," Princess Halla said, shaking her head. "It's a stupid law, but it's the law just the same."

It is possible for us to carry a human and not bind with that person. We will be more effective in defending this city if we fly with skyfighters on our backs who can shoot and throw these weapons you use in your practices.

Excited by the idea, Kie told the others, "She's arguing that it's possible for them to carry riders and not bind with them."

"I've never heard of such a thing," Topar said, "but if the rider and the skysteed don't officially recite the binding vows together, maybe they wouldn't invoke the magic that binds skysteeds and their riders."

The prince looked thoughtful. "It might be time to change that law anyway. Some greedy breeders got it passed a century ago to prop up the prices for their skysteeds."

"Humans shouldn't be owning or selling skysteeds in the first place," Kie said hotly.

"I agree," Dessie said. She turned to face N'Forth. "I would gladly fly with you to fight the Foul Ones, and I know many grooms would join me."

"So do I," Terry said.

Tell the tall girl to bring her friends here tomorrow morning, N'Forth said to Kie, *and I will bring forty of the Unbound who are willing to carry riders.*

With that, N'Forth and her companions galloped across the stadium and leaped into the air.

"The Unbound are so wild and undisciplined. I hope you aren't planning to trust them to do anything important," Ruden said, looking aghast.

"How many Unbound are there, do you suppose?" Topar asked as the riderless skysteeds disappeared into the twilight sky.

"I'm not sure anyone knows for sure," Terry replied. "There must be hundreds at least."

"They could be a huge help, but we need to be able to direct them. Which means," the prince said in an undertone to Kie after Ruden had turned away, "you are going to have to establish mental links with many more of the Unbound skysteeds who want to help us."

"Right," Kie said, her head already starting to ache at the prospect.

After another restless night, Kie rose early the next morning and went to find Trishop in his office. When she started to explain her new assignment, he frowned and held up a hand to forestall her.

"I already received a message from the palace that you and Prince Shayn will be in charge of training the cadets at the Academy."

"At least your staff won't have to groom the Academy skysteeds anymore," Kie said, trying to cheer him up.

"So Terry informed me this morning, along with the fact that the Unbound want to carry riders and help if the chimerae attack the city. It's quite amazing that one frontier girl could turn so many traditions in this capital upside down in such a short time."

Kie shifted uncomfortably in her chair.

"You might also be interested to know," the head groom continued, "that I couldn't find any mention of a skyrider in my records who could talk to other skysteeds the way you can, except for one, and that was the mage, Sian, who was instrumental in helping Prince Isen defeat the chimerae three hundred years ago."

"I'm no mage, sir."

"I didn't think you were, but I'm afraid you are going to find yourself in more dangerous situations, like she did, if our head-strong young prince has his way. Please, for your uncle's sake, be careful."

"I will. I don't want N'Rah to get hurt again."

"I don't want any more skysteeds or their riders to get hurt or die, but if the chimerae come, we'll have no choice but to fight. I've already ordered our skysteed healers to make plenty of that antidote for sand dragon venom, based on the recipes in your uncle's manual. Let me know if there's anything I or my grooms can do to help you."

"Well, as a matter of fact, sir," Kie said, relieved he had given her such a good opening, "there is one thing." She explained about the grooms who had been coming to her practices. Since they had already been training with botans and triwires and were familiar with skysteeds, they were logical candidates to present to the Unbound.

"If the Unbound will accept them, those grooms are excused from their work for me. Your cadets aren't the only ones who are going to have to start caring for their own skysteeds." Trishop's lips twitched. "I almost look forward to telling some of our Rosari nobility that they are going to have to groom their own skysteeds now that there's a war on."

A large group of excited grooms and assistant grooms, carrying flight harnesses, followed Kie, Dessie, and Terry into the new stadium a short time later. Next door, in the old stadium, Topar and the twins were already directing the cadets' practice, but Kie

wanted to make sure this crucial first meeting between the Unbound and her friends from the Imperial Stables went well. The
grooms kept glancing at the sky.

"Maybe they changed their minds," one young man said.

"They'll be here," Dessie reassured him, but she watched the
sky as intently as the rest.

"There they are!" Terry cried and pointed to the east.

N'Forth, plainly possessing a flair for the dramatic, circled
the stadium once with a herd of Unbound skysteeds flying behind
her, the morning sunlight shining on their bright wings, manes,
and tails before they landed. After she made a quick count, Kie
heaved a sigh of relief. There were forty skysteeds, and she was
almost sure there were forty grooms present. It was hard to get
a good count because the humans kept shifting about so eagerly.

A handsome black skysteed with silver wings landed next to
N'Forth. "By Great N'Rin's mane, N'Tarin has come, too," Terry
said, looking rapt.

How would you like to do this? Kie asked the big roan mare.

*Have them spread out, and we will look them over, just like the humans
did when they turned us down at auction,* N'Forth replied with a toss
of her head.

*I will ask them, but remember, these are not the rich humans who claim to
own you or refused to buy you at auction,* Kie told N'Forth sternly. *These
are hardworking people who chose to devote their lives to caring for skysteeds
because they love your species. Please tell your companions this.*

Very well, N'Forth said less stridently. *I will tell them.*

"Now spread out so the skysteeds can look you over and

smell your scent," Kie told the anxious grooms.

The grooms quickly spread out around the stadium. The sky-steeds watched with ears pricked and nostrils flaring.

They are as excited to make a human friend as the grooms are to meet a special skysteed, N'Rah said, and a lump rose in the back of Kie's throat.

She reached out and hugged his neck. "I'm so very glad you chose me as your skyrider. Even though these pairs aren't reciting the binding vows the way we did, I hope someday they may be allowed to."

As soon as the grooms were in position, the skysteeds began to mill about. Kie grinned when N'Forth chased off two headed toward Dessie and planted herself in front of the tall Mosai girl. Her eyes glowing, Dessie put her hand out, and N'Forth sniffed it delicately.

Kie held her breath when N'Tarin walked up to Terry and bowed to him in a courtly fashion. Terry bowed back, and then the black skysteed allowed him to stroke his neck. As more and more skysteeds chose their riders, Kie hurried around with N'Rah to make the introductions. Remembering Ruden's and Prince Shayn's worries about being able to direct and communicate with the Unbound, she made a point of touching each one.

"N'Tarin says he is glad to see you again," she told Terry. "He still mourns his skyrider, but he has returned to Pedarth because he wants to fight the chimerae, and he knows he will be more effective with a human on his back."

Kie winced when she spotted a small black-and-white pinto standing all alone. Somehow she must have gotten the count wrong. There were no grooms left for the little skysteed to choose. Then Hedly came rushing into the stadium, looking like he'd just scrambled into his clothes.

"I couldn't sleep most of the night because I was so excited," he said breathlessly as he ran up to Kie, "and then I slept through the morning bell. Please, please, tell me I'm not too late."

Kie smiled and gestured toward the little pinto mare, who had already pricked her ears and was studying the boy curiously. She trotted over to him, smelled his hand, and then rubbed her head against his shoulder.

"Hedly, this is N'Wren," Kie said to the boy who smiled in wonder, "and she says she would be happy to fly with you."

The grooms began to brush their skysteeds, who seemed delighted by the attention as years of dust and dirt were removed from their coats. They were more skittish when they were fitted with harnesses and saddles. N'Rah and N'Forth had to talk sharply to several to get them to settle down.

Before long, the grooms were smiling broadly as they trotted and cantered round the stadium.

"When can we try flying?" Dessie asked Kie. The Mosai girl already looked quite at home on the big roan's back.

"We have a few things to cover first," Kie said and called the group over. "Remember, your skysteed can understand your spoken words, but they will understand what you want even more quickly from the way you shift your weight."

She proceeded to demonstrate how she asked N'Rah to climb, descend, and turn by shifting in her saddle. "Now check to make sure you're clipped in properly, and then we'll take off. You will follow me on this first flight. If it goes well, I promise you'll be soloing soon. Skysteeds, fly as smoothly as you can. You don't want to scare your new skyrider."

Kie trotted N'Rah to the far end of the stadium, Dessie and N'Forth right behind them, and the rest following in a long line.

"By the Messenger's wings, I hope this goes well," she murmured to N'Rah and squeezed his sides.

He galloped down the stadium and leaped into the air. When the rest were airborne, she asked Dessie and N'Forth to lead the group to the far end of the park while she and N'Rah hovered in place and watched the new skyriders. She encouraged a few who looked pale and clutched their skysteed's manes, but most appeared thrilled to be flying.

Kie returned to the lead and began a series of gentle turns, ascents, and descents as they circled the park. After they completed three circuits, she headed back to the stadium. When her new skyriders had all landed safely, she told them, "Go water and talk to your skysteed, and we'll try some flight drills next."

My human and I are coming to speak with you, N'Talley informed Kie. Soon, N'Talley, with the Dowager on her back, and a dozen of the senior herd carrying their skyriders landed nearby. Many of the skyriders had gray hair and proudly wore old Skyforce uniforms.

"The twins told me that the Unbound had approached you," the Dowager said in her brisk way after Kie had bowed to her. "I'm glad you've given them a purpose. You, my girl, are full of surprises. N'Talley finally admitted that you can speak to every skysteed you touch—and now we're going to put that ability to good use."

Then she gestured toward the twelve skyriders behind her. "These are my sentry captains. They fly the senior skysteeds who can mindspeak the farthest, and they are in touch with our sentries with the best day and night vision. I want you to establish links with my captains' skysteeds, and they will contact you if chimerae are spotted in their watch sector."

"So their riders don't mind that I will be talking directly with their skysteeds?"

"They don't mind, or they wouldn't be here," the Dowager snapped, and Kie drew in a breath.

Do not feel hurt by her tone, N'Talley said quickly. *She is just trying to protect the people of her city, and the responsibility of that weighs on her.*

Kie certainly understood how responsibility for other's lives could weigh on one. The old woman proceeded to introduce her to the twelve skyriders and their mounts. Kie concentrated on learning the skysteeds' names rather than their riders', because the nobles' elaborate titles were confusing.

"How do the evacuation drills go?" she asked the Dowager when she had finished.

"They take too long," she admitted wearily. "We still needed two hours on the last one to get everyone underground."

"Has there been any more news from the front?"

"We're getting reports of individual scourges attacking settlements deep in the heart of the Telawa Valley. Evidently, more and more chimerae are slipping past our lines, and they appear to be headed east, toward Pedarth."

The Dowager paused, her face tight with worry. "Push your students hard, Kiesandra. I'm afraid the chimerae could be here within a matter of days."

Chapter Twenty-Six

Thanks to the news the Dowager had shared, Kie was in a somber mood when she met up with her fellow instructors over lunch.

"How is it going over here?" Kie asked as they all gulped down sausage rolls in the shade of one of the equipment sheds.

"Well enough," Prince Shayn replied. "We've already divided up our cadets into those who will attack with triwires, bows, and botans, and those we'll have drop the wing-shredders and nets."

"Do we have anything that our skyfighters can practice dropping yet?"

"Actually, I found a big stash of wing-shredders when I was poking around in the old armory last night," Prince Shayn said with a grin. He carefully handed Kie a heavy metal object the size of her hand that looked like a silver insect with six long, outstretched pointed legs. "Even though they're three hundred years old, they're still sharp as knives. We'll practice with those until we have those new ones the blacksmiths are making for us."

"And there's our first batch of nets." Princess Halla gestured toward a colorful pile of bundles. "The ladies of the court decided they were so ugly, they had to put them in pretty bags." She made a rueful face, but then her expression grew serious.

"I have an idea, but I don't know if it's a good one. I could organize three triads composed of our best archers, and our job would be to work together to hunt and kill as many of the scourge masters as we can. What do you think?"

"It's brilliant," her brother said instantly. When Topar and Kie agreed, the princess beamed at them.

"How is it going with the Unbound?" Topar asked Kie.

"Better than I expected. Most of the grooms who volunteered are good riders, but it takes time to learn how to direct a skysteed in the air." She went on to share the Dowager's warning about the scourges that were slipping past the front lines.

"If their scourge masters mass their chimerae and attack in force, we're in trouble," the prince said soberly and got to his feet. "Guess we better get back to work."

Kie spent the rest of the day helping the grooms develop their flight skills. Dessie and Terry were naturals, and Hedly on quick little N'Wren could outfly them all. Late in the afternoon, she sent her new skyriders soaring off solo with their skysteeds to get to know each other better.

She flew to the other stadium to watch four lines of cadets on the biggest skysteeds taking turns dropping wing-shredders and nets at target crosses on the ground. Kie frowned when she realized that many of the cadets were missing their targets by thirty and forty feet.

"I'm sure the drop squad will get better with practice," Prince Shayn said as he flew up beside her. "Ruden's already got the hang of it."

Just then, dark gray N'Saran swooped past, his skyrider's

brows drawn in concentration. Ruden tossed two wing-shredders that landed right in the center of the ground target.

"Let's move your drop practice into the new stadium at the end of today," Kie suggested to the prince. "My grooms are ready to join the cadets, and we don't want any of those wing-shredders landing on someone's head by mistake."

They sent the cadets and grooms off to supper, and afterward they worked on their flight skills, talked about triad tactics, and everyone pitched in to move the drop squad equipment into the new stadium. Kie's heart fell when she saw Ruden, Gunge, and Kelton talking with several third-year cadets who did not look happy. When the cadets left, Ruden and his friends walked over to Kie, Topar, and the twins.

"Some of our classmates in the drop squad asked us to talk to you," Ruden explained. "We know the chimerae are fast. The fact they've decimated our Skyforce makes that clear enough. But once we've tangled chimerae in a net or shredded their wings to slow them down, we could use our lances to finish them off. That's the weapon we've practiced with the most."

"But if we let you carry lances," the prince said skeptically, "what's going to keep you from charging straight at the chimerae and getting yourselves killed?"

"Common sense and concern for our skysteeds," Ruden retorted, sticking out his chin.

"That's assuming Academy cadets have common sense," Princess Halla said under her breath.

"Remember, during our fight in the Telawa Valley," Topar

spoke up, "skyforce fighters did a great job of killing the chimerae we'd crippled. We should let the drop squad cadets carry their lances."

"Fine," the prince said, throwing up his hands. "The cadets can have their lances, but if some of those glory-hungry fools get themselves killed, it's on your heads."

Kie was exhausted by the time she and Dessie returned to the girls' dormitory that night. Dessie, though, couldn't quit smiling as she got ready for bed. She came over to Kie before she climbed under her covers.

"Even if I were to die tomorrow fighting chimerae," Dessie said seriously, "just one day of flying with N'Forth has made it all worthwhile. Many of my friends feel the same way. Thank you for making a lifelong dream come true for us." She gave Kie a long hug.

"But I don't want you or N'Forth or anyone to die," Kie said as she stepped back, a catch in her voice. She was horribly aware that the grooms *she* had helped partner with Unbound skysteeds could very well get killed if they ended up battling chimerae. But Dessie's unbridled joy helped to lift her spirits a little.

Before Kie fell asleep, she reached out to the senior watch captains' skysteeds. They'd seen no sign of chimerae in any of their sectors.

So far.

The next day, they started practice early. Palace staff appeared at the old stadium midmorning, driving three cartloads of wing-shredders, a hundred more nets, and the first batch of real triwires.

"Grandmama has been busy," the prince said as he and Kie inspected the piles of equipment, "but how are we going to ferry all this stuff miles outside the city to where we hope to stop the chimerae?"

"I have an idea." Kie smiled and reached out to N'Forth. The big roan and Dessie left practice, and Kie hurried off on N'Rah to find Trishop.

They met back at the old stadium an hour later, about the time that a dozen grooms showed up with a cartload of saddle-bags and pack saddles. N'Forth brought a hundred more Unbound skysteeds with her.

These are the Unbound who do not wish to carry riders, she told Kie, *but they are willing to carry these nets and bags of wing-shredders to where we will fight the chimerae.*

Kie spent the next few hours meeting each of the Unbound, and with Dessie's and the grooms' help, she got them used to car-rying a pack saddle on their backs. Some hated the sensation and flew away, but many more stayed.

"If the alarm drums sound, we'll come here first and help get these skysteeds loaded up for you," an older Mosai groom named Dalton promised her. She smiled as she watched him pet a friendly buckskin skysteed before he left. Maybe more Unbound would be finding human partners before this conflict ended.

That afternoon, the warning drums sounded across the city as the mayor and the Dowager conducted another practice evacua-tion. Kie kept her grooms and cadets busy and tried to ignore the thunder of the drums. She issued real triwires to the students who had been training with their practice triwires the longest. As they started their first aerial target runs, Kie held her breath. All thirty hit the target posts, and none of them hurt their skysteeds with the razor-sharp weapons. She insisted they make several more runs until their timing was perfect.

In the meantime, Topar helped the rest of the attack group make more botans. He was demonstrating ways to dive and throw botans from the air when a beautiful dappled gray stallion carrying a Skyforce officer appeared. The officer watched Topar for several minutes before he flew down to where Kie and Prince Shayn were standing.

Kie gulped. Their Skyforce visitor was Lord General Rennart.

N'Meary, you better tell Topar to get down here, Kie said. *I think we're about to do some planning with the Skyforce Lord General in charge of defending Pedarth.*

N'Meary and Topar landed beside Kie as the Lord General approached their group. The Lord General looked tired, but there was warmth in his smile when he said to Topar, "You couriers certainly know how to fly." Then he turned to address them all.

"I've come to discuss how we can best coordinate our two forces. I just watched your cadets in the other stadium practicing with nets and those wing-shredding devices. If those succeed in slowing down the chimerae, that could be a big help to my skyfighters, even if the scourges do come at us in force."

The Lord General agreed they should try to engage the chimerae outside of the city, and he suggested that the drop squad, protected by the fleeter attack squad, would fly above the chimerae and do their best to cripple and slow down the scourges. His three hundred Skyforce skyfighters would try to stop the chimerae from reaching Pedarth. Healers for both humans and skysteeds were ready to race out to wherever the fighting took place.

"Tell your cadets that we want them to sleep with their flight gear and weapons by their beds from now on," the Lord General said grimly. "Five villages were attacked two hundred miles from here, and I've asked the Emperor to send us reinforcements."

He paused and looked at Kie. "Finally, I'd like you to establish a link with my skysteed, if you can. I understand our senior sentry captains are going to report to you the moment they spot the chimerae, and then I want you to relay that report to me. Every second may count in terms of giving our citizens time to reach the caverns."

Kie found herself staring at the Lord General as he talked. Some of his mannerisms were so like Topar's! Hastily, she nodded and walked up to the dappled gray stallion. The way he held his head and the intelligence in his dark eyes seemed very familiar. She stroked his silky neck and, after the usual tingling, she could hear his thoughts.

"Why, he says his name is N'Tyr, and that my uncle's skysteed, N'Tor, is his sire," Kie said with a surprised smile.

"So it's true, you can speak with all skysteeds." The Lord General looked relieved. "We're going to take full advantage of your remarkable gift."

After the Lord General left, they pushed their students hard and organized them into flight wings. That night passed uneventfully, and in the morning, Kie and Prince Shayn issued real triwires to every member of the attack squad. By midday, there were some sliced fingers and close calls, but at least no one was seriously hurt.

In the afternoon, Prince Shayn took Kie aside to practice communicating with the leaders of the various groups and their skysteeds. First she practiced with N'Saran and Ruden, leaders of the drop squad, and Topar and N'Meary, leaders of the attack squad. Then she worked with Dessie and N'Forth, the main link to the Unbound skysteeds carrying equipment. Prince Shayn drilled her in reaching out to each of these skysteeds until she could find each of their minds almost instantly.

Her head ached by the end of their practice session, but it wasn't as bad as it had been before. *It's like I've found a new muscle, and now I have to strengthen it*, she explained to a sympathetic N'Rah.

After dinner, Kie shared with the cadets and grooms all the advice that her uncle had drilled into her about fighting chimerae, and Topar and Prince Shayn chimed in with what they'd learned.

That night before bed, she picked up the dayan leaf she had plucked the day she left home. She raised it to her nose and caught a hint of its fresh, sweet scent. A lump rose in her throat. Right now, apples would be maturing on the branches of her trees, but she wasn't there to check them for pests or blight.

Wondering if she'd ever see her orchard and Uncle Dugs again, she fell into a restless sleep, a part of her mind listening for the senior skysteeds patrolling the night skies outside of Pedarth.

Sometime in the early hours of the morning, Kie was jerked from sleep by a desperate sentry skysteed calling out to her.

Young one, you must wake up! Over a thousand chimerae fly from the east. Rouse your forces. The Foul Ones are only fifty miles from the city and closing fast!

Chapter Twenty-Seven

Kie's heart beat triple time. Cold terror mixed with despair paralyzed her. How could they possibly stop a *thousand* chimerae with only five hundred skyfighters? They were going to be annihilated. The best they could do was delay them long enough to let the people of Pedarth reach the caverns.

She drew in a breath and pushed past her fear. Having rehearsed this moment so many times in her mind, she knew what to do. First, she told the sentry skysteed that she'd heard his warning. Then she reached for N'Talley's mind.

Tell your human that a thousand chimerae come fast from the east. Start evacuating the city.

I will tell her. Look out for yourself today, young one.

The old skysteed's concern warmed her, but briefly. She was too frightened for herself and for N'Rah and all the brave people and skysteeds she'd met since coming to Pedarth.

As she scrambled into her clothes, she contacted the Lord General's N'Tyr, and then N'Saran, because Ruden was in charge of rallying the cadets. Next she roused N'Rah and N'Forth, and then Prince Shayn and Topar through their skysteeds. After hurrying to Dessie's bedside, she shook her friend awake. She wasn't surprised to see that Dessie had slept in her clothes.

"They're coming. Wake the other grooms."

"What time is it?" Dessie asked, instantly alert.

"The four o'clock bell just rang."

By the time Kie ran to meet N'Rah in the stable courtyard with her flight gear, the alarm drums had begun to thunder. Great Cerken in his half phase bathed the dark courtyard with silver light.

How are you feeling? she asked N'Rah as she threw on his flight harness and saddle.

I am not stiff anymore. I am ready to fight, he replied eagerly.

Then Trishop was beside her, handing her the last of her gear. "May all the gods bless you and protect you this day, Kiesandra," he said and laid a hand on her shoulder. "Your uncle will be proud. Try to stay alive so he can tell you that himself."

"Thank you, sir," she said, her voice gone tight. She wanted to see Uncle Dugs again so badly. Who would look after him and make sure he took his meds if something happened to her? She simply had to stay alive today, and N'Rah did, too.

After making that promise to herself, she vaulted into her saddle. She had just clipped into her flight harness when N'Forth landed beside them.

The Unbound are already on their way to the stadium, N'Forth told Kie as Dessie threw on her flight harness and saddle. The roan's eyes flashed fire as she added, *I thank you for giving us this chance to strike at the Foul Ones.*

You may not be thanking me by the time today's over, Kie replied grimly and sent N'Rah leaping into the night sky.

The new stadium was already bustling. In the bright moonlight, cadets loaded the riderless Unbound with nets and bags of wing-shredders. When Dalton and some other grooms arrived at a run and took over the loading, the cadets mounted their skysteeds and formed their triads and squadrons.

Then the twins and Topar were beside her. "I guess this is it," Prince Shayn said, his voice remarkably calm. "How far out are they now?"

Kie reached for the sentry skysteed's mind. "He says they're thirty miles out and passing over the village of Ganor." Swiftly, she relayed that information to the Lord General's skysteed, too.

"Anyone know where Ganor is?" Prince Shayn shouted.

"I know where that is," Hedly piped up. "We'll fly right over my mum's house on the way there." His enthusiastic reply generated a ripple of nervous laughter.

"Then you are going to lead us," the prince said.

"How many chimerae do we fight today?" a cadet shouted.

"Our sentries counted over a thousand," Prince Shayn replied, and even in the moonlight, Kie could see the shock and dismay on the faces of the skyriders closest to her. "We must hold and delay those scourges as long as possible," the prince continued in a confident voice, "and give the people of Pedarth time to reach the safety of the caverns. If we work together and keep our heads, I believe we can even defeat them. Good luck to you all!"

He motioned for Hedly to lead off. Beaming with pride, the young groom sent his little N'Wren galloping down the stadium and into the wind, and they were airborne. Next, Kie, the twins, and Topar and the wings of his attack squad took off, and then the drop squad under Ruden's command, and then Dessie and the Unbound ferrying their extra weapons. Hundreds of skysteeds soared through the dark sky, moonlight gleaming on their wings and making their tails look like silver banners.

She leaned forward and patted N'Rah's neck. "They make a grand sight, don't they?"

They do, he replied, but she sensed his apprehension. Maybe he was wondering, just as she was, how many of them would be returning to Pedarth this night. A treacherous voice inside her head kept saying their untried skyfighters didn't stand a chance against a thousand chimerae.

"Has the Skyforce launched yet?" the prince asked as they flew over the eastern outskirts of the city.

"They just took off." Thanks to Prince Shayn's energy and planning, they'd beaten the Skyforce veterans into the air by several minutes.

"The scourge masters must have chosen to come from the east," the prince said, wearing his thinking look, "so the rising sun would be in our eyes. We need to find some clouds along their path, hide in them, and then attack the chimerae from behind. Then the sun will be in *their* eyes."

"It's a good plan," Topar said from his position flying on the prince's right, "and it gives the Skyforce time to catch up with us. Now we need to pray that there are clouds right where we want them."

The skies were starting to lighten, and there were no clouds ahead. Kie's stomach tightened.

"Where are the chimerae?" the prince asked Kie several minutes later, his voice more strained.

"The sentry says the chimerae are east of Towarth Village," Kie replied.

"That's maybe ten miles from here," Hedly offered after peering at the ground.

"Then we need to find some cloud cover, and find it soon," the prince said tightly.

Moment by moment, the sky grew lighter. If they didn't find a cloud to hide in, they would have to face a thousand chimerae in the open with the Skyforce still minutes behind them.

"There, off to the south. N'Meary's spotted some fine, fleecy clouds for us!" Topar cried.

"Right. I see them now," Prince Shayn said. "Kie, tell everyone we're racing for those clouds, and we all need to be hidden before the sun rises and the chimerae pass."

N'Laure sprinted forward, and N'Rah and the rest hurried after him. It seemed to take forever to reach it, but at last they plunged into the damp gray heart of the first cloud. Kie couldn't see anything but fog and the skysteeds and their riders on either side of her.

"Tell everyone to stay silent," the prince told Kie. "Chimerae have excellent hearing."

They also have an excellent sense of smell, Kie worried as she relayed the prince's orders. Resolutely, she ignored the headache building between her temples as she contacted so many skysteed minds.

The prince motioned that she, Princess Halla, and Topar should follow him out to the edge of the cloud, and there they waited, peering through white swirling tendrils of water vapor. All she could hear was the quiet *whoosh* of air passing through hundreds of wings and the pounding of her pulse in her ears. Dampness cooled her cheeks, and droplets formed on her hair and eyelashes. She glanced down at her courier timer. Only forty-five minutes had passed since the alarm drums first sounded. They *had* to stop and hold the chimerae for at least another hour if all the citizens of Pedarth were to reach safety.

N'Rah tensed. *Here they come!*

Numbly, Kie told the Lord General's N'Tyr they would be attacking within minutes. Then she shifted her bow into fighting position and checked her four triwires.

The moment she spotted the approaching monsters, she felt like someone had punched her in the gut. The chimerae host was *huge!* Hundreds and hundreds of the black-and-tan monsters flew in their scourges of six, commanded by their masters. The chimerae flew so closely together, they almost looked like a giant spiderweb spanning the pink sky, the sun's first bright rays highlighting their wings. Kie shuddered when she realized she had seen this moment before, in her nightmares.

In the past, when she had fought chimerae, she had been frightened for herself and her friends. Now she was terrified for them, plus hundreds more who were her responsibility. As the great host drew relentlessly closer, Kie found herself praying to the Messenger: *Please don't let them see us. Please don't let them smell us.*

A lifetime later, the near right wing of the host flapped by their cloud. And then the chimerae were past their hiding place. She jumped when the lion heads roared in battle fury, the blood-goat heads screeched, and the scourge masters yelled commands in their harsh language.

"Do you think they sensed us?" Princess Halla whispered in dismay, her Rosari freckles standing out against her pale cheeks.

But the host kept flying straight west.

"Maybe they've spotted the sunlight flashing off the Sky-force's weapons," the prince said hoarsely. "Let's go kill these monsters!"

Kie reached for N'Meary's and N'Saran's minds, and seconds later, Topar's and Ruden's squads streaked out of the cloud and chased after the chimerae.

Focused on attacking the Skyforce, the scourges picked up their pace. But, determined to protect their city, the young sky-riders flew even faster. Soon the eight wings of the drop squad spread out above and behind the vast chimerae host. Topar's attack wings hovered behind Ruden's drop squad, ready to protect the slower skysteeds. Kie and the prince followed, flying above them all where they could watch the battle as it unfolded.

"There are no houses beneath us," the prince said. "Tell Ruden to begin his attack, and order the Unbound carriers to land in that big field ahead. Then get some riders to help them unload and spread those nets out."

Kie relayed the prince's orders. The Unbound carriers flashed beneath her, heading for the field, but . . . they'd brought unloading help with them! Dalton and three of his friends had ridden out here on the backs of Unbound, without flight harnesses.

A silver rain of wing-shredders began falling from the drop squad, and nets twirled downward like giant moths. The lion heads roared in anger and surprise as the metal shredders tore through their wings. When the scourge masters peered over their shoulders, they stared straight into the bright dawn sun. Their confusion gave the skyfighters precious seconds to dump their entire loads, tearing more and more wings and tangling more chimerae in their nets.

But the scourge masters rallied and sent their scourges charging upward toward the drop squad. Kie's breath caught as the attack squad dove into the host, their triwires and botans spinning through the air. She spotted a blur of golden chestnut as Princess Halla and her elite archers went after the scourge masters.

Chimerae started to fall from the sky, struggling against the weapons that bound them and stole the lift from their wings. Half the drop squad attacked the tangled chimerae with lances while Ruden sent the other half diving down to the field to pick up more wing-shredders and nets.

"It's working," the prince cried to Kie and pumped his fist. "But we must kill two for every one of us who falls." Before he looked away from her, she saw the pain in his eyes.

Because skysteeds were beginning to fall. Kie's eyes burned with tears as the beautiful animals spiraled downward like birds with broken wings, either too hurt to fight on or with injured riders slumped against their necks.

"Those Skyforce healers better get here soon," Kie said thickly.

Now the tide of battle was turning against them. The chimerae had such a great advantage in numbers, they started to hunt the prince's forces in triads of their own. Kie winced as she heard skysteeds neigh and scream in pain, and the scourge masters shout triumphantly.

We should be fighting, too. N'Rah snorted.

"We talked about this," she said to him, her throat aching with grief. "Right now my job is to help the prince communicate with everyone. We'll be fighting soon enough."

But she, too, longed to help their friends. Pain lanced through her body every time a skysteed she was linked to was hurt, or the contact broke off entirely as the animal died. Desperately, she tried to ignore that pain and focus on the prince, so she would be ready to relay his next command.

Just when she was sure her friends would be obliterated, trumpets sounded, and the Skyforce smashed into the chimerae host from behind. Then it was chaos as the pale dawn sky dissolved into hundreds of swirling fights between skyfighters and chimerae, and it was impossible to tell who was winning. Lord General Rennart had kept a third of his skyfighters in reserve.

They formed a defensive net behind the aerial battle, blocking the chimerae's path to Pedarth.

Princess Halla dove past as her triad attacked another scourge master. Kie cheered fiercely when the princess's arrow pierced the man's neck, and a Skyforce fighter drove a lance to the central heart of the scourge master's leaderless chimera.

Two riderless Unbound skysteeds rose from the equipment field, each carrying a corner of a net in its teeth. They dropped it on a chimera that was trying to savage one of Dessie's groom friends. Their timing was perfect. The net caught on the beast's right and left wing talons at the top of its wing stroke. With its wings bound together, it fell from the sky like a stone.

"The Unbound watched our practices and they learned," she said to N'Rah in amazement.

Of course they did, her skysteed replied proudly.

More and more of the riderless Unbound swept down to the equipment field in pairs and picked up nets as fast as Dalton and his companions could lay them out.

Kie concentrated and reached for N'Talley back in Pedarth.

How does the evacuation go?

Too slowly. This time our city folk knew it was not a drill, N'Talley replied in frustration, *and these foolish people keep trying to bring all their household goods with them. You must hold those beasts, or they will catch half our population still aboveground.*

Kie shared N'Talley's message with the prince and relayed it to the Lord General as well, through N'Tyr. Then she noticed three bigger chimerae hovering above the center of the host, each ridden by a scourge master. A large group of scourges seemed to be rallying in front of them. Anxiously, she pointed them out to the prince.

"I believe they're commanding this host," the prince replied, "and they're gathering those scourges to punch through the Skyforce's line. Warn the Lord General!"

Kie reached out to N'Tyr. *We see them,* N'Tyr replied. *We must stop them and give the city people more time.*

Dread twisting her gut, Kie contacted N'Meary and N'Saran. *See those chimerae massing in the middle? We must keep them from hammering through the Skyforce line!*

But the cadets of the attack and drop squads were spread out over a huge area as they fought bravely against the chimerae. Few of them could reach the middle of the host in time. Even as she watched, the dense mass of chimerae charged straight at the Skyforce's center!

CHAPTER TWENTY-EIGHT

FRANTICALLY, KIE REACHED OUT TO N'Forth and every other Unbound skysteed she had linked to. *Drop your nets on that big group of chimerae attacking the middle of the Skyforce line. They are trying to force their way through. You must stop them!*

Her head throbbing from calling so many skysteeds at once, she turned to the prince. "We have to help them!"

"Agreed," he said, unslinging a triwire, "but we're too far from the chimerae attacking the line. We have to go after their leaders. Let's gain some altitude, and tell N'Seella and Halla that we need them."

As she looked away from the seething mass of chimerae and skysteeds in the heart of the battle, she caught a glimpse of bright N'Meary. Topar fought side by side with his father, trying to stop the scourges from smashing through the line.

Biting her lip, she fought down her fear for Topar and forced herself to focus on N'Seella's mind. *We need you and the princess. We hunt the leaders of the host.*

We come, N'Seella replied. *Our triad has killed many scourge masters already.*

Within moments, Princess Halla appeared along with her triad of archers, her cheeks flushed. "The second archery triad is coming. The third one . . . doesn't exist anymore."

The princess's second triad of expert archers arrived, and the prince outlined his plan. Approaching from behind, he and Kie would attack the big chimera in the center, and the princess's two archery triads would try to kill the scourge masters riding the two chimerae on either side.

"All right," the princess said, and nocked an arrow. Kie did the same, her whole body shaking. Those chimerae were *huge*.

"Good hunting," the prince cried. Kie's belly tightened as N'Rah tucked into a deep dive, keeping pace beside N'Laure.

Right as Kie came into bow range, the bloodgoat head on the big chimera to their right screeched a warning. The three beasts spun around. As she flashed past, she fired her arrow at the head of the scourge master.

But . . . the man had no legs! It was just a human torso that rose from the chimera's back behind the three necks. Fast as thought, the sand dragon head shot backward, its scaled neck deflecting her arrow. She glimpsed a vaguely human face on the torso's head, its expression twisted in hate, and then they were beyond it and climbing.

"Those aren't regular scourge masters," Kie gasped to N'Rah, trying to understand what she'd just seen.

They have no legs. I think they are humans who are fused to their Foul Ones! N'Rah shuddered in revulsion.

"Someone has physically bound humans with chimerae," Kie shouted at the prince as they soared up beside him. She tasted bile in her mouth. "H-how is that possible?"

"I don't know," he replied, looking as shaken as she felt.

"I'm afraid it makes them react faster. The sand dragon head blocked my arrow."

"I got the lion head," the prince said with grim satisfaction. Kie glanced down at the three command chimerae far beneath them now. His triwire had cut halfway through the lion's neck, and now that head dangled lifelessly next to the other two.

"These horrible things react too fast," Princess Halla panted as she and her two triads joined them. "The other heads just blocked our arrows."

"Then we have to get rid of some of those heads," her brother replied. "Tell Ruden's squad to drop some wing-shredders and slow them down," he ordered Kie.

"Right," she said, and reached for N'Saran's mind.

We just loaded up. Be right there, the skysteed promised her.

Twenty of the chimerae have broken through the Skyforce line, N'Meary called to Kie urgently. *They fly toward Pedarth. They are so far ahead of us, I fear we cannot catch them!*

N'Forth, Kie yelled with her mind, even as N'Rah veered to avoid a chimera wildly flapping its tattered wings. *Tell the Unbound they must chase down those twenty chimerae that got through the line and drop nets on them. Without riders, your friends can fly faster than any of us!*

I will tell them, N'Forth replied.

"Thanks," Kie said breathlessly to N'Rah as he soared up next to the prince again. "It's hard to concentrate with so many voices in my mind." Or think past the headache splitting her skull apart.

Shortly, N'Saran swept over the three command chimerae,

Ruden throwing a dozen wing-shredders down at them. Then he dropped a net on the left command chimera, binding the lion head to its right wing and claws. As the tangled chimera roared furiously and veered sideways, the princess and her archers went after it, and the enraged center chimera charged N'Saran. Despite the holes in its wings, the monster was still incredibly quick.

N'Saran, watch out! Kie warned him. The big skysteed made the mistake of trying to climb instead of diving, exposing his belly to the chimera. Just when the monster reached out to gut N'Saran, Hedly and fleet N'Wren shot past the chimera. The young groom threw a triwire that bit deeply into the sand dragon neck and stopped the beast midair as a fountain of purple blood blinded its human captain.

Ruden reacted quickly. While N'Wren distracted the bloodgoat head, the burly cadet drove a lance deep into the creature's chest.

"That's one down. Let's tackle the one on the right," the prince yelled at Kie. "We'll try to triwire those heads at the same time."

Too frightened to speak, Kie nodded. She took out a triwire and whirled it over her head. She sent N'Rah into a dive a heartbeat after N'Laure began his pass. The bloodgoat head screamed a warning. It and the lion head ducked, while the sand dragon head hovered over the human torso, protecting it.

Kie threw her triwire, but the beast swerved, and her weapon went spinning away. The prince had better luck. His triwire wrapped around the bloodgoat's neck, slicing its head off completely, while the lion head roared in fury.

"They *are* smarter than other chimerae!" the prince panted as N'Rah skimmed up next to N'Laure after their attack pass. "I've never seen the heads duck like that."

Kie forced herself to think past the throbbing at her temples. "They may be smarter, but they're still desert predators. Somehow we have to use that."

"Let's try another pass," the prince said. "One of us will get the sand dragon head this time."

On this pass, she caught the chimera's right wing with the triwire, tearing deeply into the skin and cartilage. The prince swept past the chimera so close, the monster reached out and clawed at N'Laure while the sand dragon head ducked under the prince's triwire.

Are you all right? she asked N'Laure.

I th-think so, he replied.

All at once, an idea came to her. *Act like that swipe caught you,* she told N'Laure. *Pretend you're terribly hurt.*

The brave little pinto fluttered and listed sideways just out of reach of the creature, as if the chimera had wounded him seriously.

Their predatory instincts aroused, the lion and sand dragon heads swiveled to watch N'Laure. Kie urged N'Rah into a dive and pulled her bowstring back. The moment they swept past the chimera, she fired at the human torso. Her arrow lodged deep in its throat, and then they were beyond it.

N'Saran, can you—

Before she could finish the thought, Ruden and N'Saran were

there, driving a lance into the central heart of the disoriented monster. Ruden barely had time to wrench his lance free before the chimera fell from the sky.

Kie wiped the sweat from her eyes. They'd killed two command chimerae now, but what about the third? She glanced around and found it below her. Although it was tangled in a net and riddled with arrows, the last one refused to die. Princess Halla and her triad kept diving at it, trying to shoot its human head. It veered as N'Seella dove past, and the monster raked her flank. As N'Seella neighed in pain and reeled back, the chimera lunged after her, trying to claw the chestnut mare again.

Out of nowhere, a black skysteed with silver wings flashed between the big chimera and Princess Halla. It was N'Tarin! From point-blank range, Terry coolly threw a triwire at the human torso, and one of the three wires caught it around the neck and partially severed it. In the same moment, the bloodgoat head shot forward and drove its horns into N'Tarin's side.

Gunge, taking advantage of the confusion, rammed his lance deep into the chimera's central heart. The creature convulsed in midair and fell. Kie dashed away tears as both N'Seella and N'Tarin spiraled toward the ground after it.

Praying both skysteeds would survive their injuries, she sent N'Rah climbing upward, where she could take stock. The prince joined her there. Beneath them, their forces still fought fiercely, but there were many fewer chimerae in the air now. Except for the twenty chimerae who had punched through it, the Skyforce line appeared to be holding.

Only three chimerae reached the city, N'Forth reported, *but the archers there and spearmen fight them now, and others ride from Pedarth to fight the ones we grounded.*

Well done, Kie said to the mare. *Twenty hungry chimerae would have killed many people and many skysteeds.*

"There's one more of those command chimerae." The prince pointed to a big chimera that hovered high over the fight.

Even as they watched, a hundred of the least-damaged chimerae left the battle and formed up around it. Kie sensed the moment the human part of the beast spotted her and glared across the thousand feet of air separating them. She trembled when a cold, angry mind touched her own. *You may have won here today, but this fight is only beginning, young Nexara.*

The command chimera pivoted and flew northwest, protected by a cloud of scourges.

"Should we try to stop them?" Kie asked, sweating even as she shivered from the contact with that horrible mind. How could he know who she was? How could he mindspeak with her? She *never* wanted to link with a mind that foul and cold again.

"As much as I'd like to, we don't have enough skyfighters left," the prince said wearily. "The good news is, I'm pretty sure they're retreating. Ask someone small and quick to tail them at a safe distance and make sure they don't turn and go for Pedarth."

After giving them firm orders not to fly too close, Kie sent Hedly and N'Wren to keep an eye on the departing chimerae. The next few hours passed in a pain-filled blur as she, the prince, and Ruden hunted in a triad, helping the other skyfighters kill the last chimerae in the air. The brutal fight on the ground lasted even longer because the hundreds of maddened, crippled chimerae blundering through farmers' fields and pastures were hard to kill. Archers and spearman arrived from Pedarth, and with their help, the last of the chimerae were finally slain.

Black dots gathered around the edges of her vision by the time Kie and N'Rah landed next to a stream near the equipment field. Her head splitting, she slipped from his back and fell to her knees, fighting off a wave of dizziness.

Then Topar was there, kneeling beside her. "Kie, what is it? Are you hurt?" he asked urgently.

"Not hurt—just dizzy. Linking with so many skysteeds is tough on my brain. You two all right?"

"We got lucky. Neither of us was injured."

When the first wave of her dizziness had passed, Topar gently helped her stand. He hovered nearby as she checked N'Rah for injuries. Her skysteed was sweaty and spattered with dark purple blood, but amazingly he had no new hurts.

N'Meary and N'Rah drank deeply from the stream while Topar and Kie washed up in the cool water. After drinking her water bottle dry, she felt a little better and forced herself to look around. The once-green fields were strewn with chimerae carcasses and dead and dying skysteeds. N'Meary and N'Rah huddled side by side now, their muzzles almost touching, as if they were drawing comfort from each other's presence.

Dessie stood nearby, her hand on N'Forth's withers. The young groom had a bandage around her arm, and N'Forth had gashes on her shoulder and side that had already been stitched. As she drew closer, she heard Dessie reciting the Binding Oath that Kie had recited with N'Rah years ago. Kie waited until Dessie finished.

"N'Forth asked me to bind with her, and I said yes," Dessie said defiantly. "If the Pedarthian Guard tries to arrest us, we'll run away."

"Well, I'm not going to arrest you. I'm too grateful to you both." Kie bowed to the roan mare and tried not to wince. Bowing made her head pound more. "N'Forth, we owe you a great debt for what you and your herd did today. But I'm looking for Terry and N'Tarin. Have you seen them?"

Dessie's face clouded. "They're over there, behind that big bawa tree."

His heart will not beat much longer, N'Forth warned Kie with sorrow.

With N'Rah, N'Meary, and Topar following on her heels, Kie hurried around the tree. Beyond it, the big black-and-silver skysteed lay sprawled on the grass. Tears rolled down Terry's cheeks as he stroked N'Tarin's neck.

"He was so terribly hurt," Terry said to Kie, his voice rough with sadness. "But somehow he got us safely back on the ground."

Although the valiant skysteed was weak, she could still hear his words. Kie had to clear her throat before she could speak. "He wants me to tell you it was an honor to fight with you, but he is glad to be joining his skyrider at last."

Princess Halla appeared with N'Seella. The mare had a long

wound on her flank that would scar her forever.

The princess knelt by N'Tarin's side. "Thank you for saving our lives," she said softly to the dying skysteed. "When you see my brother in the green fields and blue skies of the High Valley, please tell him that I miss him."

Kie bowed her head as the light faded from N'Tarin's eyes. Then she walked to N'Rah, buried her face in his mane, and finally let herself cry her heart out for all the brave skyriders and skysteeds they had lost today.

CHAPTER TWENTY-NINE

SEVEN DAYS AFTER THE BATTLE of a Thousand Chimerae, as people already were calling it, the Emperor was holding a banquet to celebrate. He and his reserve forces had raced back from the Telawa Valley after they awoke to find their chimerae adversaries had vanished. Fearing for Pedarth, they arrived the day after Lord General Rennart's skyfighters and the motley squads under Prince Shayn's command had saved the city.

Now that event was to be celebrated in grand Imperial fashion, and Kie was doomed to be a part of it.

"But I don't want to go to a banquet or a ball. I just want to go home and take care of my uncle and my trees and fly my courier route again," Kie grumbled for the hundredth time.

"You have to be there tonight because you're one of the guests of honor," Princess Halla said unsympathetically. "Now, quit squirming so I can finish your hair."

Kie made a face, but she did try harder to stay still as the princess and her maid braided her hair and jabbed pins into it.

While they worked, Kie smoothed the shimmering skirts of her dress. The Dowager had insisted that Kie needed a proper gown for the occasion, so she'd boldly asked the court seamstress for something in courier blue. The woman and her helpers had created a lovely dress far finer than anything Kie had ever worn.

"There," the princess said at last. "You didn't make it easy for us, but for once you don't look like a grubby groom or a courier. Take a look."

"But I am a grubby groom and a courier," Kie protested as she turned to Princess Halla's dressing table mirror. She blinked in amazement. She hardly recognized the slim girl staring back at her, her golden skin glowing in contrast to the royal-blue silk of her dress.

They'd pulled her thick brown hair up and back from her face and braided it with silver ribbons. The hairstyle made her eyes look bigger and emphasized her cheekbones. Tonight, she was almost pretty. And she very much liked the fact that she looked taller.

"You two are miracle workers," she said to Malli, the princess's smiling young maid, and to Princess Halla herself, who looked particularly beautiful tonight in a flouncy emerald-green gown.

Someone knocked, and there was Prince Shayn, resplendent in a green-and-gold embroidered tunic, his red mop almost neat for once, and Topar, looking dashing and grown-up in his dress courier uniform. They both wore black armbands to honor the hundreds of skysteeds and skyriders who had died in the recent fighting.

"How come you get to wear your uniform?" Kie asked Topar.

"Because I'm not the Nexara and the heroine of the hour." Topar grinned back at her. "You look the part tonight," he added with a light in his eyes that made her oddly breathless. "If only Betta and the rest of her awful friends at your old school could see you now. Are you ready for this?"

"I'd almost rather fight chimerae," Kie muttered as the prince offered her his arm and led them from his sister's bedchamber.

They walked through a maze of corridors to the doors of a vast hall lined with tapestries and mirrors. The Emperor was already there, wearing a Skyforce dress uniform and standing next to his mother and Lord General Rennart.

"Chin up and shoulders back now, girl," the Dowager whispered as a palace official announced their arrival, and everyone in the hall promptly stood.

Kie took a deep breath and followed the Emperor and his mother into the grand chamber. She smiled when she spotted Terry and Dessie waving at her from the tables of the grooms who had survived the fight, and then Gunge and Ruden, who did the same when they walked by the cadets' tables. Her smile faded when she realized they were seating her on a raised dais where *everyone* could watch her eat. The prince led her to a chair on the Dowager's left. Lord General Rennart sat in the place of greatest honor on the Emperor's right.

"That's where you should be sitting," Prince Shayn said under his breath, "but for political reasons, Father has to pretend that the Skyforce saved the city, not us."

As she worked her way through multiple courses, Kie mostly concentrated on not spilling food on her pretty gown. She almost wished that she were wearing the dress she'd worn for the mourning ceremonies. The dark gray color of rainclouds, it would have hidden stains way better.

In those ceremonies, held in the heart of Tavalier Park, the Emperor had read out the name of every skysteed and rider who had died fighting the chimerae. They'd placed a feather saved from each fallen skysteed and a lock of hair from every dead skyfighter in a grass basket that would be taken to the Makar Mountains, the legendary home of the skysteed breed. There, the feathers and hair would be given to the wind from the back of a skysteed flying high over the peaks.

Kie had held her tears during the ceremony, but afterward, she and N'Rah had slipped away into the park, and she'd cried her eyes out for N'Tarin and sweet Kelton, who had died when the chimerae tried to storm through the Skyforce line, and all the other skysteeds, grooms, and cadets she'd trained who were gone.

Afraid she'd start crying right now, she decided to focus on the Dowager, who was sharing amusing gossip about the grand people all around them. Topar, she was glad to see, had been seated on Lord General Rennart's right, and the two were deep in conversation. At last, servers cleared the final dishes away, and the Emperor stood. Instantly, everyone hushed, and Kie sat up straighter in her chair.

"There are many people I need to thank tonight for defending this great city," the Emperor began, his deep, rich voice filling the hall. "Lord General Rennart, please stand. You and your skyfighters fought bravely against a host twice your size. I'm grieved that we lost our valiant Lord Generals Stygurt, Furin, and Virsart during the fighting out west, but I am glad to name you Supreme Commander of all our forces." He took a glittering medal from a tray held by a steward, pinned it to the Lord General's chest, and everyone cheered.

Next the Emperor turned to his mother. "There is no medal worthy of my capable and wise mother. Her senior sentry system gave our forces crucial warning of when and where the chimerae would strike, and her coordination with Pedarth's mayor ensured our people reached safety in time." As he kissed her cheek, applause broke out once more.

The Emperor raised his hand, calling for silence. "There are also many valiant young people who came to the defense of our city whom I would like to recognize. Princess Halla, your archery triads killed or wounded over thirty scourge masters. I, as both your father and your Emperor, am so very proud of you, and name you a Protector of the Empire." He smiled, kissed her forehead, and placed an amartine medal on a blue ribbon about her neck.

Then he approached Topar. "Topar Singu of the Lsari clan, I am indebted to you for teaching our cadets how to use the botan, a weapon that has proved its worth many times over now. I am also grateful to you for saving the life of Lord Commander Rennart. You also are now a Protector of the Empire."

As Topar leaned forward to receive his medal, Kie smiled and clapped. She wasn't surprised that in the midst of the intense fighting, Topar had found his way to his father's side. He'd spent time with the Lord General over the past few days, getting to know his father and his Rosari family. But Topar still wasn't ready to serve as his heir.

"Prince Shayn and Captain Nerone," the Emperor said next, "I credit you both for seeing that the best way to defeat our remorseless enemies was to use the most effective tactics from the olden days, combined with the strength of our modern skysteeds. My son was also instrumental in organizing the young skyfighters who helped the Skyforce defend our city. For these brilliant deeds, I make you both Protectors of the Empire."

Kie clapped long and hard along with the rest as the two received their medals. She was so glad that Captain Nerone's career in the Skyforce obviously wasn't in jeopardy any longer.

"Kiesandra Torsun, stand please," the Emperor said, and Kie felt her grin vanish. She almost panicked as she fought to get her feet clear of her long skirts.

"Stand up straight, girl, and don't fidget," the Dowager whispered.

Kie's cheeks heated as the Emperor smiled, took her hand, and helped her to stand. He was quiet for a long moment as he stared out at his guests.

"You should know that Kiesandra's uncle sent her to our capital with an impossible mission: to make us understand that the old ways of fighting the chimerae had value. Despite the fact that few here would listen to her, she persisted, and Pedarth is safe today because of her efforts. Even more importantly, she made us take a long, hard look at our relationship with our skysteed allies. She listened to the Unbound and allowed them to join our forces, and that decision helped to save our city. A brave and able skyfighter and courier, Kiesandra Torsun saved my son's life twice. Finally, our young Nexara's remarkable ability to speak to all skysteeds made a crucial difference during the Battle of a Thousand Chimerae."

The Emperor paused to pick up another medal from the tray. "For all these services, I am delighted to make her a Daughter of the Empire."

Cheering broke out as the Emperor placed the ribbon bearing the gold-and-amartine medal about her neck. Kie's lips twitched when she heard some very undignified whistles and yells from the cadets' and grooms' tables.

"And I hope you will consider yourself an honorary daughter of our family," the Emperor said with a warm smile as the applause washed over them, "for truly, you have won all our hearts."

Trying not to cry, Kie smiled back at him. His words meant so much to her. Her family had been getting smaller and smaller, and now it felt bigger in the nicest sort of way.

Then he faced the room again, and Kie tensed, hoping this was the moment he would announce the deal they'd struck after a long talk together. When the Emperor and his skysteed N'Thiren had wanted to know how to thank her, she knew exactly what she wanted.

"Out of gratitude for the Unbound skysteeds' bravery," the

Emperor declared, "no breeder in all Prekalt, from this day forward, may prevent skysteeds from binding with the rider of their choice."

There was a shocked silence, and then the grooms who had flown with Unbound skysteeds into battle burst out cheering. Kie looked for Dessie. Her friend was crying and smiling at the same time. Now she and N'Forth wouldn't have to run away, nor would any of the other grooms who had already secretly bound with their skysteed partners.

The Emperor turned to Kie again. "My only regret is that your uncle Duggan Torsun was still too frail to make the trip here. Prekalt owes him a great debt, and I have already named him an honorary instructor at the Skyforce Academy, with a substantial lifelong stipend to accompany it. We would be honored if you would accept an instructorship there as well."

"Thank you, Your Supreme Highness, for your generous offer."

At last, Kie was allowed to sit while the Emperor went on to recognize the efforts of Pedarth's mayor and others who helped to save the city. Kie stared down at the shining folds of her dress. Embarrassed warmth still heated her cheeks, but happy warmth filled her heart. She hadn't known the Emperor was planning to offer Uncle Dugs a teaching position with a stipend. Her uncle would never have to worry about paying for his meds again. She didn't want to teach at the Academy, but she could see Uncle Dugs relishing such a position.

Carefully, she cupped her medal in the palm of her hand. Shaped in the form of a flying skysteed, the medal was intricately inlaid with with enamel and semiprecious stones. She traced the skysteed's wings, the same glorious golden shade of N'Rah's mane and tail. Whoever would have thought Kiesandra Torsun, fruit farmer, junior courier, and part-time Imperial groom, would someday be named a Daughter of the Empire? Uncle Dugs was going to be so proud. Kie found herself grinning. She looked over at Topar, and he was grinning, too.

The dancing started after the medals were all given out. Princess Halla had insisted that Kie learn a few of the simplest court dances, but even those had fiendishly complicated steps. Blushing and smiling, Terry, Ruden, and Gunge were brave enough to ask Kie to dance, and she only stepped on their toes a few times. She enjoyed two dances with Topar who, of course, was disgustingly light and graceful on his feet and made the most complicated dance steps look easy. Even Prince Duren asked her to dance, and proceeded to tell her in great detail how the triwire she'd lent him had saved his life.

But as soon as she could, Kie slipped away from all the people, the mirrors, and the music and headed for a quiet window. Prince Shayn was already there, leaning his elbows on the window ledge. Standing beside him, she, too, looked out into the moonlit night.

"I'm afraid it's not over, you know," Prince Shayn said after they'd shared a companionable silence, "even though no one's seen a head or a tail of a chimera since the battle. Our first wars with these beasts lasted almost thirty years, and we know what that creature said to you. We are going to have to figure out who is creating the chimerae, and why, and how big a threat these new, smarter chimerae are to Prekalt. I have a hunch we will need the Nexara again to manage our alliance with the skysteeds."

"I hope you're wrong. As far as I'm concerned, the war is *over* for me," Kie said firmly. "I appreciate your father's offer, but I can't wait to get back to my orchard and my uncle."

Prince Shayn sent her a rueful look. "I knew you'd stick to your plan. I wish you could take me with you." He screwed up his face and gestured at his fancy tunic. "I hate this part of being a prince."

"You'd get bored of pruning dayan trees after a day, believe me."

"I suppose you're right. I can say that to more people now. I used to be so sure I was right while everyone else was wrong. I'm glad the captain said I was too focused on fighting chimerae with smaller skysteeds. Because I was trying so hard to prove that our skysteeds were the answer, I lost track of what really matters."

"At least you were open to a new idea, unlike your father's commanders. And I learned that to make friends, you have to trust them, even with some of your most embarrassing secrets," Kie said, remembering their battle against the chimerae scourge in the Telawa Valley, where her secret-keeping had almost gotten her skysteed killed.

The palace clock chimed, and Kie straightened eagerly. "It's time."

Looking resigned, the prince led her back through the endless corridors to Princess Halla's bedchamber. There, Malli helped her out of the beautiful dress, and Kie smoothed its shimmering fabric one last time.

"Are you sure you don't want to take it with you?" the maid asked as she hung it carefully.

"I've no need of it where I'm going." By the time Kie had changed into her courier uniform, the princess waited beyond the changing screen.

"You wretched girl," Princess Halla said, her eyes swimming with tears as she hugged Kie. "I finally make a friend I can trust, and you go running off to your apple orchard and leave me."

"You and N'Seella could always come visit, you know," Kie said as she stepped back and tucked her medal into her saddlebags. She couldn't wait to show it to Uncle Dugs, along with ten gold dashins, which represented an advance on Uncle Dugs's new stipend.

"We just might come visit you," the princess said, brightening.

Kie smiled, trying to imagine her elegant friend in her tiny farmhouse in the frontier foothills. "I hope you do. You'd be most welcome."

She caught up her saddlebags and stepped out into the garden shared by the Dowager and her grandchildren, and then she halted in surprise. Right now, it was very full of skysteeds and people!

"You and Topar have lots of friends who wanted to see you off," the prince told her with a smile.

As she looked around, her heart seemed to swell. She had made good friends in the short time she'd been in Pedarth, and most of them were here. N'Rah trotted over and lipped her hair.

Look, you have a fine herd of your own now, he said happily.

You're right, I do, she replied. That curl of warmth deep down inside her returned. But with it came a sharp pang of sadness. She was going to miss her new friends very, very much.

Because Terry stood closest to her, she turned to him first. "I'm so sorry about N'Tarin."

"I am, too, but he's happier now that he's reunited with his skyrider," Terry said, his brown eyes touched with sorrow. "I'll miss you at senior sick call, but I'm off to the Torgaresh next summer to find a wildborn of my own. Unless one of N'Forth's friends claims me first."

Dessie stood beside Terry, N'Forth behind her. "I refuse to get all mushy in front of everyone," Dessie said, her eyes suspiciously shiny. "Thank you, and you'd better write. I hear couriers get a discount on their mail."

"I promise I'll write," Kie said as Dessie hugged her hard.

Nexara, N'Forth said, *thank you for giving the Unbound back the honor, respect, and freedom we were due.*

You won it for yourselves a week ago. Take good care of Dessie.

Beyond Dessie, she found Gunge, Ruden, and Hedley standing together. It hurt not to see Kelton with them as she said goodbye.

"I'm glad you taught me never to judge a skysteed by its size," Ruden said to her. "I wouldn't be standing here tonight if it weren't for Hedly and his N'Wren. Already I can mindspeak with N'Saran much better, and that's thanks to you as well."

She was startled when he performed a formal bow to her, a gesture of respect she guessed he'd rarely given a Mosai before.

Beyond the cadets, she found the head groom waiting for her. Trishop's lean face lit with a smile. "Well, at least it wasn't dull having you around my stables. Tell your rascal of an uncle that he should take that teaching position the Emperor offered him, especially now that you've shook up Pedarth and much of what Duggan hated here is going to change."

"I will," she promised, "and thank you for giving me a job and looking out for me here in Pedarth." Last, she came to N'Talley, and Kie's throat went tight again.

I am going to miss you, the old mare said, *and my human will not be happy when she finds out you have slipped away.*

"I think she knew what we planned. Your human doesn't miss much. I'm going to miss you, too," Kie said. Ignoring court protocol, she stepped forward and gave the plump old skysteed a hug.

If you ever need us, youngling, you know where to find us, and we know where to find you.

Yes, ma'am.

"Are you ready to leave?" she asked Topar as she settled her travel bags behind N'Rah's saddle.

"I'm more than ready," he replied, and they both vaulted onto their skysteeds' backs and clipped into their flight harnesses.

N'Meary and N'Rah rose up on their haunches, their wings swept downward, and they were airborne.

"Fly safe, fly free!" their friends called after them.

As soon as N'Meary and N'Rah had climbed above the palace turrets, shining in the wash of moonlight from great Cerken, Kie and Topar turned their skysteeds west, toward home.

Acknowledgments

First of all, I would like to thank my incomparable agent, Rosemary Stimola, for taking me on as a client and making the sale of *Skyriders* happen despite a global pandemic!

I also would like to thank my brilliant editor, Jenny Bak, for her enthusiasm for flying horses. She grasped the heart of Kie's story and was a huge help in making these characters come alive. Thank you, too, to everyone at Viking Children's Books for taking a chance on my skysteeds.

I'm so very grateful to the uber-talented Brandon Dorman for creating the most gorgeous cover EVER! Horses are hard to depict, flying horses even harder, and your concept of a chimera is cooler and more terrifying than anything I imagined.

I also want to thank a host of beta readers whose comments improved this book. Those readers include Reid Wilson, Nancy Brown, Hannah A., Amy, and Matthieu Guerin. I'm particularly indebted to Antoine Guerin for pushing me to describe skysteeds and chimerae more clearly.

The members of my critique group also gave great input as this story was taking shape. My thanks to Robert Eilers, Pam McWilliams, Lanie Nielson, Melanie Sumrow, and Hema Penmetsa. Karen Harrington and Marci Peschke, two of the finest writers I know, I so appreciate your constant friendship and support. I miss you all!

I would like to give a special shout-out to Laurie Kuelthau for being such a good friend and for letting me ride her sweet, funny Chico, a former BLM mustang, on many occasions. Chico provided much of the inspiration for N'Rah's personality.

I am so grateful to my husband, Joseph, for supporting my writing, for tolerating my piles of books, and for moving us to Steamboat Springs!

Finally, thank you to my parents, Edith and John Holyoke, for giving me so many books in my childhood that fired my imagination. In particular, I spent hours reading *Pegasus, The Winged Horse*, retold by Nathaniel Hawthorne and illustrated by Herschel Levit. Levit's illustrations of the cruel chimera made me shiver, and his glorious illustrations of Pegasus made me long for a flying horse of my own.